POLISHED HONEY

Gary Steel

ISBN-9798702523453

Cover design by: Art Painter
Cover Photograph by: Gary Steel
Library of Congress Control Number: 2018675309
Printed in the United States of America

CONTENTS

INTRODUCTION

Characters merge in dreams that intersect with reality. Disasters destroy lives and create new ones. Pain and loss are linked. Punctuated with humor, Polished Honey explores loss, loneliness and home.

Stan lives in Seoul, South Korea where he works as a freelance English teacher. His dreams are journeys of self-discovery and he attempts to make meaning of them while hanging out in bars with his friend. Stan eventually spirals into loneliness and starts to question his life in Seoul; finally, events conspire to have him return to Australia where bushfires rage.

Jinni's story runs parallel with Stan's although in a different time and a different city. The Sampoong Department Store collapse inspired her to flee her abusive husband. She falsified her death and found sanctuary working in a bar in Busan. Eventually timelines merge and events peak in Melbourne during the Black Friday Bushfires.

CHAPTER 1

Where it all Began

Stan is between dreams, lying on his back staring at shadows sliding across the ceiling, his mind in stubborn wakefulness. The bed sheets are in twisted disarray as he trials one position and then another. Finally, the distant hypnotic drone of Seoul's traffic has his eyeballs trembling under their lids as he again descends into REM sleep and dreams jostle for focus.

He stands by the bed looking back at the confusion of sheets. He is in his running gear but he cannot remember putting them on. He shrugs his shoulders and drifts to the bathroom where he throws water on his face before peeing as quietly as possible into the toilet bowl. Then, he is back in the bedroom where he lingers at the bedside studying a woman's face. Her closed eyes tell him nothing and her skin is the hue of polished honey. He has to run.

Stan opens the door to a gray morning of dust, and lingering diesel fumes. Hawk kites circle. Plastic kites hang lynched and abandoned from indifferent trees. This is not Seoul. New Delhi? The polluted air closes around him as he moves forward. He runs past perpetually never finished building sites and amongst the tangled scraps of rusted reinforcing lie wire-thin, dark-brown, homeless families intertwined and sleeping. His feet move forward and his thoughts blend real and unreal. He turns at the first intersection and keeps running. A sleeping, legless beggar raises his eyes but not his interest. Stan lengthens his stride. He runs past the Yatri Nervas Hotel, the hotel he stayed in when he first visited New Delhi so long ago. He runs toward Connaught Place; there is a need to keep moving. He runs past stores selling Tibetan artifacts, stores selling Kashmiri rugs, stores advertising treks and travel; he passes clothing stores and gold stores. He passes them all and they lose shape as he passes. There is a lingering atmosphere of bargaining, of raised voices, of half lies, of total fabrications. The fumes of old sweat from yesterday's people and yesterday's transactions mingle with the fresh sweat beginning to leach from Stan's pores. He is surrounded by distortion and fronted by clarity and he continues forward. The kites watch him running.

Jinni lies sleeping. One leg has found its way out of the sheets while the other remains covered. Her pillow embraces the left side of her face. Her right eye moves slowly beneath its closed lid. She is facing the window and she is dreaming.

Stan strides into Connaught Place. Around him, feral children with limbs interlocked sleep as one and Stan runs and waits. He is waiting for the dawn and, in the meantime, he has no choice but to circle.

The pre-dawn gray lessens and the soupy atmosphere becomes tinged with orange. The dawning encourages a light breeze that stirs the lynched kites. The groups of feral children become individual urchins. Snake charmers rouse their toothless cobras from drugged lethargy. An old man's gray hair and beard is stained with henna and his skin melts like chocolate; he is organizing his shoeshine box. His fingers are stained black and cracked from a lifetime of boot polish, the whites of his eyes reddened from a lifetime of hashish and his body bent from a lifetime of hardship.

Stan runs toward Connaught Place, a large roundabout, almost two kilometers in circumference. Under this roundabout is a market shaped like a bicycle wheel with a central hub intersected by corridor spokes intersected by corridor rims. During the day it is a hot, airless, sweaty, mad, maze of energy. Bargains can be found and then lost; whole shops can be found and then lost and people can be found and then lost. Above ground, the once grassy circle is now compressed dust. Connected and disconnected people eddy through time. The ear-cleaning wallah proudly displays his affidavits and recommendations. Doe eyed fortune tellers seduce the unwary with practiced acts. Dirty children with dirty babies touch dirty fingers to their lips in an effort to procure alms. Scabby skinned old men and scabby skinned young boys drag lifeless legs behind them; they beg for small change. Macchiato colored teenage girls with green eyes offer watercolors on silk. Haggard old women in stained saris offer modern versions of the Karma Sutra. The images merge and melt. Stan is running through a mirage of Delhi and the dream is expanding. The unexpected and unknown have become expected and known. There are shoeshine wallahs everywhere and their faces are melting into their bootblack. Day is replacing night as light advances and spreads its tendrils. Now, Stan is sprinting and gasping. He sprints across Connaught Place and the blind beggar watches him pass. He rises over the chaos. Auto trishaws, bicycles, buses, cars and trucks have lost their definition. Delhi's anarchic noises have become familiar choruses. The putrid smells of raw sewage, old curry and stale humanity has become a potpourri of known scents. Stan sprints over it all, floats through it all until he is sitting on the side of his bed watching Jinni wake.

Jinni's sleeping face is calm and as she stirs, Stan watches. A smile lights her face without her eyes opening. Stan reclines beside his vision and he stretches his arm behind her neck and she is not there. She is standing by the bed looking at Stan.

"Been far?"

Stan reaches for the bedside radio. DJ Hyun is playing K-pop on the Korean English language radio station, Arirang. The undemanding sounds vibrate and he allows the rhythms to flow over and through his sleeping mind. His fingers pick up the rhythm of a K-pop girl band and Jinni's vision joins the chorus. The high pitch harmonies soften around him and he watches her moving to the beat.

He rolls over in his sleep and one dream fades and another takes its place.

"Mister do you want a nice Bangladeshi girl?" And Stan is sitting on the plastic, sparingly padded seat of a pedal trishaw.

"A what?"

"I take you, sit tight."

"But where am I?"

And, Nazir rises out of the saddle, pushes on the pedals with the left side of his body and then the right side. His muscles flex and his body, built like a ship's rope, strains to push the trishaw. This is no racing bike. The chain hangs loose like a mad man's smile; the seat is a plastic swirl of color; the trishaw itself is decorated like the contents of a confetti box and this kaleidoscope coalesces into faces that could be gods or movie idols. Stan closes his eyes in search of Jinni but she does not return and his ears ring with the sounds of trishaw bells and good-natured squabbles in an unknown language. He keeps his eyes closed, willing himself from one dream to another but he can't make the crossing. He opens his eyes and he is looking into the large, brown eyes of a posse of Bangladeshi schoolboys.

"Mister, mister, where you from?"

"Mister, mister, do you play cricket?"

Stan closes his eyes again and when he reopens them, the trishaw is stopping outside a construction site. Teams of two lift buckets of cement, sand and bricks onto the heads of boys who could be twelve or twenty years old. The laborers wear loincloths of dirty rags and their skin can't be seen for cement dust. Their eyes are emotionless.

"Ok mister, nice Bangladeshi girl in here."

Stan looks at the partially finished building and closes his eyes, but when he opens them he is inside a room that is lit by natural light that filters through a haze of dust and a torn hessian bag that has been nailed to the wooden window frame. A woman sits in a chair with her face lifted to the light. Stan can only see her from behind and her black hair flows over the back of the chair. Dust motes play in the filtered sunlight that strikes the top of her head.

He stands inside the room separated from the woman by a single bed that sports an off-white mattress that aches with stains. There are no sheets and no pillows. The walls have never been painted and the sound of a door closing has him reaching behind searching for the doorknob but there is none. He turns to face the door and it morphs into a wall. He looks back to the woman and she has risen from the chair. She paces along her side of the bed always turning away from Stan. The spotlight of sun follows her, as do the dust motes. She is in profile and her sari of pinks and blues hide her body and her hair falls across her face. When Stan senses a light breeze brush his face, he looks up and watches a ceiling fan stained with fly-shit fight each revolution and when he looks down again, the woman is beside him and her black eyes beckon him to the mattress.

He lowers his body onto the mattress and closes his eyes. When he rolls onto his side and opens them, Jinni is rising from the bed and the K-pop rhythms of *Wonder Girls* hit "Nobody" fills the room. She smiles at Stan and the girls continue to sing, "Nobody but chyew." Stan rises to stand with her but she is back on the bed.

Morning sun slides through the open slats of the cane blind. The breeze moves the blind a little so that fingers of light play across Jinni's nakedness. DJ Hyun is back raving about the K-pop wave and Stan catches glimpses of past, present and future.

Jinni's face pulls in and out of focus. Cities, houses, cafes, mountains, forests, roads, beaches and faces all wrestle for time and space. Some of the visions he has already visited but others are new. It is impossible to make sense of what he is seeing. The wave is too large, too uncontrolled and the visions clash; then, Stan is floating free of the visionary debris.

He rolls to the edge of the bed, stands and looks back for a moment. He pulls on a pair of shorts and a t-shirt and pads into the kitchen and fills the kettle with spring water. While the water is boiling, he pours whole coffee beans into the electric grinder and flicks the switch. The sound of grinding coffee clashes with the K-pop rhythms but it releases a bittersweet aroma. Stan likes his beans ground ultra-fine.

The aroma of coffee can lure anything and Jinni appears in the doorway of the kitchen. Her slender limbs, upright breasts and delicate creases fill Stan's vision, but the vision soon twists and fades. Stan is alone sipping his coffee and the kitchen is overflowing with its smell but there is only one cup. The apartment is alive with the sound of K-pop but Stan is the only one listening. The bed sheets are tangled but the bed is empty. The telephone is ringing.

Stan replaces the cup on the table and picks up his phone.

"Hello."

"Morning Stan. Vince here"

Vince is hoping for an afternoon coffee but Stan has an appointment and suggests a beer in the evening.

"I'm Tango dancing between six and eight so let's make it around nine."

"Tango dancing. This is new?"

"I'll tell you about it over a beer."

"Right, see you around nine, *Scrooge* ok with you?"

"Yeah, see ya."

CHAPTER 2

The Day After

Stan has known a lot of people in Seoul, a lot of people. They are varied in nature and the friendships varied in intensity. But lately, he has begun wondering, "Why him or why her?" People come and people go; it is the nature of life. Groceries are not the only thing with "use by" stamped on them. At present, Vince is one of few men in Seoul sporting a valid "use by" date. One reason for this freshness is because they don't meet often, once a fortnight would probably be just about right. But, when they get together, the conversation is eclectic and cathartic. But, he still wonders why Vince. Vince comes from a big working-class family. He grew up in poverty and kept winning scholarships to get through university up to a PhD. Stan, on the other hand, is an only child from middle class wealth with a private school education. You add two odd numbers together and you get an even.

Vince is a visiting professor of Information Technology at a University in Seoul. And, a chat about campus politics is common fodder over a beer. It is good to have a quick whine before moving on to other topics. This doesn't mean that the campus politics are not interesting; it just means that life for them both moves beyond work.

Stan looks forward to the evening conversation and deliberates on Vince and tango before he drains the last of his coffee, being careful not to siphon coffee grains into his mouth. This morning, his mind is distracted by visions of Jinni. The action should be automatic; the result should be liquid only. Stan runs his tongue over his teeth as he stands and walks toward the kitchen sink where he spits a few offending grains before continuing towards the bathroom.

Showering, Stan senses recollections of last night's dreams. He bends his head forward so that the warm water can slap the back of his neck as he tries to remember. There is landscape but little detail. He tastes dirt, diesel and dust. Involuntarily, he runs his fingers over his lips and he looks at his fingertips for any residue, but there is nothing. He pictures Jinni. He sees a stained mattress. He remembers twisted concrete reinforcing and broken concrete. He shakes his head to clear his thoughts and he concentrates on the shampoo.

"Enough is just enough and never too much." He tries to sing the words with a K-pop beat but fails. He massages his scalp with his fingertips and begins to think of Jinni. Jinni with the lips like quartered peaches, peeled; Jinni with the midnight hair; Jinni with the skin of polished honey. But, a vision of dust motes playing in the hair of an ephemeral Bangladeshi woman interrupts these thoughts.

"Not now." Again, he looks to harmonize with the K-pop band playing on the radio and again he fails. He concentrates on the job of showering. He uses the shampoo foam from his head to lather one armpit at a time. Another heaped handful of foam is used to cleanse his shoulders, another his back (his right shoulder is a little stiff and he wonders if he has done a complete job left of center). Another handful of suds cleanses his chest and then a next to last one is used on his legs. Finally, he scrapes the remaining bubbles from his hair with both hands and massages his other parts. He wants to linger and think of Jinni but the sun has already risen too far in the sky for this. With the shower turned to cold, Stan braces his feet and accepts the water that pounds away at his flesh as it rinses the remaining soap from his hair and skin.

Stan lives in a small, tired one bedroom, one living room, and one kitchen/dining room apartment in Itaewon. It has a broad balcony that he must walk across to get to the steps that will take him down onto the street. This morning he pauses on the balcony and looks south toward the mountain range of Gwanak-san in the far distance and at the greening of Seoul. An early spring morning in Seoul sees the air crisp and cool. The winter hibernation is ending. Color is returning to the plants; young green buds are forming on the deciduous trees and the conifers are cloaking themselves in new, green, youthful needles that quietly confirm life. The smells of spring and pollution fight for supremacy. And, the young Korean teenagers, fresh from the dark clothes of winter, have clad themselves in color. They have awoken from the darkness, into the uncertainty of almost adulthood. Stan thinks of young kangaroos that leave the pouch for the first time and cannot control their leaps; the power of the Achilles tendon too frightening as is the open space so they gather in supportive groups and soon return to the security of their mothers' pouch. The world can be a scary place when the trainer wheels are removed. The youth on the streets of Seoul seek strength in friendship groups and these clusters jostle for space on the pavement.

Stan is dressed in his usual skinny, navy-blue pants; white, cotton, collarless shirt and a navy-blue sports coat. And, on his feet, he is wearing a pair of his extensive collection of sneakers. He just cannot do shoes. He is proud of his fitness, and proud of his 45-year-old body. He tells Vince that his mid-section spare tire is nothing more than a mountain bike tire and he wants to reduce it to a racing bike tire. Vince usually laughs, throws out a, "Whatever," and chides him with a minor lecture on the properties of beer and middle-aged hormones.

Morning sounds confirm that the day has begun. "Com-pu-tor, Rad-di-o, tel-lee-vee," is scratchy morning music, almost melodic, loud and insistent. The amplified voice of an electronic goods rag-and-bone man calls out for trade. His blue *Bongo I* works its way through the confused lanes that make up Seoul north of the Han River. North of the river is old Seoul, and since Armistice was declared to halt but not end the Korean War in 1953, it has been rebuilt and developed with limited urban planning. Outside of Stan's apartment the lanes accommodate pedestrians, motorcycles, small vehicles and the occasional outsider in a car larger than these lanes' capabilities. Itaewon has become a popular destination for modern Koreans looking for a touch of the cosmopolitan but this morning, the *Bongo I* driving rag-and-bone man has the lanes to himself.

Bongos come in three sizes I, II and III and they are ubiquitously blue although white seems to be creeping onto the carmaker's palette, but these lanes can only accommodate the *Bongo I* and this one is blue and aged. In fact, the weathered exterior of this *Bongo I* mirrors the driver's weathered face. "Com-pu-tor, Rad-di-o, tel-lee-vee."

Stan looks at his watch before descending the stairs two at a time. He opens the rusted, blue gate and watches the Bongo truck snake its way along the lane and he shakes his head and smiles at the same time; the sight is one of those contradictions that first frustrated but now validates his life in Seoul.

Stan spends two or three hours a day instructing wealthy businessmen, and sometimes their wives but rarely their children, in the intricacies of the English language. He commands a premium return because he has cultivated a gregarious nature that he can turn on or off and he has learned to laugh along with his clients. He turns away more work than he accepts. He is not in search of friendships but, for the most part, he enjoys the superficial contact although some experiences have left him lost for words. Today, he has an appointment with a businessman who wants English lessons and they have arranged to meet in a café in Gangnam to talk about strategies, times and money. He decides to walk up to Namsan Botanical Gardens before catching the 402-bus into Gangnam. It is a walk of about three kilometers and it is a solid climb before a cruise through the gardens. For the first two kilometers Stan walks up through lanes and narrow streets behind Itaewon. He passes the Samsung family's architecturally designed massifs. These accommodations are spread along a ridge and they lord over Itaewon. After "Samsung Ridge," he continues on past the Hyatt Hotel and across the footbridge to Namsan Botanical Gardens and Namsan proper. Stan enjoys the automatic footfalls and the colors, shapes and smells of both the natural and manufactured. It is a beautiful early spring day and the garden is filled with color. He is enjoying the morning walk and he plans what to say to this new client. He has decided to increase his fee to 90,000 won per hour. On one hand, he doesn't want the work but the equivalent of 90 dollars an hour will be hard to refuse. The sounds and sights of insects, birds and squirrels is a nice change from the *Bongo* truck.

He sits down for a while on a park bench and tilts his head to sun. He can feel the sun's warmth on his eyelids and he allows his mind to amble towards last night's dreams. He doesn't want to think much about the Jinni dream; it is a little too difficult to decipher at present so he reflects on Bangladesh. He traveled there last year and he recognizes some of the visions. He certainly saw trishaw peddlers like Nazir and all the trishaws looked pretty much alike and the traffic jams of these vehicles were chaotic at best and unmoving at worst. He also saw building sites, which could have either been construction or deconstruction sites. Like India, which he has been to several times, it was always a bit difficult to tell what was going up and what was coming down. Or, what was finished and what was not.

His mind drifts:

"But, a brothel in a construction site, a little odd ...

... Was it a brothel?, If not, what?, Maybe not a construction site, A hotel? ... seedy ... I've seen seedier ..."

Stan smiles as he remembers a night in a hotel in Gulmag in the mountains of Kashmir.

"Filthy sheets, I tried to levitate and sleep at the same time ... Vince would like that story ..."

Stan sits for a while longer and plans a tale of failed multi-tasking before he needs to get moving. His plan is to get to the agreed upon café in Gangnam at 12:30 and eat a sandwich before the businessman arrives. He doesn't like eating with strangers because middle-aged Koreans, whether men or women, tend to chew their food with their mouths open and the noises of mastication and lip smacking make him uncomfortable. He walks back through the Namsan Botanical Gardens and back across the footbridge to the Hyatt Hotel. From there he walks down to the bus stop and stands waiting for the 402-bus. This bus begins its journey in the north of Seoul at Gyeongbok Palace. On its way south, it travels along the road that is cut into the side of Namsan before crossing the Han River.

"'Soak up the sun laddie, Forget the dreams ... think about the teaching gig ...'

... Who is this Scottish voice in my head?, Is that you Granny? ...

...What book?, I'll show him the one in my bag ... we'll supplement it with newspapers."

Like all buses in Seoul, the 402 is frequent and when it arrives, it is standing room only. He squeezes through bodies hanging from hand straps or holding onto the backs of seats. The bus driver swerves out into the traffic before Stan can settle anywhere and he apologizes for the collisions with a whispered "*Chosahumnida*" but no one seems to care. He finds a space that is not big enough but space in Seoul is rarely big enough and he is soon hanging from a hand strap of his own with strangers brushing and bumping him. He swings with the motion of the traffic and he tries to ignore the accidental intimacy of some of the touches. A young boy looks at his arm and begins to pat him like a dog. The mother smiles at her young son and encourages him to stroke the "foreigner's fur." Stan tries to smile but it comes out as a sneer. The boy keeps stroking while the mother keeps smiling and the bus motors down the mountain and across the Han River into Gangnam. "Gang" translates to "river" and "Nam" translates to "south" and it is new Seoul. The arterial roads are five lanes each way. The modern grid plan makes navigation easy and it takes 10 minutes for the 402-bus to reach Stan's destination. The passengers do not make way so he pushes towards the door. With solid ground under his feet, he stands at the bus stop and looks around. The road is a salmon migration path, every car going in the same direction. But, if seen from space, the pedestrians would look like ants swarming on multiple tracks, in multiple directions, sometimes crossing paths and the motion is all business and speed.

Stan stands for a while and observes the androgynous nature of Korea. Slender young women with perfect skin dressed in body hugging fashion move purposefully by as the slender young men with perfect skin dressed in body hugging fashion do the same. They have no interest in Stan even though he tries to make eye contact. And, he keeps seeing Jinni in the crowd.

"Strong connection ... she smiles at me ... but she keeps her distance, She's just so real ... I need to talk to Vince."

Paris Baguette cafés are ubiquitous throughout Korea and eventually, he walks into the one selected for this meeting and selects a chicken sandwich with cranberry sauce and orders an iced café latte. He stands patiently as his coffee and sandwich is being prepared and then he takes a seat in the window to eat and wait for his new client. While he is eating, he looks through the ESL textbook. Most of the time he shakes his head at the dullness of the exercises, but he also realizes that the exercises are a good stepping stone to more interesting conversations about real-life topics, if the guy's English is good enough.

1pm comes and goes and Stan figures that he'll give the new client until 1:30pm. 1:30pm arrives and he is still sitting alone.

He is not disappointed; in fact, he is relieved and he quickly rises from his seat and walks out. As he hits the street, he is already thinking about going for a run.

CHAPTER 3

The Collapse

In June 1995, Jinni stepped off the train at Busan Rail Station and into a new life. She was 25 years old, tall, slim and with midnight-black hair. She slept a few nights rough in the Busan Railway Station while she worked up a plan to get a new identity.

In 1992, as Mejung Oh, Jinni graduated from Ewha Women's University with a Business Degree. She had also spent two years at a private girls' middle school in Australia so her English was excellent. Her father, Wontae, was a moderately successful small businessman and her mother, Inhee, spent her time shopping and gossiping. Mejung was the eldest child and her brother was four years younger.

In his business dealings, Wontae met wealthy men of Seoul and he shopped his daughter around to their sons. Ewha is a prestigious women's university and his daughter was tall. He had made sure that Mejung had plenty of skin bleaching products in her toiletry and he insisted that she use this cream regularly. He was able to describe Mejung as a tall, slim, pale-skinned, Ewha graduate. He knew a height challenged son of a wealthy businessman would take the bait. And, he was right. Wontae Oh felt his family needed a dash of prestige, and Sungyu Kim's family definitely needed height. It was a match made over soju and beer. Neither the daughter nor the son of the emotionally impoverished businessmen knew how to resist the tide and neither knew how to care. They just let the marriage happen; it was inevitable. There was no point resisting. The wedding took place in November of 1993.

The wedding was expensive and ostentatious. White envelopes filled with money were handed over and donors' names and amounts were duly noted. Mejung sat in a small open room, alone. Guests looked in and admired or faked admiration. Her dress had cost her father enough for him to dine out on the price for years; he liked to tell people about how much he spent. Her make-up was excessive and her hair was curled and drawn-up in a ridiculous caricature of a bride's hairstyle. She sat in the "admiration room" for a good hour, and as she sat alone, she thought that—she hoped that—aloneness would not be part of her future. She also thought about her time in Australia as a middle school student. She had been free and carefree and now she was caged in a room being displayed like a zoo animal. But, she endured the stares; she thanked the guests for their "kind" words. She did what she was expected to do.

The wedding night was to be spent in the Grand Hyatt Hotel before the couple flew to Los Angeles for their honeymoon. Apart from a flirtatious, fumbling attempt at intimacy with a female university friend, Mejung had not tasted sexual pleasure. Sure, she had kissed a man here and there but these contacts were almost hands free. Unbeknown to Mejung, her new husband, Minho, had spent a lot of his father's money on gambling and prostitutes. The gambling was usually unsuccessful and the couplings bitter. He had never experienced sexual sharing; he had only experienced sexual power. Minho was physically, emotionally and sexually stunted but he had learned to wear a charismatic public face. He was gregarious and he was a Seoul National University graduate, so he had prestige. And, his father was rich.

After the wedding reception, Minho dragged his new wife

off to a soju bar. He met two of his gambling companions and the three men drank six bottles of soju in under an hour. Mejung, in her honeymoon clothes, sat silent and confused. The men laughed and joked about sexual conquests. The men's eyes undressed her. Again, she was alone.

It was after midnight when the newly married couple opened the door to the honeymoon suite of the Grand Hyatt Hotel. Minho stumbled in first and Mejung hesitantly followed.

"Undress."

Mejung struggled for a reply, "What? Come-on honey let's sit and talk for a while."

"Undress now."

Mejung sat on the sofa and put her hands in her lap and stared at them. Her soul flew out of the closed window and hovered outside as she unbuttoned her coat.

Minho opened the mini-bar and took out a miniature bottle of whiskey. He unscrewed the cap and swallowed the contents in one draught; then, he opened another bottle.

Mejung fumbled with her clothing, wishing her husband of 5 hours would fall over drunk. He didn't; he stared at her. "Hurry up." She was down to her briefs and bra and she was sitting on the sofa again looking at her hands. Her soul still hovered outside the closed window. Minho put the whiskey bottle on the top of the fridge. He moved to the bedhead and picked up a bottle of complimentary moisturizer. Mejung continued to stare at her hands and she cried silently. Minho took a strong grip on her upper arm and lifted her roughly to her feet. He spun her around and bent her over the back of the sofa. He fumbled with his belt and zipper, and then tore off her briefs. With his pants around his ankles, Minho roughly slapped moisturizer between Mejung's legs and mounted her from behind. He pushed with his semi-erect drunkenness and grunted, pushed and grunted.

Ten minutes later, Minho was collapsed on the bed, snoring.

Mejung was sitting on the sofa wearing a hotel issue bathrobe. Her soul had returned and her eyes were dry.

She had been a confident and well-liked middle school student in Australia; she had been a confident and competent university student; she was intelligent. How did it get to this?

It only got worse.

June 29, 1995, Mejung Oh stepped out of a taxi just a block away from the Sampoong Department Store in the wealthy district of Seocho-gu, Seoul. It was 5:45pm. She had spent most of the day talking aimlessly with a couple of friends while drinking coffee. She liked to reminisce about her middle school years at Penleigh Girls Grammar School in Australia and her friends had similar experiences in other foreign countries. They were all escaping the present. One of her friends related a story she'd read about the gangs of Busan and their move into forged identity documents. All laughed at the unreality of starting a new life in Busan with forged documents.

Before she left, she told her friends that she was going to the department store to buy some groceries. She needed to get some food for dinner. Her husband demanded that dinner be on the table at 7:30pm. He sometimes attended; he often did not come home for days. She had no way of knowing if he would be home this evening but deep bruises on her upper thighs and buttocks had trained her to have dinner ready. And, she was running late. She was thinking about bulgogi for dinner with melon for dessert. She could get these things from the supermarket in the basement of the department store.

What Mejung didn't know was that the executives and owners of the building had hurriedly exited a few hours before she stepped out of the taxi. Cracks had appeared and quickly widened in the supporting columns of the executive offices and the walls of the fifth floor, which housed an illegally built food court. Rather than warn the workers and shoppers, these men quietly but hurriedly fled. The owners would later say that they didn't want to close the building because they didn't want to lose the revenue from the thousands of shoppers who would pass through that day.

The building was doomed from its beginnings. It was built on a landfill and shortcuts were taken in construction. Instead of 16 reinforcing bars in the support columns, only 8 were used. Bribes were paid for inspectors to turn a blind eye. Bribes were paid to government officials to allow flawed designs to be approved. The original construction company refused to construct the building without significant changes to the design. They were fired and the Sampoong Construction Company completed the work. The family owned company was fabulously rich, owning varied and diverse companies. Sampoong Department Store stood for five years before it collapsed as though a demolition crew had done a perfect job. 502 lives were extinguished in a matter of minutes, all for the greed of the already rich. Mejung missed this fate by a few minutes.

She exited the taxi and stood on the pavement across from the department store. The taxi drove away and the building came down. The crashing concrete and buckling steel partially deafened her and she watched the horror with dull eyes. Dust and death clung to her face and clothes; she stood and watched. Before the sirens of emergency vehicles began to wail, she pulled her ID Card from her purse and walked to the edge of the desolation. She hesitated for a mere moment before throwing the card into the confusion. She watched it fly out before spirally down; then, she slowly walked away.

As she walked, she pulled her cell phone from her bag and turned it off and she headed to the nearest ATM and withdrew the Korean equivalent of $3000. She hoped it would last for a month or two. At a small local market, she bought a cheap pair of jeans, a few shirts, underwear, a peaked cap, running shoes and a backpack. No one asked about her dustiness; no one seemed to care; everyone was listening to radios and talking about the Sampoong disaster. Some had been to the site to get an understanding of what had happened; some had stayed to watch but others, the ladies who sat around the radio, had found the horror too much to stomach. Mejung changed into her new clothes in a public toilet at a subway station and washed her face. Before exiting the toilet, she stuffed her dusty clothes into her backpack, piled her hair up on top of her head and pulled her new cap low. She walked out of the toilet feeling very alone and she bought a subway ticket to Seoul Station.

At the entrance to Seoul Station, a middle-aged man covered in Christian symbols with a lightweight, plastic cross strapped to his back was proselytizing about the Department Store collapse. He held a bible in his left hand and a megaphone in his right and he ranted about the devastation being the wrath of God. "SINNERS WILL DIE AND BELIEVERS WILL BE SPARED. IT IS THE WORD OF GOD. HEED THE WORD OF GOD. REPENT THY SINS AND LIVE IN THE EMBRACE OF JESUS. JESUS LOVES YOU; RETURN HIS LOVE AND LIVE WITHOUT SIN OR DIE IN CHAOS. EMBRACE THE LOVE OF GOD BECAUSE GOD LOVES YOU. JESUS LOVES YOU."

Mejung moved past the man without looking at him and approached the ticket counter where she bought a train ticket to Busan.

The overnight train took 5 hours and she slept little and cried in tearless silence. She arrived on the morning of June 30 and it was Jinni who stepped off the train. The first thing Jinni needed to do was discard all evidence of Mejung. In the Busan Railway Station toilet, she removed her driver's license, credit card and phone from her purse and stuffed them into the bottom of her pack. She folded her dusty clothes and stuffed these into a plastic shopping bag. She was tempted to just discard the cards and phone but she figured they could be of value. She needed a new identity and she might be able to sell her old identity to buy the new one.

As Jinni walked through the station, she dropped the shopping bag of dusty clothes into a rubbish bin and she stopped in front of a TV being watched by a crowd. Scenes of destruction, excavators digging into the broken concrete and twisted metal, and the sirens drowned the reporter's sincere sadness. Black body bags, some bulging and some almost empty, were being loaded into ambulances. Middle-aged women were squatting in groups watching and wailing while men stared blankly at what was once Sampoong Department Store. Jinni moved on and placed her backpack into a station coin-locker.

The sun was shining as she exited Busan Rail Station, and she headed across the road to the nightclub area of Choryang Dong. She ignored the three ajumma at the entrance to Gogwan Street and they watched her enter with little interest. They were listening to a radio tuned to the news. It was just approaching noon so life on the streets of this nightclub district known as Texas Street was quiet. Jinni needed this quiet time to explore so that when she returned at night, she would not look out of place. She needed to look comfortable and assured if she was going to avoid trouble.

She stepped around a small pancake of vomit just beyond the group of ajumma. Cigarette butts lay abandoned and a disheveled homeless man crouched low and selected the most smokable. Jinni turned into Choryangjung Street and nearly tripped over a US Soldier collapsed in a doorway. Spew stained his shirt; his left hand lightly gripped an empty stubby of Budweiser; a cigarette, burned to the filter, hung from the limp fingers of his right hand; his eyelids hung heavy and he tried to focus on the passerby. He failed and fell back into his stupor. "Ayego" She spoke aloud this Korean exclamation that roughly translates to "Oh my God" or "Shit." And, she walked on noting where nightclubs were, where salon bars were, where bars were. The cooking smells of kimchi chigae, budae chigae and soondae guk hung limp in the air. And, Jinni remembered everything. Jinni had a fantastic memory, trained by the Korean education system that rewarded memorization. Jinni possessed an almost photographic memory and a creative and inquisitive mind from her middle school years in Australia. But, for more than a few years, these qualities had been neglected as she just tried to survive her married life. She had felt hopelessness and helpless and it had taken 502 deaths to give her a second chance. We worship a cruel and violent God.

After a day of exploring the seedy side of Busan, Jinni returned to the Rail Station. She thought about staying in a hotel; she had the money but she couldn't bear the thought of being alone. She certainly didn't want to talk or interact with anyone but she didn't want to be alone in empty space, not just yet. The hustle of the rail station and the anonymity of the crowds suited her for the time being. She removed her backpack from the locker and washed in the bathroom. She sat with travelers waiting to depart, but she was going nowhere. She just pretended she was but she had arrived at her destination; she just did not know how to stay. The night closed around the station but it did not penetrate the fluorescent interior. Jinni slept on and off. She dreamt of her mother, the woman who refused to listen to her pleas for assistance and protection. Inhee claimed that a husband must be obeyed. She had always obeyed Mejung's father and her life was fine. She did not have to work and she enjoyed shopping and gossiping although she claimed that she was not gossiping but talking over important issues with her friends. Jinni knew that her mother's "important issues" revolved around the lives of others: whose daughters were marrying whom and whose sons were working where. Jinni hated all this and all it stood for; she hated herself for having submitted to that lifestyle, but her desire to make a phone call left her in tears, real tears. She walked a little distance to be amongst a large group watching the Sampoong horror on television. Some of the women in the group were sobbing in empathy with the shattered families and not all the men were dry eyed. Jinni sat with them and allowed the tears to flow. She wept for the lost souls and their shattered families; she cried for her own family.

She shed tears for almost all she had left behind, but not one tear fell with Minho's name on it. An hour passed and the names of the dead flowed from stranger's eyes and Jinni walked away.

She spent another night on a bench in the Busan Rail Station. She slept some; she wept some; she stared into the vacant future and she woke with a start and opened her eyes to a foreigner kneeling beside her. His hand was on her backpack, but he quickly backed away when she woke. She looked around but there was no one within complaining distance and what was there to say? Jinni picked up her bag and stood on unsteady feet. She returned her backpack into the coin locker before walking to the railway station exit, but she almost stumbled and it was then she realized that she had not eaten since lunch with her friends in Seoul an epoch ago. "Friends" she said out loud. She needed to taste the word and it tasted bitter. It was 9am and the exit was a river of people coming and going. On the sidewalk, she stopped at a street vendor and bought a small plastic bowl of *tteokbokki*. She tried to eat slowly but she scoffed down the rice cakes in hot chili sauce. She was just one of many workers grabbing a quick snack. She moved onto the *oden* food vendor and ate three sticks of the fish cakes. Finally, she crossed the road to Paris Baguette for coffee and a sandwich. She also took the time to sit and think.

CHAPTER 4

Running and Thinking

Stan is a regular runner and while he runs he thinks about things that have happened and he plans variations to his future. He has several running routes but his favorite takes him up to the Hyatt Hotel and then north along the 402-bus route before entering Namsan Park.

As soon as he arrives at his apartment, he changes into his running gear and it is not long before he is pushing up the hill away from his dwelling. He runs strongly up to the Hyatt Hotel. It is a steep climb and he concentrates on his breathing and his footfalls. His sports watch beeps each kilometer and as he turns left at the Hyatt, it beeps for the second time. He checks his time and smiles to himself. The next two kilometers are pretty flat as the road follows the bus route to the north. Stan is in a solid rhythm and he is able to give his mind freedom.

"Just a dream?, Don't think so ... It wouldn't bother me, probably wouldn't even remember it, rarely remember dreams ...

... Can't remember any dream I've had before these Jinni dreams, memory failing like my mother's, nothing to do with the quality of the dream, wonder how mum's getting along ... sharp mind, failing body ...

... Home care is really good, Visiting nurses like her, She doesn't

complain, She's funny, She laughs at herself ... And other people enjoy laughing with her."

Stan's watch beeps again and he looks and sees that he is on a solid pace.

"Reality in this dream? ... too spooky ... Dreams affecting reality?, Dreams are not predictors of the future, Jung says fragments of the past distorted by subconscious ...,

... Feel this dream is a predictor of possible future, Many possible futures ... this dream is looking down one route ...

... A bit like running, can choose any route but today, this one, Might change direction at half way mark, at any point really, Running strongly, I think ... want to maintain pace ... Beautiful day, I do like the Garchy ... quirky like the Australian magpie, but Korean quirky"

And he smiles and enjoys the sun on his shoulders.

"Hope for a tan, Being brown makes me stronger, Just a mind thing ... is this Jinni dream my mind playing tricks, How vivid can a dream get and still be a dream...?

... Freud said a cigar was a penis substitute but he also said that a cigar can be just a cigar, A dream just a dream?, Can be substitute for reality?, An alternative reality?"

Beep, and Stan checks his time as he turns off the 402-bus route and heads up a steep hill that will take him past the Yongsan Library and through the Namsan car park. His time has dropped off. He empties his mind and returns his focus to his breathing and footfalls. He is pushing it hard up the steep hill and at the top of the rise he gives himself 15 seconds to drink from the water fountain before he picks his way down the steep stairs.

"Never counted these steps, got to be a hundred maybe 75, maybe 130 ... Careful, steps are steep, would be nasty fall, Good the bottom ... build the rhythm again."

Stan runs 200 meters and enters Namsan Park and onto the rubberized running track from the western end. It winds gently up and down for three and a half kilometers.

"Good the track, love the light filtering through the trees, Should be cooling down in Australia now, Nice time of year in both hemispheres ... The bark on the beech trees look like skin, I've seen girls with beautiful skin in this country but Jinni's was spectacular, darker than amber, browner, not so orange ...

... I don't understand the Korean fixation with white skin, Wish my skin was darker ... but I want to keep my blue eyes, 'Ah laddy ye want all I see,' Well yeah, what's wrong with a wish here and there?, I wish I wish, I wish I wish ..., 'For what does ye wish laddy?,' I wish to see Jinni in the flesh, Or dream ... but to see her in reality ... to touch her skin for real, As Vince would say, Jaysus that'd be special, like real special."

Stan's watch signals the five-kilometer mark and his running has become a bit ragged.

"'Now don't get ahead of yourself laddy,' I know, I know, What do I know about what?, Nobody knows what nobody knows said the Garchy to the worm, Squirrels, great, gather all you can, spring is short in this country and winter is long and bloody cold ... Should get myself a new quilt while they're on special in the market ...

... I feel like singing, just like Leo Sayer, Actually I don't want to sing like Leo Sayer, Jinni oh Jinni with the long brown legs, Oh jinni with the great big smile, Shut-up, that's pathetic, Concentrate on your running for a while, Come on empty your mind, A little bit of Zen-running is needed."

The six-kilometer mark and then the seven-kilometer mark are signaled by beeps and Stan has 500 meters to push hard to the end of the running track and the little, free, open-air, gym. But, he sees Jinni walking along a gravel track parallel to the running track. Trees obscure his view. And then, he is on the ground and a young child is crying and a mother is yelling. Stan ran over the top of the kid and now both are on all fours and both are bleeding from scraped knees.

"Chosahumnida, I'm sorry, I'm sorry"

The mother fusses over her child as Stan gets to his feet and looks over to the gravel path but an ajumma is looking back at him and shaking her head. There is no Jinni. He turns back to the mother and bows to her. She picks up her kid, turns her back and walks away; the child's cries turn to whimpers and Stan looks around at other faces staring at him.

His breathing and heart rate return to normal but shame keeps his face flushed. Everyone is looking at him and every look is an accusation.

He walks off in the direction of the gym with his eyes on the ground. By the time he gets to the natural spring near the gym, no witnesses remain. He washes the blood from his knees; the damage is minor. And, for 30 minutes, he punishes himself with weights and he tries hard not to think but he keeps seeing a vision of Jinni holding a child with bleeding knees.

Finished with the punishment, Stan decides to take the short route back. It is a four-kilometer run back to his apartment, and after a steep climb of about 700 meters, it is downhill all the way. He limps along at a sad pace and his Granny lets him know all about it.

CHAPTER 5

The Boys and Beer

At 9pm, Vince and Stan greet each other on the street below Scrooge Tavern. On the way up the stairs to the fourth floor they talk about family back in their home countries. Vince talks about his mother's failing mind and Stan tells how his mother's mind is razor sharp, although her memory is creatively selective, but her body is failing. Once they are seated and have ordered a beer each, Stan remembers Vince's tango class, "So tell us about the tango."

"It was good ... enjoyed myself ... got to interact with people. You know, I've spent a lot of time in front of the computer working on different programs and assessing my students' program writing; I needed a break. And ... I've been going to a little café lately and I got talking to the girl who works there."

"A woman?"

"Jaysus, mate," Vince regularly channels his Irish ancestry through his use of language, "Give us a break. Anyway, I was talking to her and she invited me to her tango class and I just thought I'd go."

"So."

"I'm loving it."

"You loving the girl?"

"Back off."

Stan can't hold back any longer. He needs to talk about his dream, "I've been having weird dreams."

"What? That's a quick change of direction. I hope you don't want to go into a moment by moment recounting of this dream. I don't need to be bored stupid by someone else's nighttime visions ... Jaysus, you've got to give a bloke a bit more warning when you change direction." Vince downs the remainder of his beer and orders another. "I hope I don't regret this; in fact, ... fuck it, get on with it. But I warn you, bore me and I'm out."

The music in the bar is a little loud but it surrounds the two friends like silence. Stan doesn't even know what the music is; it is just sound to him. He raises his glass of beer to his lips and drinks deeply, swallowing twice, before he returns the glass to the bar top. He starts by musing about the possibility of his dream being a crack in the universe.

Vince is quick to reply, "Are we talking a Star Trek crack or a Dr. Who crack?"

"I'm serious Vince."

"Stan, Stan, mate; it's a metaphor, a metaphor; get on with it before I walk out."

Stan tears at the edges of his beer coaster, "Not sure, I told you it's pretty weird. I am here and then I'm somewhere else. I think I am with someone and then I am not. I think I am awake but then I wake-up."

"Sounds like a dream to me."

"No, it's deeper. Sometimes I wake-up and my feet are sore. I can almost feel blisters. And, this girl that I am in love with in the dream..."

"Back-up a bit. You said 'love' like loving love?"

Stan ignores the interruption. "Her skin has the quality of polished honey and I feel as if I know her, like really know her, but I don't ... I don't think I do, but I feel like I should know her."

"Should know her? Do love her? Explain Mr. Spock."

Stan looks at his friend and shakes his head as he answers, "Yeah, I should but I don't ... I don't know what's happening but the reality of the meetings go beyond a dream. But she doesn't let me touch her."

Vince drinks from his beer and the sounds from the pool table compete with the music and Stan's dream. He absently watches the old, drunk Korean guy clear the table and Stan's tale continues while Vince's interest is taken up by the pool game. Mr. Kim staggers; he sways and he rarely misses. The young Westerner waits impatiently for a shot but he never gets a chance. The two pool players shake hands. The old guy shrugs and grins broadly while the young guy shuffles back to his seat and his cheerless beer.

Stan finishes retelling his dream while pool balls collide and drop and Vince brings his mind back and asks, "You drinking much? I've never seen you really drunk but I know you drink alone at home. How much are you putting away in the evenings?"

"Not much."

"What does that mean?"

"You know ... I drink often, but I'm never shitfaced. I drink a glass or two of wine or whiskey while watching television but that's about it."

Vince looks at his friend pick his second coaster to bits, "Do you think these dreams have anything to do with alcohol?"

And, the two friends continue speculating without resolution over several more beers until Stan says, "Ok, I'm out."

"Me too."

And with that Stan and Vince walk toward the door. Mr. Kim is in the stairwell returning from the bathroom and he smiles and challenges Stan to a game of pool. The offer is declined with a returned smile and the two men continue down the stairs and out into the open air. They do not shake hands in farewell. There is a mutual, "See ya." And both turn heel and wander off in opposite directions.

Vince heads off knowing that he will stop off somewhere for a few more beers.

Stan walks up the steep hill toward his apartment where he will do exactly as he told Vince he does, drink wine and watch TV, before bedding down to dream or not to dream.

Mr. Kim, on the other hand, will continue to play pool and drink. He has been playing pool and drinking for a long time. He enjoys besting the young foreigners. He used to work on the local US Military Base. He worked there for 30 years. He learned to play pool; he learned English; he made friends. The US soldiers were always coming and going and most thought of him fondly. The local Korean Base workers shared the experience of being foreigners in their own land. They were a strong clique of shared uniqueness; they understood each other. But then, he turned 55 and he was told that his services were no longer needed. "Retire and enjoy your life," the US Soldier said to him. But, the Base was his life. He had status, friends and an income but the US Military is not compassionate and they took away his Base Pass. For two years, he pined for his old life. He drank soju and was bored with his wife; actually, he had always been bored with his wife, and the boredom was mutual. Their marriage had been arranged a lifetime ago and they had never learned to communicate, but he misses his daughter.

In an attempt to fill the vacuum of loss, he sat alone in Pagoda Park with the other *ajeoshi* and these middle-aged men endured a mutual solitude, together in their loneliness. He tried his hand at paduk without much success. If new faces came to the park, he bored them with stories of his "life with the Americans." No one was interested in the other. No one asked about the other and no one offered self. These men protected their loneliness as if it was something worth protecting. Then, he discovered the bars of Itaewon. He staggered in one night desperate for attention. He was looking for the familiar. He was looking to replicate his old life. He put his name on the pool players' chalkboard, won his first match easily and he has been a fixture in several bars since. He has not built friendships, he drinks too much for that, but he has built a begrudging respect amongst the Western pool playing community. Rarely is he beaten, and he drinks free and drinks often, and he remains bored with his wife and he continues to think about his lost daughter.

CHAPTER 6

A Dream not Remembered

Stan Dreams.

Stan looks down at his mother. She is lying in a hospital ward populated with three other old women. She is surprised to see him and says, "What brings you back?" He tells her that he came to see her and she quickly volleys that back. She lets him get away with some vague explanations before they move to safer territory. They talk about how dry the weather has been and the test cricket series and the upcoming football season, territory that both feel comfortable in.

One of the other patients in the room interrupts their comfort, "Why did you leave Australia? "Stan looks at his mother and she shrugs her shoulders and her eyes call him in. He obliges and puts his ear close to her mouth, "Nosey bastards."

"Boredom, I was just bored with life. You know how it gets?"

"I don't know 'how it gets.' Life is inherently boring. We sleep; we wake; we eat; we shit. That's life. It's what we do around life that makes it interesting."

Stan again looks at his mother, and she tells him that the old lady reckons she is a philosopher but, in fact, she was just an old primary school teacher.

"Shit a 'wanna be' philosopher, that's all I need."

"She's got a point though; you've been running this line every time you come back. You had a good teaching job. You did lots of things outside of work. You played tennis with Robert and you canoed and bushwalked and rock climbed with other friends. You were far from leading a bored life." She looks at the other patients and says to them, "He even spent time in the Himalaya leading treks."

She returned her eyes to her son, "Don't throw the 'I was bored" line at me again."

"You know how boring teaching is mum."

She turns on him and she is ready to tear him apart. She points out very clearly that she was a hard-working teacher for 25 years and a principal for 10. Teaching was never boring to her. She threw herself into it completely. She cared about people's lives and she points out that she has had more visits from her former students than from her only son.

The retired primary school teacher chimes in with, I still sleep, wake, eat and shit."

"What?"

Stan's mother pushes him a little further before giving up. Finally, she asks, "Have you visited your father?"

"He's dead."

"Unnecessary, son. Visit his grave ... it might help."

Stan sleeps on and his body recreates the old depressions of his childhood single bed and, when he wakes, he has no recollection of his dream but he feels a residual anger directed at his parents.

CHAPTER 7

Mr. Kim at the Tipping Point

It is past midnight when Mr. Kim slips the key into the lock of his dingy, two-bedroom apartment in Bokwang-dong. He won his snooker games and drank too much. He talked at people but listened little. He had been amongst people, but he was alone. As the door slides open, he hopes his wife is asleep but she is not; she is sitting in the living room, in the dark. Only the moonlight filtering in through the curtainless window illuminates her profile. Mr. Kim begins to walk around her to the bathroom and as he passes, his wife reaches out and clasps his arm. "Sit for a while, yobo." She has not used the honorific, "honey," for more than 10 years.

"What? Why aren't you in bed?"

"Sit a bit, please."

Mr. Kim just wants to get away. He does not want to talk. "Need to pee."

"Do you know what day today is?" She asks.

"Need to pee."

"I'll wait for you."

Mr. Kim maneuvers his way to the bathroom. He looks into the mirror and he does not like the man who looks back. He shakes his head. Mr. Kim pees into the bowl, flushes the toilet, washes his hands and throws water on his face. Since October 21, 1994 he has not spoken with any depth to his wife. They cohabitate, but they do not communicate. They rarely speak. There are nods and grunts and the occasional, "Pass the kimchi" but not much more. He walks out of the bathroom unsteady from alcohol and shaky from emotion. He sits across from his wife and looks at her like he has not looked for 10 years. He really looks. He stares at her for several minutes and then he starts to speak.

As though from a long-rehearsed script, Mr. Kim speaks, "Today is the 21st of October, exactly 10 years since the Seongsu Bridge collapsed, exactly 10 years since our daughter died, exactly 10 years since we made love. At the hospital, I stared at our daughter ... she didn't look dead ... her hair was damp ... she was in her school uniform. A deep cut ran the length of her face but she looked calm ... she looked like she'd rise from the table and smile. There were tears but I wasn't crying; you sobbed and covered your face with your hands, not that I took much notice of you. I said to her; I begged her, 'Come back Kim Miji,' but she didn't move; her face remained a greying mask ... I couldn't walk away ... I loved her. I still love her."

Mr. Kim stops talking and glares at the naked fluorescent globe on the ceiling as if looking for it can give him strength to go on. The light offers nothing.

"That day, I lost my only child and I built a wall to protect my weakness from everyone and from anything. *Yobo,* I am not the man I was before October 21 ... I don't know what I am, who I am; I only know that there is a hole deep inside and I can't fill it; nothing can, nobody can."

He sits on a straight-backed chair. His wrinkled hands enclose a knee each. He holds his wife's gaze for as long as he can. He is shattered, his rawness exposed at last. His head drops and the tears flow, at first a rivulet and finally an overflow of emotion. His shoulders heave, and he weeps for his lost daughter and he cries for lost love. Finally, there is nothing else to do. "I'm sorry, *yobo,* I'm just so sorry. Miji didn't have to catch the school bus. I should've driven her to school like I usually did. If I hadn't drunk myself senseless that night, she'd be alive today. I killed her."

"No, *yobo,* her death is not yours. Her death is God's. You're not God. You are Kim Doksun; you're human. You're fallible, and you have paid with 10 years of aloneness ... I don't blame you." Mr. Kim raises his eyes and looks at his wife, his eyes filled with self-recrimination. "I don't blame you. I never did. You blamed yourself and you retreated. On the night of October 21st our mutual guilt coupled. You probed for my life, for any life. You searched for a life to replace the lost life. We hadn't made love in years and I cried for the gift and for the loss, and we haven't made love since."

Silence, and then Mr. Kim says, "It was my choice to drink."

Almost on top of the final word, the wife says, "Enough, it is my choice to drink now. Get me soju."

"But..."

"NOW."

Mr. Kim rises, wipes his eyes with the sleeve of his shirt, turns toward the kitchen and moves away. The wife sits and looks down at her hands, the hands that had washed baby Miji, that had wiped Miji's bloodied knees, that had wiped Miji's tears, that had comforted Miji's pain, that had caressed and raised a reluctant husband. Back then those hands had the power of a wizard's wand. Today, they are as limp as her husband's masculinity. On October 21, 1994, after the death coitus, her hands lost their wizardry. Now, they just hang from the bottom of her arms; sure, they can grasp and hold, but they can no longer inspire, heal or comfort. She stares at them.

Mr. Kim returns to the living room with a bottle of soju and two shot glasses. He hands a glass to his wife and fills it for her. He then gives her the bottle and she fills his glass, ritualized customs don't die. "Cunbae," And they both throw back the liquor in one gulp and refill each other's glass. Mr. Kim's emotions have sobered him and he is ready to drink more and he is ready to open to his wife.

"Miji would have been 26 years old. We would have been grandparents... Before the night of October 21, I didn't drink that much, just an occasional drink with workmates." Mr. Kim's wife nods but remains silent. "Since October 21, the night Miji died, I haven't stopped drinking ... I think about how it could have been different ... I dream other endings and I wake to the same reality."

The old couple drink deep into the night. They move through guilt, anger at themselves and anger at Dong-ah Construction but, for the most part, they share their sadness and they share their loss. For the first time in their 28 years of married life, they talk to each other and they listen to each other. They share the horror of a daughter dying.

During this time, Mr. Kim and his wife sit across from each other. They alternate with who rises to get another bottle of soju and they alternate with toilet breaks. At no time do they rise together and at no time do they touch. But, they are more connected than they have been for many years. Their tears are the same and they flow for the same cause, mutual loss and self. The sun is not far from rising when Mr. Kim pushes himself off his chair and stumbles into the bedroom. His wife watches him leave but she says nothing; she thinks the night is over and she sits inside her personal sadness, and she feels lightened. A few minutes later, Mr. Kim returns with his arms filled with a sleeping '*yo*' duvet and pillows. As he drops them onto the living-room floor, his wife stifles a sob and drops to her knees beside her husband and the two of them arrange the bedding. They do not speak.

"I'll get our pajamas," says the wife.

"No," and Mr. Kim lets his hand fall on his wife's arm.

"Just lie down," and the two of them do. Fully clothed, they lie on their backs and hold hands until sleep takes them ...

... Mr. Kim calls to his daughter. "Are you ready?"

"I've been waiting for you, ..."

Mr. Kim smiles as his daughter brushes by him, her shoulder rubbing against his. She is taller than her father and she is only 16.

"Let's go; I don't want to be late for English class."

"Ok, let's talk English as we drive."

"Ahh, come on dad, you speak English with an outrageous Korean accent."

"Whadaya mean? My American soldier friends say I speak English good."

Miji looks across at her father and feigns horror, "Whadaya? What kind of English is that? And it is, 'Speak English well'"

Mr. Kim smiles at his daughter and tries to sound hurt, "It's American English and 'good/well'... same-same."

"Dad, my English teacher is from Melbourne, Australia and he would spit the dummy if he heard 'whadaya' and 'speak English good'"

Mr. Kim is genuinely puzzled, "Spit the dummy, what does that mean?"

"Maybe for your American English it should be 'Spit the pacifier.'"

Mr. Kim's expression remains the same. He mouths the expression a few times but he shakes his head. "No, that doesn't help."

"Idiom dad, idiom, think about it."

Mr. Kim's brow wrinkles. "Come on Dad, get in the car. You can think about it as we drive."

Father and daughter sit side by side in the family car with their heads turned toward each other. They smile and the father starts the engine and off they go ...

... Mother and daughter walk arm-in-arm toward the entrance to the yoga studio. Miji is 20 and filled with life. She is long limbed and lithe. Her skin is pure and alabaster white. Her hair is black silk. Her eyes are naturally big, full and almost black, only a hint of brown in her irises. "Are you ready for this, mum?"

"Of course, my flexibility is superior to yours."

"Dream on, old woman." And, Miji shares a big smile.

"What? Come on girl, get into those tighty, tight shorts of yours and let us see who does the 'downward dog' with the better form."

"Me, me, me." And, mother and daughter slide open the door, have their membership cards swiped and head to the change rooms ...

... Miji is 21 years old and her father thinks it is time to find a good man.

"Kim Miji, this is a special guy. He is a graduate of Sogang University. His father is the CEO of a large company. You'll like him. Please, give him a chance."

"Jees dad, don't take life so seriously. I just want to hang out with my girlfriends. 'Girls just gotta have fun' you know."

Mr. Kim looks at his daughter and his voice is serious when he says, "I was 25 when I married your mother and your mother was 21."

"So ... what's that got to do with my life?"

"Please give him a chance, Miji ... for me?"

"Look, I'll meet him but I promise nothing. If he bores me, I'm out. Dad, I love you, but I love what I am doing and I'm very happy with my friends; I don't need a man."

Mr. Kim pulls the car up to the Hyatt Hotel. "Enjoy yourself Miji."

"I will because I'm not staying if he's not fun."

With those words hanging in the air, Miji opens the door, gives a little wave to her father before bouncing off toward the hotel entrance...

... Miji is 26 and she meets with her mother in Starbucks.

"Mum, I like a man."

"That's nice dear. How old is he?"

"I am not sure."

"You're not sure ... well, what university did he go to?"

"Melbourne University."

"I don't know that university; is it in Deagu?"

Miji pauses before she says, "It's in Australia."

"Oh, it's nice that he was able to get a foreign education. What high school did he go to?"

There is another pause before she answers, "Essendon Grammar School."

CHAPTER 8

Prepare to be Weirded-Out

Some days Stan's teaching experiences throw up unusual moments and today's moments have been stranger than most. He uses speed dial to call Vince, and after a few rings, Vince answers. "I need a beer; I've got something weird to tell you."

"More dreams?"

"No, although today's experience may invoke nightmares."

"Ok, meet you at *Scrooge,* one hour."

"Sounds good, maybe a game of pool?" It has been a while since the two friends have played.

"Maybe, but not if Mr. Kim is on the table."

"Fair enough. See you in an hour"

Stan has had a few peaceful weeks. He hasn't met with Vince; he hasn't drunk too much; he has been eating well and most of his dreams have been uneventful, just dreams, not memorable and not remembered, although Jinni continues to make the occasional chaste appearance.

An hour later the two men are seated at the bar and ordering beer. Vince orders San Miguel and Stan orders CASS and they are soon drinking their first draught.

"Be prepared to be weirded-out."

And, Stan starts:

"I've been instructing a 55-year-old woman for a few months who calls herself Bette after the actress Bette Davis, but today I knocked on the door of her luxurious apartment in the wealthy district of Apkujong-dong to find that she had invited three of her middle-aged friends. This was not a concern because I had told Bette that if she wanted to have group classes, it was ok with me. I did let her know that the fee would double but money was not an issue for people like Bette.

The four women were much alike. They all wore sophisticated, designer clothes. All wore their dyed black hair short with a designer wave. All wore their make-up light and comfortably. They were good-looking women, sophisticated women. They were women of wealth, style and culture.

The living room, where the women were seated on leather sofas, was a good 15 square meters. The carpet was plush in understated beige and the women rubbed their bare toes through the luxurious pile. I was shown to a familiar well-padded armchair and I nodded greetings as I sat."

Stan explains to Vince that Bette speaks very good English and he suspects her lessons are more of a social event than a lesson. They sometimes meet in her apartment but they often meet in cafes or restaurants. She does not want to use a textbook. He enjoys her company, and she enjoys his. The three new women had also adopted English names from famous actresses. They were introduced as Grace (Kelly), Julia (Roberts) and Audrey (Hepburn).

"Lame, yes but not weird."

"Mate, every good story needs a strong exposition. I am just setting the scene."

"I got it: four rich old ladies in an expensive apartment."

Stan swallows a gulp of beer before going back to his story:

"I was offered my customary cup of green tea and while Bette was preparing the tea in the kitchen, I asked Grace, Julia and Audrey a few basic 'get to know you' questions. Their English level was advanced and it was an easy conversation and I couldn't help thinking about the easy money. Bette returned with five cups on a tray and handed the tea around, offering me a cup first. We all sipped tea and chatted aimlessly but comfortably. Grace spoke for the group when she said that they had all studied in US when they were young but they rarely practiced English here in Korea. She told how they traveled abroad at least once a year and they wanted to keep their English proficiency high. I tried to put the women at ease by letting them know that I would be happy to help them."

Stan turns to look at Vince before saying, "And then, it got weird. You won't believe what they asked me to do."

"Has the exposition finished?"

"You bet; the crisis is on us."

Stan downs the rest of his beer and orders another, and Vince has a few centimeters left in the bottom of his glass but orders a refill in anticipation of being finished by the time the new beer arrives.

Stan waits for the beers to arrive before returning to his story. While he is waiting, he asks, "So Vince, you going to tango again?"

"Jaysus, you can change tack quicker than a racing yachtsman. Anyway, I think so. I want to go out with the girl again and I actually enjoyed the dancing. I enjoyed the non-obligatory physical contact and the movement. I'm not going to say I had rhythm but I enjoyed it ... Yeah, I want to do it again. And yes, before you go asking, I still like the girl."

The beer arrives; both thank the Pilipino bartender and Vince pays before he encourages Stan to continue his story. "Come on, you're at the crisis, get on with it."

Stan drinks half his beer in one dose, places the glass back on the bar and continues.

"Your tango and this story have a bit in common because Bette asked me if I wanted to earn a million won for half an hour's work."

"Bejaysus Mary and feckin Joseph, a thousand dollars for half an hour? Are you kidding? You said yes, right?"

Stan fumbled with his beer and continued to tell his tale.

"Bette handed me a folded note and asked me to go into the bathroom and read the instructions. The bathroom was as big as my bedroom; actually, it was bigger and I sat on the edge of the bath and unfolded the note."

If you wish to earn a million won in 30 minutes, this is what you have to do.

We want you to vacuum the carpet in the living room.

This sounds like a simple enough task, but we want more than just vacuuming. We want you to vacuum while wearing only underpants. We want you to vacuum with dance moves.

If you choose to accept this job, open the package on top of the toilet.

Before exiting the bathroom, flush this note down the toilet.

"I opened the package and inside was a new pair of Calvin Klein underpants and an envelope filled with 20 x 50,000 won notes."

"Vince, I stood looking at myself in the mirror. I didn't know what to do."

"So, what did you do?"

"I flushed the note as instructed, stripped off my clothes, slipped into the new Calvin Klein's—they were peach and fitted me perfectly—and I boldly went where no man had gone before."

"Before I exited the bathroom, I heard the Bee Gees' "Staying Alive" being played at moderate volume. I rolled my eyes, took one last look in the mirror and bounced out of the bathroom doing an impression of Mick Jaguar's chicken strut with pout. I noticed a very expensive looking vacuum cleaner in the middle of the room and I strutted toward it. I bent over straight legged and pulled the cord from its recess. I Michael Jackson moonwalked to the wall socket and plugged in the cord before gliding back to the middle of the room where I performed a few Elvis knee shakes and air-guitar arm swings. The four women sat on their sofas eating crackers and nuts and drinking green tea. They chattered away as if it was a normal social gathering and they dropped crumbs at their feet. I maneuvered the head of the cleaner around the women's feet. Every now and then, one of the women would put her toe on a nut or a crumb. I needed to bend and lift the foot to vacuum under it. I gently caressed each foot as I lifted it and placed it back on the plush piles some time later. And, I moved back to the wide spaces of the living room after every foot excursion. I danced with my vacuum cleaner partner and Barry Gibb's falsetto helped me disappear into the moment."

"Are you serious? You've got to be making this up."

"I'm not creative enough to make up shit like that."

"So, what happened in the end?"

"The music ended; my time was up. I walked—I did not dance—back to the bathroom and I did not look at the women. When I got into the bathroom, I locked the door. And then, without thinking I ran the bath. I filled it with warm, almost hot water."

"Vince, the water pressure was fantastic; in fact, I haven't seen water pressure like that since I was hanging with a Taiwanese cellist whom I kept dating because her shower had great pressure, far better than my shower in Itaewon has."

Stan goes back to the story, "The tub was filled in no time. So, I slipped out of my peach colored Calvin Klein's and merged with the water. And, for the first time in a long time, I soaked in a bath? There was a knock on the door but I ignored it. They called my name a couple of times but then there was silence. I just soaked. I soaked away my shame; I tried to soak away my dreams and my life. I soaked for a good 15 minutes and, eventually, I took a deep breath and submerged for as long as he could. I held on and held on; I tried not to come up but I came up hurting for air. Then, I pulled the plug and stepped out of the bath. I felt kind of cleansed and I was ready to move forward. The towel was the softest towel I've ever used and I dried myself slowly and then, I slipped back into my clothes. When I exited the bathroom, there was no one to be seen. The women had left the living room and a backpack was sitting in the middle of the empty space, right where the vacuum cleaner had been ... it too had disappeared along with the women. I stood in the middle of the room for a few minutes before picking up my pack; I put my hard earned million won and my new peach colored Calvin Klein's into it and walked toward the door. Before opening the door, I took one last look around; the place was definitely empty. I opened the door, walked through and closed it quietly behind me."

"Jaysus, I don't know what to say."

"Neither do I."

"Do you think you'll hear from this Bette woman again?"

"No idea, absolutely no idea. To be continued ..."

Both sit in silence for a few minutes; both men's thoughts drift until Vince interrupts the silence.

"So, why'd you do it? Did you need the money?"

"No, not money. I don't know ... I felt compelled."

"Compelled? What does that mean? The bath tells me you felt dirty."

"Don't know; I just went with it." And Stan tries to change the subject, "Snooker?"

"You need to think seriously about the 'why.'"

"Snooker?"

"Yeah, fine ... typically illusive. Sometimes you can be a total wanker."

Stan's reply is, "Let's get a few games in before Mr. Kim arrives."

They play two games and during that time they laugh at Stan's vacuum cleaner dance routine. Stan moonwalks around the table; Vince tangos with his cue as his partner, dipping her regularly. Stan tries a Mick Jaguar Pout, and both laugh some more. And then, Mr. Kim arrives and writes his name on the white board.

"I play winner."

"No, no Mr. Kim, Vince and I are finished. Table is yours. We know your talents far too well. I wouldn't play against you if you gave me four balls start."

"I give you six." Responds Mr. Kim.

This is the signal for the two of them to move back to their bar stools where they talk for a while longer covering varying topics, but they almost always return to vacuum cleaner dancing.

"If you'd taken tango lessons, you might have been left a tip."

"Yeah right, the gig's yours next time."

While Stan and Vince drink and talk, Mr. Kim makes a mess of two Western boys in quick time. He drains his first victory beer and moves onto his second. Four victories in and four beers down, he takes a rest and leaves the table. He goes to the toilet and when he returns, he settles down to some serious drinking. He chases his beer with Jack Daniels and ice.

"Ok, I'm done." Says Stan.

"Yeah, I'll stay for a few more. Can't say I'll ever look at a vacuum cleaner the same; in fact, don't want one in my apartment anymore."

"Yeah, yeah, see ya," And with that, Stan is out of the door and heading for home.

Once home, Stan pours himself a glass of single malt whiskey, sits on the sofa and sips in silence until the glass is empty. He keeps thinking of Vince's "Why" but he can't come up with a reason.

Eventually he rinses the glass in the sink, brushes his teeth and retires for the night. As he lies in bed, just before sleep takes him, a vision of Mr. Kim passes behind his eyes. He struggles to shake the vision and sleep does not come easily.

CHAPTER 9

Miji Arrives in Lisbon

Stan finds himself sitting in a café in the shadow of Castelo de São Jorge in the Alfarmer district of Lisbon, Portugal. He is sitting alone but he chats with the waiter while sipping an espresso. He watches people; he tries to make eye contact but arouses little interest. He is not as young as he once was. He is not even sure if the passers-by actually see him; they appear to look straight through him. In fact, the only person who acknowledges him is the waiter. He remembers the waiter and the waiter remembers him from a visit a year ago. The waiter is an aspiring photographer who still uses film. He wants to own the great shot, not fluke the one good shot on a flash drive of hope. Stan orders another espresso and a pastel de nata. He has a thing about these little egg tarts.

With dusk come the swallows. They are free to move from one side of the castle wall to the other. Stan would have to pay to enter the castle. These swallows have recently migrated from Africa. They are silhouetted against the cyan blue of the Lisbon sky, and they are nesting in the eaves and other crannies of the castle and its wall. He envies the freedom of movement. But, he does not envy the hardship of migration. A long flight in a plane is nothing to a swallow's flight across the Sahara. Stan can order a glass of wine, a glass of water; a meal is delivered to his seat but a swallow must fatten up before the flight. The swallow does not even have a choice of flight or no flight; instinct drives it and death takes many on the journey.

The sun has left the sky and continues its never-ending westward journey and a Fado band begins its mournful melody. Stan is drawn to it. He rises from his chair, fumbles in his pocket for more than enough euros to pay his bill. He leaves the coins on the table and walks into the night drawn by the music. He approaches a Fado tavern and the band is set up on the open-air terrace. On the microphone is *Amália da Piedade Rodrigues*. She is singing of loss, of poverty and resignation to this loss and poverty and she is singing in black and white. Fado is all about fate. It is a Portuguese shrug of the shoulders, a musical "What will be will be." And, *Amália da Piedade Rodrigues* was the queen of Fado in the mid 1900's. *Amália* was of poverty. She grew up on the streets of Lisbon and sang on those same streets from the age of 5. She sold fruit and did whatever she could to bring food to the mouths of her family. Her Fado laments were her laments. Her beauty was unquestionable and her red lips contrast with the black and white of Stan's vision. And, she died in 1999.

Amália da Piedade Rodrigues' image twists and fades; the audience is enthusiastic. They applaud; they stand; they whistle, but she continues to fade and is soon no more. But, in her place, growing more solid by the note is *Maria Severa Onofriana*. Stan takes a seat in the back of the black and white audience. He looks around at the fashion and looks down at his own clothing, and *Maria's* voice trembles in the Fado way. *Maria Severa Onofriana* was the first Fado singer to rise to fame, and tonight *Artur Paredes* accompanies her on Portuguese guitar. *Maria* was born in 1820. She was a tall and gracious prostitute, a lover of many including *Francisco de Paula Portugal e Castro*, 13th Count of Vimioso. And, she died in 1846.

Stan watches as the charcoal sketch images of *Severa* and *Artur* fade to nothing. Soon he is alone walking the streets of Lisbon. His walk is casual, loose and purposeful. He is gliding across the paving stones rather than stepping on them. He does not know where he is going but there is no hesitation in his steps. His subconscious has no doubt and he follows his subconscious. The castle remains on his right as he glides past the Lisbon Cathedral and the Santo Antonio Church where beggars of varying enthusiasm and dishevelment offer their empty hands. He glides north on Rua da Madalena past Praca de Figueira where a Roma family is draped over their horse drawn carriage. They offer large brown eyes filled with generations of disenfranchisement. He glides past the National Theatre de Maria II where buskers of varying talent ply their trade. He glides north on Avenida da Liberdade past the beggar and his dog (a recent trend among Europe's beggars). The mark may not want to give to the beggar but a sad eyed dog is hard to walk away from. Stan drops a euro at the feet of the dog and, before long, he is gliding up to the entrance of the *Heritage Avenida Liberdade, Boutique Hotel.* The doorman greets him with a nod and a "Good evening Senhor." The door is opened and he finds himself moving toward the reception.

"Good evening Senhor Stan. Your friend is already in your room."

"Jolly good."

He orders two gin and tonics to be sent to his room and takes his key. In the elevator, he realizes he has no idea what room is his room. He has no idea why or how the staff know him, and who is this "friend?"

He looks at his key; it is an old-fashioned heavy metal key, Room 33.

The elevator doors open on the third floor and Stan quickly finds his room. The key slides into the lock with a clunk and he feels the metal key work on the metal tumblers and the door opens. The floors are polished oak and the room, indeed, has a heritage feel. On the queen size bed reclines an Asian beauty. She is on her side; her right elbow rests on the mattress and her right hand supports her head. Her black, silken hair cascades over her hand and onto the sheets. Stan sees her as though he is looking through a special effects lens.

He stands just inside the door for quite some time just looking and ... "Who are you?"

"You know my father," she says.

"That does not make me feel more comfortable."

"I am Miji." And the bed sheet slips but does not reveal her breasts, not quite. "Take a bath; it's big." Stan has no choice but to obey and he turns toward the bathroom and as he turns Miji's image liquefies but he quickly looks back and her image solidifies again. He shakes his head in a weak attempt to clarify his thoughts.

The bath is filled with water at a perfect 39 degrees Celsius. Stan removes his clothes and places them on the bathroom chair. He tries to empty his mind; he doesn't want to think and he slips into the water. He rests his head on the back of the tub and closes his eyes. "Miji? I know her father?"

The doorbell rings, "Room service."

Stan calls out, "Leave it at the door." And, he opens his eyes to the sound of bare feet padding on polished wood.

Miji steps into the bathroom and she is draped in the hotel dressing gown; her robe sash is loosely tied. "Very thoughtful, Stanley, the gin and tonic."

The gin has been served in large wine glasses. A cinnamon stick wrapped in lime peel is semi submerged and a few dried juniper berries float on the surface. Miji hands Stan one of the glasses.

"To meetings," says Miji.

"To Lisbon," says Stan. They clink glasses and sip ice-cooled freshness. Stan sorts through his memory and wonders whether he ought to pinch himself. He finds nothing in his memory and dares not pinch himself.

... Silence ...

Miji stands and lets the bathrobe slip to her ankles. She is narrow hipped, small breasted with coal black hair and her skin is alabaster white, polished milk but not sour, definitely not sour, but not sweet either. There is a scar that runs from her right temple down the length of her cheek and it looks fresh. She steps over the rim of the bath with her gin glass in her left hand and the water does not ripple as she slides beneath the surface. Her skin melts into the water. Stan watches her milky skin merge with the water. Her definition clouds beneath the surface even though the water is crystal clear. She takes a slow sip of her gin before placing the glass on the broad bath edge. She smiles across the water and her scar blazes in the fluorescent light. Stan drinks his gin like it is beer.

Miji reaches below the surface of the water and finds Stan's foot. She lifts it out of the water and Stan is forced to slip down in the tub; the water licks his chin. She holds his foot in the palm of her left hand and with her right fingers she grabs Stan's big toe and gives it a twist; she is not gentle. "This little piggy went to market."

"Shit."

She takes a hold of Stan's next toe and twists a little harder. "This little piggy stayed home."

Miji returns Stan's foot to the bottom of the tub and says, "To be continued."

"Shiiitttt."

Miji rises from the bath and the surface of the water does not ripple but water blends with her skin and slides off her body as she steps onto the white tiles of the bathroom floor. She turns to look at Stan. Her legs are spread; her thigh muscles are lean and defined; water hangs on her sparse pubic hair—reluctant to let go—her stomach is flat; her nipples are erect and her lips hint of a smile. Stan can only stare. She turns and with a lift of her chin, beckons him to follow.

Stan soaks a little longer. He cannot decide between exit and erection. He rises from the bath with a splash and as he walks out of the bathroom his erection wins over exit. And then he remembers the gin. "Do you want your gin?" There is no answer so Stan continues into the main room. His eyes are fixed on the bed but Miji is sitting on the chair at the writing desk. Water drips from her hair; her shoulders are delicately muscled and another angry scar creeps down her spine.

"Lie on the bed, Stanley; I'll be with you in a minute."

Stan does as he is told, taking his erection with him, and Miji picks up a pen and writes on the hotel stationary.

Stan is fumbling with the bedding and he turns around when the room fills with the music of Jethro Tull. Miji is standing in the middle of the room. She is standing on her left leg and her right foot is resting on the inside of her left knee. She is playing flute al la Ian Anderson—the flautist and lead singer of the 70's rock band, Jethro Tull. Her hair floats around her shoulders, down her back and across her face and, with her eyes and chin, she conducts Stan to the bed. Stan reclines but his erection does not. He watches. Miji is marblesque, white, muscled and androgynous. Her shoulders are wider than her hips. Her ribs show beneath a coating of pectoral muscles. Her breasts are shadows and her nipples are triggers. She is a child; she is a teenager; she is mid-twenties; she is indefinable. The flute disappears and she steps onto the bed, one leg either side of Stan's hips. She looks into Stan's eyes and sings with gusto the lyrics to Jethro Tull's *Aqualung*.

"**Sitting on a park bench,**

Eyeing little girls,

With bad intent."

And, she bends her knees and slowly lowers herself down

onto Stan's erection. She takes him in and holds him in. She arches her back and she thrusts her hips forward and down. She throws back her head and sings with abandon, without ego, with force,

"**Oohh, Aqualung my friend.**"

Her voice shatters on the ceiling. Broken treble clefs, sharps and quavers rebound around the room.

"**Do you still remember**

December's foggy freeze."

Then, the music changes, Freddy Mercury is singing,

"**I want to be Free.**"

And Miji sends more notes flying around the room and she rides Stan as if he is a rodeo bull. Her left hand has a firm grip on his pubic hair and her right arm is extended high in the air. Is that a Stetson in her hand? Miji rides him hard. She grabs and twists his right nipple and then his left nipple and he moans in pain and pleasure. Stan reaches for her breast and twists full force and Miji growls and throws back her head and releases more treble clefs, sharps and quavers. And, she pushes her hips down. Her vagina clenches and rubs his erection raw until he can no longer deal with the contradiction of pleasure and pain. He grits his teeth for a final buck. He thrusts, twists and explodes and it is over. Miji steps off as he climaxes and is gone. The room is dark; Stan struggles from the sheets and stands, feeling for the light switch. The blinding light reveals the familiar surroundings of his little apartment in Itaewon.

As he pads toward the bathroom he looks to his writing desk and there is a sheet of paper covered in a stranger's handwriting. ***Talk to my father. You can help them.***

CHAPTER 10

What's in a Dream

Stan calls Vince and tries to line up Vince for a drink but Vince wants nothing to do with it. He fobs Stan off with the excuse of meeting with his soccer team. Stan tries to explain his need to talk about his dreams but Vince continues to stall, using tango dancing as another apology. Finally, Vince agrees to a drinking session on Friday at Rose and Crown.

After hanging up, Stan puts a few things in his pack and leaves his apartment. As he walks across his balcony, Gwanak-san is covered with clouds and the sky threatens rain. He thinks about going back inside for an umbrella but he doesn't and it is not long before he is walking along the lanes of Itaewon. Once on Itaewon Road, he passes Paris Baguette and waves to the manager. He is thinking of having a coffee with the owner of Itaewon's first French restaurant if Jacque is there. And, he is. Jacque is a little rotund caricature of a French man. He has a waxed mustache, and he is on hugging and kissing terms with all who walk by. He and his partner have owned several restaurants in the neighborhood but now they are concentrating on this one. In the heady days of success and money, Jacque partied until late most mornings. He showered friends with Champagne. He was generous to friends and strangers; he still is. When Jacque sees Stan, he thrusts his stubby arms into the air,

"Monsieur Stan, sit on the terrace; I'm sure it won't rain. I'll be with you in a moment. Coffee?" He turns to his Korean Maître de, "Capitainne, get Stan his usual; you know how he likes it." With that, Jacque waddles into the restaurant to discuss something with someone. He is forever opening his briefcase and pulling out files or sketches. Stan reclines in the humid air, closes his eyes and tilts his head back, offering his face to the sun gods in the hope of bringing them out from behind the clouds. And, his mind turns to last night's dream. He rewinds the tape and plays bits back. He pulls the folded paper from his pocket, unfolds it and stares at the writing. ***Talk to my father. You can help them.***

A young waitress places a long macchiato in front of Stan with a, "Good morning Stan."

"Morning Insuk ... beautiful morning?"

"No, I have to work." And she briskly turns and walks back inside. Stan watches her leanness recede before lifting his coffee to his nose. He enjoys the delicate aroma of the French Roast ... he sips ... he sighs ... he replaces the cup on its saucer and reclines toward the anticipated sun. His nipples hurt.

"Mon'Amie, how goes it? Would you like eggs? I'm having some." And, with that, Jacque sits beside Stan also facing the hidden sun. "Capitainne, eggs for Stan and me."

The Maître de asks, "How would you like them cooked?"

"Sunny side up and soft for me." Says Stan.

"Mine, I want the sun out of my eggs and some bacon, too; do you want bacon Stan? Put some bacon on Stan's plate"

"Sun out of your eggs?" repeats Stan.

"Yes, how do you say it in English. Sunny side down?"

Stan laughs, "'Eggs over easy' is the expression but I like your original word play. Sunny side down will do or take the sun out of my eggs is just as good." Stan laughs again. "In fact, I like the expressions."

"So, what has been happening Stan?"

"Not much, same old thing, you know, teaching business people some English, drinking too much, sitting in cafes, having weird dreams." And, Stan gives an abbreviated version of his visions.

Before Stan finishes, Jacque slips into a long monologue about the meaning of dreams. He paraphrases Freud and Jung. He explains that their ideas were similar but different. Both believed dreams were important but for different reasons. Freud thought that dreams were representations of unfulfilled wishes and Jung believed they were not distortions of reality but a different language of reality that needed interpretation. Jacque also loosens the rein on his own thoughts.

He tells Stan that Freud would interpret his dream as a wish, a desire to find love. Whereas Jung may interpret it as loss; he may put more emphasis on the experience rather than the woman.

"You've just got to decode the language."

Stan sits and listens. These conversations with Jacque usually see Stan allowing his mind to drift to other thoughts, daydreams if you like while Jacque talks on but today Stan really listens.

These conversations are never equal exchanges; they are barely a sharing of thoughts. They are often lectures and they are repetitious. But Stan is surprisingly ok with this. He has known Jacque for more than 5 years and their conversations have never gone any other way. It is not something Stan can do every day or for long on the days they meet, but there is a warmth and understanding in the relationship. The eggs come and Stan tucks in while Jacque moves the conversation onto education. This is a pet topic of his lately as he tries to find a school where his daughter feels comfortable. There is always something wrong with the school and the system, never anything wrong with his daughter.

"The teachers are too restrictive. They have no understanding of Antoinette's creative needs. They make her play table tennis and they grade her ability. They chastise her when she sketches in her mathematics book. They understand nothing."

After an hour, Stan stands and reaches for his wallet.

"No, no Stan, I've got it." So, Stan throws his little pack over his shoulder and ambles away. He has a class with a businessman in Gangnam in an hour.

The day drifts along like flotsam on a calm sea but Stan's thoughts are in a storm. The businessman finishes the class after 15 minutes because of the need to get to a business meeting with government officials. Stan would bill Wontae Oh for the full hour. He has been teaching him for about a year now, and he is beginning to lose interest in the job and Wontae. His English is not as good as he thinks it is and he does not want to, or does not have the time to study. His only practice comes during the one-hour meetings with Stan once a week. And, Stan is getting bored with the embellished stories of wealth and potential business deals. He is bored with the complaints about the lack of respect shown by the husband of his deceased daughter. Stan is even bored with, but saddened by, Wontae's daughter's death. How many times can a person feign interest and horror when the story of the Sampoong Department Store collapse is repeated and repeated? Stan has certainly had enough of the complaints about the insufficient compensation. The 100 million won Wontae's family received helped him stabilize and expand his furniture supply business. He was able to procure a contract with the US Military to supply office equipment. He removes the "Made in China" stamps on the furniture he imports and substitutes "Made in Korea" and sells the furniture at an inflated rate. It was and continues to be a lucrative contract. The problem with Wontae is that he cannot keep his mouth shut. He considers his deception clever or cunning. Stan suspects a downfall is coming.

No amount of money can compensate for the death of a daughter but Wontae was only interested in the $100,000 for what he could use it for. In fact, he was only ever interested in his daughter for her marriage prospects. He married her off to the son of a wealthy business associate in the hope of tapping into the in-laws' wealth. His daughter's death put an end to that. The in-laws were not interested in continuing the relationship and the son-in-law soon remarried.

Wontae was not interested in the trials or the convictions or the jailing of the department store owners and corrupt government officials. He just wanted money. He was not interested in the fact that his daughter's body was never found. The ID Card and anecdotal evidence from her friends was sufficient evidence of death for the insurance company and that was enough for him. Stan has no problem taking 80,000 won for the 15 minutes' work. But, he needs to end this gig.

CHAPTER 11

Who is Miji?

Stan takes the early end to his working day as a chance to go for a run. He exits the Itaewon Subway and walks briskly home. He changes into his running gear and straps on his sports watch. He puts his credit card in the little zipped pocket of his knee length running shorts, just in case. He locks the door and hides the key in plain sight and stands still on the balcony with his arm outstretched for his watch to establish contact with orbiting satellites in order for its GPS to function.

As soon as Stan starts running, he almost stops and returns to the apartment. His nipples hurt as they rub on his singlet, and his dick is sore.

"Shit, not fun, Got to keep going, got to clear my mind, 'Zen the pain away laddy, Zen the pain away.'"

So, Stan heads up the steep climb to the Hyatt Hotel. He fights to keep his mind away from his nipples and onto his foot-falls and breathing. He only partially succeeds and at the one-kilometer mark his watch beeps and Stan sees that his time is not good.

"Shit, no personal best today, May as well take a less used route.

When Stan gets to the two-kilometer mark in front of the Hyatt Hotel, instead of turning left onto the 402-bus route, he turns right and runs over the footbridge that takes him into the Namsan Botanical Gardens. He runs along walking trails that sometimes follow alongside artificial streams. During the recent economic downturn, Korea increased its public works. This gave people jobs and beautified the country. Seoul's polluted rivers and Namsan Park were beneficiaries of this spending.

"Love what they've done with these old drains, Love what they've done with this park, Shit my nipples hurt, Who is this Miji chick?

... Thought ghosts were spiritual, not physical, Did it to myself?, Nah, twisting my own nipples ... you've got to be kidding ...

... Sure masturbated plenty of times, like most men, probably like most women, but never been into this masochism thing, Don't even like porn ...

... Porn, porn go away come again another day, Hah a little accidental play on words, come as in come, 'Pathetic laddy, pathetic, stick to teaching and leave the poetry to the professionals,' What about the note?"

Stan's watch signals three kilometers and he is pushing up to the Namsan access road. If he turns right, he will run downhill to the running track and open-air gym. If he turns left, he will wind his way up to the top of the mountain. He turns left.

"Shit what a slog, Pant, pant, push, push, heading up, Up, up and away we go to the top, to the top and us, they will not stop ...

... 'I warned you laddy,' Hey Granny you've been dead a long time, do you know a ghost called Miji?, Miji with skin like polished milk, Miji who could be anything from 15 to 25 years old ...

... And what was with the Jethro Tull thing, must have been 18 when I last listened to that music, 'Come on laddy, push yourself, You're slowing down a bit,' Shit Granny, give us a break, nipples hurt, thighs are beginning to scream and I'm breathing too hard to talk to you ... And the note?"

Beep, and Stan has passed the four-kilometer mark and he is

400 meters from the summit.

"'One last push laddy,' Ok, ok I'm pushing already, Just shut-up and let me concentrate, Shit my dick hurts."

At the top, Stan slows to a walk. He feels good for the effort. The exercise has released a few endorphins. He doesn't feel like punching the sky like Rocky Balboa after reaching the top of the stairs in "Rocky" or like Kevin Bartlett after kicking one of his seven goals in the 1980 Grand Final but he does feel better. He wanders around for a while admiring the views over North Seoul and over South Seoul.

"Right, time to head on down."

The road Stan is running on loops around the summit and down to the entrance of the Namsan Car Park and back onto the 402-bus route.

"Slowly now, find the rhythm, watch the knees, heavy load on the knees with the gradient, 'Breathe, laddy, breathe,' I am breathing and while you're here Granny, do you know anything about Fado music? ...

... No answer eh, Prepared to talk to me, but don't answer questions, good onya Granny, Why was I in Lisbon and what was with the black and white Fado performances? ...

... Fado is about accepting fate, Am I supposed to just let these dreams happen without thinking too much?, Don't worry about them?, Shit, tell that to my nipples, Tell that to my still aching dick, And who the hell is Miji's father ...

... Dad, you've been dead a few years, what do you know of this ghost?, No answer from you either, Guess I've just got to ask all the middle aged Korean men I know."

He turns left onto the 402-bus route heading south and his watch beeps the five-kilometer mark. Now, he is running the bus route from north to south.

"Three kilometers to go, not too far now, Zen the mind, Zen the

mind, And what about the 'them,' Who are the 'them?,' Father and mother maybe, Yeah, that's possible, Thanks dad, You know mum's doing ok don't you?, Her body's failing and her memory is still selective but you probably know that too ...

... Look at the view down over Yongsan, Sometimes Seoul is really pretty, Melbourne's flat, these hills are beautiful and I like the rolling running, It's just so hard plodding along the always flat ...

... Yes the Hyatt, 'You're almost home laddy,' Granny you're still here, You won't answer questions but you like to editorialize, I'll take it from here."

And, Stan runs the final short uphill stage past the Hyatt and then it is a relaxed cruise downhill to his apartment, if only his nipples and dick didn't hurt.

CHAPTER 12

Another Dream not Remembered

Stan's nights continue to be clouded with dreams; some he remembers and others are shadows that leave him disappointed and angry but he doesn't know why. These unremembered dreams are a continuation of a single dream that sees him talking to his mother and other patients in a hospital room.

Stan is standing in the ward looking at the old women in their single beds, he holds a block of Toblerone in his hand.

"Are you going to share the chocolate?"

Stan looks around and into a gummy smile. He peels off the wrapping and offers his mother the first piece. He then approaches each bed and helps each patient break off a section before returning to his seat and silence.

"So why did you leave home?" Asks the old teacher again and a chorus of support backs her up.

His eyes lock on his mother's and they plead for mercy.

"Life's as good as over son."

Rising from the chair, he walks over to the window and stares out at the park across the road.

"You really want to know?"

His mother accuses him of not visiting very often but she was still surprised to receive his postcard from Seoul, Korea. She initially thought he must have been on holidays but the note mentioned trying to find a teaching job. Over the years, there had been no discussion and his mother reclined in the 'bored' claim as much as Stan did. But, her ward mates are now pushing for more truth then she ever did.

Stan stares into the distance for several minutes, "I had an epiphany."

"About as good as 'bored.'" And the patients continue to suck on their chocolate.

Stan continues to stare out over the park. His vision catches a few old men sitting on a bench dressed in hospital pajamas attached to IV drips, smoking. And, he thinks back to his father's death. He suffered for 12 months just waiting for the inevitable. He had oral health nurses brushing his teeth when all he needed was a good dose of whisky and oxycodone.

"Did I ever tell you about the time I was climbing Mulkila IV in the Indian Himalaya?"

"Remember you in India, vague about the climb."

"It's a big story ... did I tell you about the body I found abandoned on the glacier?"

"No details."

"When did I leave Australia?"

"A long time ago."

"I was on a plane two months after I got back from that climb. I resigned my teaching job and organized my affairs. I needed to go somewhere, anywhere. Life in Australia had become unthreatening, too predictable. There was no edge to my life. The future was a known and India had shown me the profligacies of the unknown."

"What's wrong with a known future? Isn't that what humans strive for? Don't we work and put money away for the future? Isn't that the concept of superannuation, life's worth?"

"It's one way to go forward."

"Other possibilities are?" Asks his mother.

"On my earlier trips to India, I often consulted with fortune tellers to try to get a glimpse into my future. I figured if I could see it, I could relax and let it happen. My future had been predictable but I was trying to find another predicable future. But, Mulkila IV changed many things."

There is silence in the room and Stan walks back to the bed and picks up the jug of water and pours himself a drink. Before replacing the jug, he asks his audience if they need a drink. They just tell him to get on with the story.

And, the ward becomes an Imax cinema ...

The Indian support group got the climbing party as far as they could. Yuvraj (Bobby) Singh had assembled the usual team of ponies and camp wallahs who provided for all the climbers needs until they moved beyond base camp. The bottom of the glacier was covered in moraine and it was a pretty impressive effort on the part of the pony boys to get their horses and mules to go as far as they did. On the last night together, the tents were pitched and Bobby Singh had managed to buy a goat off one of the shepherds the day before. He assured everyone that it was a young beast and the cook made a stew out of local potatoes, carrots, and this young goat that had actually died of old age, or that's what it seemed like to Stan. The meat had boiled for hours but it needed another day on a slow simmer. It was tough. Everyone was sitting around in silence as they tried to chew the gristle and meat and then, one of the climbers shone his torch into the ice. He just shone the light down on a clear patch of ice and the light ran through the glacier and it sent sabers of light up hundreds of other gaps in the moraine. The camp wallahs ran around trying to catch the light. It was crazy, like starlight from the ground joining hands with the starlight from the sky. Other team members did the same with their torches and thousands of light shafts headed skyward. Somehow it made the goat taste better. At least apprehensions

concerning the climb were released for a while.

The scene loses focus and Stan looks out of the window and watches two dogs play in the park; their owners are talking and laughing. He takes a few sips of water. And, the film begins again.

The next morning, after a breakfast of porridge and tea, the four climbers waved goodbye to Bobby Singh and his crew. Climbing is a hard slog with a heavy pack, carrying ropes and wearing crampons and they were always roped together as they negotiated the crevasses. The first day went without a problem although it was slow going; the glacier was more disfigured by crevasses than expected. They crisscrossed the ice looking for the safest way forward. The temperature hovered around freezing yet their bodies were slick with sweat and, just before nightfall, the small group set up camp. Water was heated and towels used to dry sweaty bodies. After checking-in with Bobby Singh via two-way radio, they ate rehydrated food, drank tea and talked. The conversation was not philosophical or anything like that, just shooting the shit but laughter at the tough old goat and the reactions to the light show the previous evening proved a salve for weary minds but it was still early when they retired more fatigued than they thought possible. It is hard sleeping at altitude and Mulkila IV is a good 6,500 meters. Stan woke every couple of hours thirsty for breath; there just never seemed to be enough oxygen. The next morning, they exited their tents at dawn, breakfasted and headed higher up the glacier.

They tried to keep as centered on the glacier as they could manage. The Mulkila Glacier has, over the millennia, formed a classic U-shaped valley and the sides were prone to rock falls. Rumblings of the occasional displacement could be heard in the not far off distance and they didn't want to get tangled up in one such event. And, that night, they again camped as centered as possible. Stan was more drained than he had ever been in his life. He pitched

his tent in a blur and cooked and ate in nothing more than semi-awareness of the stark peaks and star filled night that surrounded him. Everyone was beat and the conversation was stilted at best and sleeping bags soon won the battle over sociability. That night, Stan dreamed of being impaled by a laser that burst from the ice and he woke up parched for oxygen.

The next morning the climbers rose with the sun and the sound of tents unzipping broke the silence. The sky was a navy blue, no sky blue here as the altitude drains that color from the atmosphere. Nobody had slept well; Stan's muscles still retained some lactic acid but he dragged himself down the glacier a bit to pee.

The scene fades and Stan is standing in the middle of the hospital ward.

"Have you ever tried to pee while in full mountaineering gear?"

Four old heads move from side to side.

"It's worse trying to shit but that's not a story for today. Now's a good time for a pee break." And, he walks out of the room.

Stan wakes with a full bladder. He climbs out of bed, heads to the bathroom and as he pees, he tries to recollect the dream. He knows his mother was involved but he can't get a grip on the gist.

CHAPTER 13

Polished Liquid and Beer

And finally, it is Friday. Stan has been running and flexing his mind trying to figure out the meaning of his dreams and the note. What Korean men does he know? The business people he teaches, of course, and the other day he asked Wontae Oh his daughter's name; it was Mejung.

Stan arrives at the *Rose and Crown* a little before 7pm and orders a Red Rock from the barman. Max has worked in a few of Stan's watering holes and they greet each other warmly but the conversation never goes beyond the order of beer and food and a banal, "How are you?" and tonight is no exception to that routine. Stan is halfway through his first beer when Vince arrives.

"What are you drinking?"

Vince responds with, "Hey Max, London Pride, please."

The conversation begins with banter about Vince's Soccer team. He is not completely content with his role and the commitment of his teammates. Stan counters with comments on the recreational level of the competition and suggests that Vince is taking it too seriously. He tells Vince that the competition is lower than the table they are sitting at. There is nothing riding on the games. He tells Vince that he can't expect his teammates to play with professional commitment. They just want to run around a bit, have a kick and finish with a beer.

"Stick to tango, mate."

"Jaysus, I know the competition is pretty low grade ... but competition is competition. Mary and feckin Joseph, why get involved in a game if you don't play to win. Why get involved if you don't go flat out. What's the point? I just don't get it ... Shit, maybe I ought to give it away."

"Or, lower your expectations ... and there's always tango."

"Shut up about the tango will you ... very different motives and very different expectations. Soccer and tango don't belong in the same sentence."

Both take long draughts of their beers and sit in silence surrounded by their own thoughts until Vince shakes his head and starts in with, "Enough about my pathetic soccer team. When I play, I want to win. That's all ... so Stan, the dreams continue?"

"Yeah. They're so real." He hands Vince the folded note. "Check this out. When I woke from my dream the other night, this was sitting on my desk"

"You wrote it in your sleep?"

"Not my writing."

"Jaysus, you're kidding." Vince turns the paper over and holds it up to the light looking for nothing in particular before adding, "Ok, give us the story."

And, Stan begins relating the dream. When he gets to the description of Miji, Vince interrupts.

"What's with the polished liquid thing?"

"What do you mean?"

"Last week it was polished honey and this week it's polished milk. Is it even possible to polish a liquid?"

Stan has his head down as he twists his beer around on its coaster. "I'm bereft of solids. Both had skin like liquid; both seemed polished. And Miji has this raw scar that runs from her temple down her cheek." When he looks up, Vince is smiling.

"Stan, Stan, Stan, you reckon I take my soccer too seriously?"

"I think they are serious. Look at the note," Stan says without smiling.

Vince again turns the paper around in his hands, looking at it from all angles and Stan continues relating the dream. When he gets to the part about the nipple twisting, he pulls up his T-shirt to show Vince his swollen and reddened nipple.

"Stan, put that thing away... Jaysus it looks pretty nasty."

The retelling of the dream comes to an end, and Vince rereads the note. *Talk to my father. You can help them.* "Ok, so you reckon this is not your writing? You're not doing a multiple personality thing, are you?"

Vince is smiling but Stan just looks into his beer.

"This is really bothering you; isn't it?"

"Wouldn't it you? It's got physical; it's gone beyond a Jungian interpretation of a dream."

"Yep, guess it has. Do you think there is a connection between the two dreams?"

Stan doesn't know but he does know that the two women are very different as is his relationship with each.

"Are they real ... you know, like real living human beings? Do you think that they actually exist in this world?"

"Good question ... the first woman ... the polished honey one ..." Stan pauses to drink some beer and gather his thoughts. "Her name was ... I think 'is' Jinni."

"Get a grip mate, 'is?' You really reckon she exists?"

"I don't know who she is ... Mate, I know this sounds stupid, like really stupid, and I hesitate to verbalize this thought, this emotion ..."

"Go on"

"I wasn't dreaming ... I was living a dream; it was real ... I felt the emotional ..." Stan looks at his friend and his face shows strain. "... I loved Jinni ... I haven't touched her in a dream or in the flesh ... but ... I love Jinni."

"Jaysus Stan, do you want to repeat that?"

"No I don't. It scares the shit out of me to think it, but now I've said it ... and it scares me more because I know it's true."

It takes a while for Stan to continue, "She controlled me ... no that's not right ... she directed me. I was running through Delhi and I felt as though she was directing me, like a conductor ... moving the orchestra forward to the next movement."

"But, you've been to India several times, haven't you? It has a pretty strong pull on you."

Stan is thoughtful but silent.

"So, you could have just dragged it up it from your own subconscious ... Lonely man meets beautiful woman in exotic location. Sounds like a dream to me."

Stan lets the thought hang heavy in the smoky atmosphere of the *Rose and Crown.*

Vince starts in again, "So you think she's real?"

"I think she's waiting for me. Shit, I sound like a nut case."

"Asylum fodder, I'd say."

Stan stands and stares down at Vince, he's not feeling the humor. And, Vince laughs until Stan sits back on his stool and both brood separately.

As they drain their beers, their silence mingles with the cigarette smoke and they order two more. Max deftly pulls the two beers with a practiced ease and sits the glasses on the coasters. The bar is filled with voices (both raised and whispered), laughter, smoke and cannoning pool balls and this rich mix cloaks the noisy thoughts of Stan and Vince.

"Ok, so Jinni is a living human, what about the polished milk girl?" The noisy silence stretches. Stan looks at Vince and then lowers his head and looks deep into his beer.

"I think I fucked a ghost."

CHAPTER 14

The Birth of Jinni

After sitting for almost an hour in the Paris Baguette just outside the Busan Rail Station, Jinni settled her bill and walked out. She stood on the street and scanned the third floor of the buildings looking for a PC Bang. These Korean Internet cafes are smoky dens where people of all ages play computer games. Jinni just wanted anonymous access to a computer. PC Bangs are ubiquitous in Korean cities, towns and villages, so it did not take long for her to find what she was looking for. She climbed the steps and opened the door and was confronted by a wall of smoke. She may as well have walked into an ashtray, but she approached the pale teenager at the front counter. He reluctantly lifted his eyes from his computer screen; he said nothing.

"I want an hour on a computer," Said Jinni.

"Number 33."

Jinni found computer number 33 and sat down. She opened the Korean search engine, NAVER, and typed in, "Busan gangs."

Like most countries, South Korea has an organized crime presence. China has its Triads; Japan has its Yakusa; Italy and the USA have its Mafia; Australia has its Mafia and motorcycle gangs, and so on. South Korea has three main crime organizations with the *Chil Sung Pa* (Seven Star Mob) being the strongest and most ruthless of them. The *Chil Sung Pa* has its roots in Busan and it gets its name from its seven founders. Members of this mob have seven stars tattooed somewhere on their bodies, and the Mob controls drugs, prostitution, gambling, smuggling and protection. There are politicians and police officers that owe allegiance, in some cases their very existence, to the *Chil Sung Pa*. This was the world Jinni wanted to connect with.

After a solid hour of research, Jinni stood up from computer 33 and with a memory filled with information, she paid her tariff and walked out the door, down the steps and back onto the street. She smelled her clothes and they reeked of stale cigarettes. She walked back toward Choryangjung Street and its surrounds for another day of observation and research. Jinni walked around for a while before hunger pains stabbed again. She chose an almost clean but appetizing enough restaurant with a roughly painted sign saying *MYONGHEE'S*. She sat alone in a corner. The old lady, the halmoni, ignored Jinni as she continued to watch a live report of the Sampoong department store collapse; she did not even raise an eyebrow. Jinni stared at the menu printed on the wall before selecting Bibimbap, which was one of her staple lunch meals. The rice and mixed vegetables in a hot stone pot was her comfort food and, right now, she needed comfort. Jinni called the halmoni over with a, "Yoggy yo."

Reluctantly, the halmoni looked toward her lone customer, "Whadja want."

Jinni had forgotten how aggressive and loud the Busan dialect was. Busan is a port city, founded on fishing. Small and large boats would, and still do, head out in small seas or large, high winds or light breezes. The Busan dialect is born of the sea; words can be blown away by the wind, hence the need for the sentences to be short, clear and loud.

Jinni tried to dredge up some emotion toward the scenes on the television but failed. She responded meekly, "Dulsop bibimbap, please."

"Ayego, have ya seen this stuff about the department store?"

Jinni looked away.

The halmoni continued, "Who's to blame? Probably greedy rich bastards, not to mention corrupt politicians. Bastards. Give me the CSP any day. At least they do what they say they'll do. At least we know where we stand.... Whadya say ya wanted?"

"Dulsop bibimbap, please."

The halmoni slowly righted herself from her cross-legged position on the floor and opened the refrigerator. She removed plastic containers of varied foodstuffs and placed them on the table. As she did so, she kept glancing at the TV.

"Ayego, another body bag. Wait, they've found a live one. Look, a miracle. Her hand's movin'. How many days has it been now?"

Jinni did not look at the television and she tried not to listen.

The halmoni had made bibimbap thousands of times so she could watch the TV and throw the ingredients together with ease, and soon the stone pot was surrounded by flame and the smells of cooking filled the little restaurant.

The halmoni talked as she roughly dropped small saucers of kimchi, black soya beans, odeng, and seasoned seaweed on Jinni's table.

"Ayego, this country's crap. What's goin' on. The rich have everything and they just want more. They cut corners for profit and who bloody suffers? Us poor buggers that's who."

Soon after the side dishes arrived, the bibimbap followed. It was good, hearty, honest food and Jinni tucked in. As she ate, the sounds of the reporter at the disaster scene plus the persistent emergency sirens almost cracked her veneer.

"Halmoni, do you know where I can find a waitressing job or anything?"

"A job? Ayego, the CSP control everythin' 'round here."

"CSP?"

"The *Chil Sung Pa.* Ya need to contact them. But ... ayego ... don't, just don't."

Jinni let the silence linger as she worked on a different approach.

"If I wanted a few drinks tonight, where would you suggest I go?"

"A few drinks?"

"Yeah, meet some people and discuss work possibilities; you know, just get to know people."

"If ya'r askin' what I think ya'r askin', ya oughta git yaself back to Seoul now. Ya accent's goin' to tell everyone that ya not from here. Ayego, it sounds like ya went to some posh school or somethin' ... It's not worth it girl."

Jinni said nothing. But her silence was persistent.

"Ayego, I don't know why I'm telling ya this. Try the *Love Always* bar up the road on the left ... ask for Mr. Park ... he's known as Blue Park ... tell him you're a friend of mine. Ayego girl, go back to Seoul ... And, my name's on the front of the restaurant."

Jinni slowly navigated her way through the bibimbap before she asked, "Halmoni, do you know a safe, cheap place to spend a few nights?"

"Girl, what's happened to ya? What ya runnin' from?"

Jinni went back to the side dishes and ate some more without responding.

"Ayego, try Choi's Inn; it's two streets up on the right. And, girl, if things go wrong ... I'm hear 'til 2am. I hope I don't see ya."

"Thanks halmoni."

The halmoni went back to the TV and the rescue efforts, and Jinni finished off her meal. She ate every last grain of rice and by the time she was ready to leave, the plates were almost clean enough to put straight back into the cupboard. She pushed her chair back from the table and rose to her feet. "Thank you halmoni."

"Yeah, yeah ... look at the mess on the TV. Ayego, getta look at it. What a mess."

"Thanks halmoni." And Jinni moved toward the door.

"Hey girl." Said the halmoni as she looked up from the TV. She forced Jinni to make eye contact with her. "Remember, I'm closing this dump at 2am."

Jinni's emotional bank was nearing bankruptcy as she walked toward Choi's Inn. She did not register the summer humidity; she did not notice the sweat running down her back; she did not know what month it was. She pulled her cap low as she approached the inn. The automatic door slid open and she entered. Reception counters are a rarity in Korean Inns and Choi's Inn was not rare. A 20-centimeter square window at navel height gave access to the proprietor. Jinni did not bend down, and the proprietor did not seek eye contact. "I want a room for three nights, please."

"30,000 won per night. 90,000 won in advance. Third floor."

She handed over the equivalent of $90, took her key and headed toward the elevator. The inside of the elevator smelled like the love child of cheap aftershave and cheaper perfume. She wondered if she could hold her breath for three floors. She exited the elevator and gasped for breath before walking down the corridor looking for room ... she looked down at her key ... room 33. She smiled to herself and she enjoyed the coincidence and repetition of the number 33. That tiny, facsimile of a smile was the first upward turn of her lips in three days. She allowed the smile to grow to 50% before shutting it down. But, for that short moment, a fresh breeze ruffled her soul.

She opened the door to room 33 and stale cigarette was the dominant smell with cheap scent on the mid palate and old sex deep in the back. The room was adequate. A small TV squatted ninja like high in a corner opposite the queen-sized bed. The window was half a meter by a meter and it looked down on a dingy lane filled with overflowing garbage bags. She opened the window as far as it would go and the air-conditioner labored against the mid-summer heat. As simple and adequate as the main room was, the bathroom was grand. It was almost the same size as the central space. It was tiled in white with an ocean blue feature running around its circumference and a large spa bath took center stage. For the second time in 10 minutes, Jinni smiled. Like the previous smile, it was a lip curl rather than a full-blown smile but the fresh breeze blew again. She turned on the taps and the bath filled slowly.

While the bath filled, she removed her clothes, wrapped herself in a freshly laundered bathrobe and fell onto the bed. She emptied her mind, fought sleep and waited for the bath. It took a full ten minutes for the bath to fill. She reluctantly pushed herself off the bed, dropped her robe on the floor and padded up to the side of the bath. She turned off the taps and was about to test the water temperature when she glimpsed herself in the full-length mirror. It was a contradictory sight. Her face was drawn and grey; her eyes were hooded and empty but her body was lean and toned from exercise and diet. And, the bruises on her upper thighs were yellowed and fading. She stared at her mirror image. She did not recognize the face and could not remember the body. She raised her left eyebrow half expecting a different response from her reflection. She was almost disappointed when her image copied her movement.

Jinni slid into the hot water, sighing as she sank to her neck. She needed a good scrubbing but she chose to soak first, to hell with convention. After becoming accustomed to the temperature, she sucked in a deep breath and allowed herself to sink below the water. Her thick, black hair floated on the surface and bubbles leaked from her nostrils. She tested her lungs before tilting her head back and pushing up. She used her hands to keep her heavy hair off her face and she rose to where her small but upward tilting breasts broke the surface of the water. The used air flowed from her lungs and she sighed with uncertain pleasure. Mejung Oh was washing away; Jinni Lee was emerging wet and new. Her smile was a little stronger this time.

After a good soak, she stepped out of the bath, picked up the shampoo and squatted on the low stool. She lathered and soaped herself until she had scrubbed her skin raw and then she rinsed her skin and hair and looked at her shiny new self in the harsh fluorescent light. She dried herself before walking into the main room to pick up her underwear. They needed washing as much as she had and she accomplished this task quickly and hung her briefs and bra on a hook to dry. She was still naked when she collapsed back onto the bed. She did not have time to organize her thoughts before she was asleep.

It was 7pm when Jinni dragged herself off the bed. She slipped into her old, but now clean, underwear; she pulled on her jeans, shirt and cap and walked out of the room and back into the elevator. She needed to retrieve her backpack from the station.

CHAPTER 15

From one Bar to Another

Stan and Vince have settled into some serious drinking. Most of the time, the two men sit in brooding silence. "Let me paraphrase this for you. One girl is real enough to love and the other is a ghost with a vagina that can grip a dick in a death lock. Jaysus mate."

"I've shown you my nipple; I'm not going to show you my dick. But if you can imagine..."

"Stop ... enough."

"I'm going to *Scrooge,* I'm ready to take on Mr. Kim."

"I might see you there but first I've got things to do."

"What?"

"Jaysus, if you must know, I want to talk to the tango girl."

And with that, glasses are drained and Stan and Vince move toward the door, down the stairs and into a beautiful Seoul evening.

CHAPTER 16

Jinni meets Blue

It was 8pm when Jinni collected her backpack from the coin locker at the station. She threw it over her shoulders, straightened her back and walked out into Busan's growing night. As she walked back to Choi's Inn, she looked for a place to grab a snack. She didn't want to return to the same restaurant she had lunch at. She stopped at a street vendor selling chicken sticks. She stood among a few others and picked chicken chunks off the stick with her perfect teeth. No one spoke to her and she was happy for that. She ate one stick of chicken and sipped on a cup of hot oden juice before heading back to Choi's Inn.

She rested on the bed in her room and watched a little TV. The scenes of the Sampoong Department Store collapse left her dry eyed. She was distancing herself from it and from Mejung. At 10pm she brushed her teeth before struggling into her new tight jeans and new tight, white T-shirt. She looked at her face in the mirror and was surprised to see the greyness gone. The soak in the bath and the sleep on a soft bed, not to mention the food, had brightened her skin. She applied eye shadow, but not much. Before leaving her room, she picked-up her New York Yankee's cap and pulled the peak low. She left the room with no money and no identification.

Jinni had checked-out "*Love Always*" from the outside during the daylight hours, but the night scene was quite different. Neon lights bounced their colors off bare brick and concrete. Shadows masked dirty corners and human features. Two chunky, neckless men with earphones stood on either side of the double-door entrance. Men approached the entrance and nodded to the two doormen. The nods were returned and the doors were opened. Some of the men had women on their arms, but not many. Jinni slipped off her cap and struggled to get it partially into her back pocket. She pulled her hair back into a ponytail. She figured that this exposed her cheekbones and full lips to their best advantage. She approached the door.

"Do I know ya?" Asked the doorman on the left.

"No, but you will want to." Replied Jinni.

"She's fakin' it," Said the doorman on the right.

"I'm here to see Mr. Park."

"Are ya now? Is he expecting ya?"

"Maybe. He should be."

The left doorman spoke into his sleeve, "Boss, there's a chick out here who says ya could be expecting her." There was silence as he listened to the reply. Eventually he looked at Jinni and spoke into his sleeve again. "Stylish, Seoul accent, hot, about 25, beautiful lips, thick hair pulled back, not much make-up, tight T-shirt, nice body boss, real nice body, real clean like ... Yeah boss ... ok boss." And Jinni was in. The bouncer on the right opened his door.

"Thank you Left and thank you Right."

Private booths surrounded an empty dance floor. There was a curved bar at the far end of the room with stools on the outside of the curve. On the inside of the curve was a mirrored wall with shelves of alcohol bottles. Two skinny boys in black suits and skinny black ties busied themselves amongst the bottles. Girls wearing limited clothing and unlimited make-up carried trays of drinks from one corner of the bar to the private booths.

At the other corner of the bar sat a middle-aged man dressed in blue. His suit was deep blue; his shirt was also deep blue; his tie was sky blue; his socks were also sky blue and his shoes were blue suede. He was a big man with broad shoulders. His skin was tanned. His black hair was streaked with grey and it had a delicate wave. He watched Jinni move toward him. He did not smile; he did not twist his head. He just followed her with his eyes.

Jinni tried to look confident but she couldn't help staring at the scantily clad girls and their full smiles. Her failing shoulders betrayed her uncertainty. Men stared at her from most directions and by the time she got to the bar, she felt undressed and alone.

Blue Park was hard not to miss, and she managed to pull back her shoulders and her timid breasts strained against her T-shirt. She sat down on the stool next to his, crossed her legs and tried to be cool as she nodded to the bartender who slid up close.

"Lemonade?"

The barman looked at Blue who shrugged his shoulders and Jinni rested her elbow on the bar and looked at her reflection in the mirror behind the bar.

Blue Park's gnarled hands toyed with his glass of soda water. Three knuckles on his left hand sported tattooed stars, as did four knuckles on his right hand. His thoughts seemed to bubble up through his soda water. Without taking his eyes off his glass, he spoke, "Do I know you?"

The bartender placed a coaster on the bar in front of Jinni and on top of the coaster he sat a glass filled with ice and a clear liquid. Half a lemon floated on top and slices of lemon were arranged around the rim. She slid the lemon slices to one side and lifted the glass, pursed her lips and sipped. The bartender watched. Blue Park did not. She replaced the glass on the coaster and lifted her eyes to the bartender. She allowed a hint of a smile to cross her lips as she gave him a nod of approval. He smiled and moved back to his bottles.

Jinni uncrossed and re-crossed her legs so that her body was open to Blue Park, but she continued to play with the ice in her glass. "I am Jinni."

"Not familiar."

"Give it time."

For the first time, Blue looked at Jinni; it was not welcoming, "Manners girl."

Both returned to their drinks. Both prodded their ice with red plastic sticks.

Blue Park broke the silence, "Are you here to drink or do you want something?"

"For now, I think I'll drink."

"And later?"

Jinni took another sip of her lemonade. "Your bartender tries hard."

Blue did not reply.

The bar was filling. Conversation, the occasional laugh and cigarette smoke drifted about and socialized, but silence surrounded the two people at the corner of the bar. Jinni played at being relaxed and cool but the minor tremor in her hand every time she picked up her drink betrayed her efforts. Blue Park was relaxed but alert. There were shadows with weapons nearby. He was never really alone; he was always alert.

Silence reigned until the glasses were empty. The bartender approached holding Blue Park's gaze. Park nodded and before the bartender could engage Jinni, Park tapped the bar top and nodded again. The bartender backed off toward his station where he began work on another awkward attempt at lemonade.

Before long a soda water was placed in front of Park and lemonade in front of Jinni.

Jinni looked directly at Blue Park for the first time, "Thanks"

"You are most welcome."

Jinni went back to prodding her ice cubes and Blue Park signaled to one of his attendants. The black shadow was soon by his side and the two conversed in whispers, "Yeah boss, will do." And he retreated back to the shadows.

Blue Park swiveled his stool ever so slightly to open himself to Jinni. "I have cancelled all appointments for the next 45 minutes. You've got my attention."

Her body tensed. She searched for an entry into what she needed but she couldn't find an open door. In the end, she said, "I need a job."

"That's it?"

"For now."

Blue Park looked up from his drink and stared at the strange new woman sitting to his left, "Big show for a small ask."

"For now, this is all I can ask."

The two sat quietly for a while before Blue Park broke the silence. "Your accent tells me that you are not from Busan. You have a Seoul accent."

"Your accent is also Seoul. Actually, it's a bit Seoul and a bit Busan."

"That's a long story and not a story for you right now."

"Fair enough."

"But, you need to give me a little more of yourself if you want to work for me. Or, I could have my boys remove you from my bar."

"Also fair enough ... Look, I will not lie to you ... but, right now, the truth is illusory."

"Big word."

Blue Park's prose and manners were at odds with his tattoos and appearance. He was a product of the streets of Busan, but his IQ score was 130 plus. He breezed through school and passed the university entrance exam in the top 2 percentile and he was offered a scholarship to Seoul National University. He took up the offer and studied law. The study was easy; the scholarship paid his tuition and the *Chil Sung Pa* paid for his housing and lifestyle. But, at the end of his study, the legal profession wanted nothing to do with him. Even though he passed the bar exam at his first attempt, the legal fraternity closed ranks. He was excluded.

CHAPTER 17

Blue Park

Sangho Park was 12 years old when his mother died of TB and his father disappeared into a crowd. He was poor before he was orphaned but he was resourceful. The family had lived in a small village outside of Busan and soon after his mother died, his father took him to Chigulchi Market in Busan; he said it would be a nice outing. Young Park was wearing blue jeans, a navy-blue shirt, dirty blue sandals and, on his head, he wore his treasured, faded, battered, royal blue New York Yankee's cap. The heady smells of fish, both fresh and sour, mixed with the sounds of bartering, the sounds of laughter, loud conversations and the salty sea air. Fishing boats were having their catch offloaded; auctioneers called for bids and the crowd pushed past the young Park. He held tight to his father's hand but as his father pushed deeper into the crowd; he found it more and more difficult to hold on and keep pace. The crowd became an entity that worked to separate son from father and the father conspired with the crowd. The father loosened his grip; he let his son's small hand slip from his and he became one with the crowd and young Park stood still, alone. The crowd no longer pushed him; they parted around him as though he was a rock in a stream, and his little brow wrinkled as he peered through gaps in the human mass. But, his father was gone.

Park worked his way to the dock where he found space among the fishing boats. He sat on a stanchion that held one of the boats fast to the dock. He was a small kid, a dirty kid dressed in blue and his eyes brimmed but he refused to allow the tears to flow. He kicked at the thick taut rope that ran from dock to boat and his thoughts flowed without beginning or end. As he sat, his mind a maelstrom of eddies, an ajumma passed by and handed him a banana. She walked on without looking back. Park looked from the banana to the disappearing woman and back to the banana. He had seen this exotic fruit before but he had never eaten one. He didn't know how to eat it so he just looked at it, running his fingers over its smooth flesh. It was a distraction from the reality he knew. His father had deserted him, melted into a crowd and left him alone. He was twelve years old and alone.

Park sat on the stanchion until the crowds thinned and the setting sun made silhouettes of the boats and buildings. He held on to a fading hope that his father would find him and take him home but by the time he decided to move, his hope had faded to an ever-weakening ache. He still held the banana in his small hand when he stood, but fatigue weakened his grip and the banana slipped from his hand and bounced once on the edge of the dock before splashing, almost gently, into the diesel rainbow on the surface of the water. Park watched the rainbow break, warp, wobble and reform as the water swallowed his banana like the crowd had swallowed his father. With an empty stomach and taste buds still unfamiliar with banana, Park walked slowly away.

After leaving his lonely stanchion, Park found more loneliness. The crowd was thinning and the remaining people were too busy with their own difficult post-civil war existence to acknowledge his needs. Eventually, he discovered a mound of waste cardboard and papers behind an overflowing refuse bin and he burrowed in, taking his hunger pains with him. The smells were irrelevant and hunger was no stranger so he was soon wrapped in fitful dreams. Park's father drifted through his sleep and made a feeble apology. His mother spoke of love and encouraged him to be better than her, to make something of his life. His sleeping mind found these visions baffling at best, teasing at worst. *If you are sorry why disappear into a crowd? Better than what? What were you anyway? What do I know of life? I'm twelve.*

He woke to the sound of arguing. An unwashed old man dressed in a dirty brown shirt and green plaid pants was fighting with an equally dirty and disheveled gray-haired woman. The man pushed the woman and the woman pushed back. The woman slapped the man and the man threw a punch that caught the woman on the side of her head and she fell onto Park's makeshift bed. The man moved in and kicked her in the kidneys. She did not move and the man started gathering up the cardboard and loading it onto his homemade cart. Park scurried out of the paper and cardboard like a large rat and kicked the man in the shin before running away.

This was the beginning of a hungry few days. Park stole food where he could. Mostly, the stall owners were aware of the theft and allowed it to happen. He stole food and collected food scraps and soon the market people were taken in by his smile and cheek, and it was not long before he acquired the nickname, Blue. And, with the nickname came acceptance and belonging.

"Hey Blue, ya want fish?"

"Hey Blue, ya want kimchi?"

"Hey Blue, ya want apples?"

"Hey Blue, ya want ...?"

And, it did not take long for him to see a profit in the products on offer.

At the edge of the market in a ship repair yard, the young Blue Park made himself a slum dwelling of wooden boxes, cardboard and old blankets. He wasn't the only person living rough but he was the youngest. The Korean War had left the cities and people shattered and destitute. One had little time for another. It was survival first. Some men, homeless or not, tried to molest him and others protected him; some women tried to mother him but he kept his distance from all without losing support. What was the point of relying on others when reliance led to weakness? At the age of twelve, he preferred independence. He had created a place to sleep and a place to store his gains. And soon, he took his cheeky smile and confident bravado to grimy restaurants where he ate free in return for supplying them with almost fresh produce. By the age of thirteen he was quite the entrepreneur. Rather than swapping produce for cooked meals, he began to take cash. His cash tins were multiplying and he could now afford to buy new clothes but he only bought blue clothes. And, the nickname remained.

Blue's career moved sideways when he was doing his usual rounds on a fine autumn day. He noticed a woman drop a card from her bag. He sauntered over, bent at the knees and scooped up the card. It was an ID Card. He slipped it into the pocket of his blue hoody and continued on his rounds. That night in his little dwelling, by the light of a kerosene lamp, he stared at the card and his little brain spun.

The young Blue Park had observed stall owners slipping money to hard looking men, protection money. He decided to follow one of these men. Back then, the streets were a crush of people, trucks and buses, but mainly people. Private cars were a rarity. It was easy for Blue to follow the man dressed in pin-striped pants and plaid jacket carrying a briefcase. After a walk and bus ride, which he did not pay for, Blue found himself outside the back door of a dodgy nightclub in the red-light district opposite the Busan Rail Station. He did not hesitate; he pulled open the door and walked in and tough men soon surrounded him. They prodded him and laughed at him and he stood firm and asked to see the boss.

One tough tried to hold him by the scruff of the neck but he broke away and stood with legs apart fronting three CSP goons.

"Ya got big balls little fella."

Park was not intimidated, "I wanna see the boss."

"Ya wanna keep those balls?"

His confidence began to waver but his resolve did not, "I wanna see the boss."

The three goons were beginning to tire of this game, "Do ya now, and why would the boss wanna to see you?"

"I've got somethin' he'll want."

The toughs laughed loud and long and began to push Blue back toward the rear exit, but the action was interrupted by an opening door and a soft voice demanding to know what the commotion was about.

Blue was quicker than the men pushing him. "Boss, I've got somethin' to offer ya." The old man looked at the small boy dressed in blue and then at the men surrounding him.

"Ya do, do ya?"

Blue did not reply; he just looked at the boss and smiled.

"Ya betta come in, then."

The toughs began to protest but the old man silenced them with a look before he turned to reenter his office. Blue quickly followed. The old man sat behind his desk and motioned for Blue to sit in an armchair that almost swallowed him. "Ok, so what ya got?"

Blue felt inside his pocket, retrieved the ID Card and dropped it on the desk.

"That's it kid?"

Blue hesitated only momentarily, "Well, no ... that's the beginning."

"Tell me more."

And with that, Blue spoke about his market produce business and offered the Boss exclusive rights to all his produce. He also offered more ID Cards. The old man listened gently, smiled occasionally and encouraged this feral kid dressed in blue to tell his story. Blue found the old man irresistible and he talked about his mother's death, his father's disappearance and his life on the streets. He talked and talked.

The Boss finally asked, "And school?"

Blue thrust out his boney chest, "Haven't been inna few years. Not interested."

"It also smells like ya not interested in washing either."

Blue smiled at this remark and unconsciously sniffed his armpit.

The Boss thought for a while, "I'll take ya offer, but ya gotta go to school."

"But ..."

"And ya not to cheat the market people. And don't steal. And have the occasional bath."

"But ..."

"That's my offer ... ya want it?"

Blue struggled out of the oversized armchair, stood facing the Boss over the desk and bowed low and long.

The Boss pushed one of three buzzers on his desk and waited. Silence filled the space between the boy and the old man until a knock on the door broke it.

"Come ... Myonghee, look after this boy, will ya."

CHAPTER 18

In the Kitchen

At 11pm, Blue Park stood up from his bar stool; he nodded his head toward the girls shuttling drinks and sex, "You reckon you can do that?" Jinni's face betrayed her. "I didn't think so."

"Can you wash dishes?"

"Of course."

"*Jenjang* woman, mind your manners."

"Sorry Mr. Park. Yes, I can."

Blue called over one his bouncers, "Take her to the kitchen and see what she's got."

Jinni breathed hard; she was afraid. Blue remained standing and watched as she followed the bouncer into the kitchen.

The kitchen was marginally clean. Stovetop burners lined one side and an ajumma worked away at boiling pots of stew. Another woman was at a cutting station slicing vegetables and fruit and two ajumma were at work among a pile of dishes and food scraps. One scraped leftovers off plates while the other was elbow deep in soapsuds. The bouncer spoke to the women and left. All the ajumma stopped what they were doing and looked at Jinni and began laughing. Jinni stood rooted to the floor and tried not to cry. One woman came forward with an apron and placed it around her neck. The ajumma deep in soapsuds stopped laughing and took off her rubber gloves and handed them to Jinni. No words were spoken. Jinni put the gloves on and got to work and as she did the laughing stopped. The others went back to their work while the spare woman supervised Jinni's work.

At 1:30am, the women had seen enough. They did not praise Jinni's washing. They just told her to be back in the kitchen at 8pm the next day.

When she exited the kitchen, the bar was full. Couples were dancing; the boys behind the bar were flat out as were the hostesses. No one noticed her as she slid along the wall to the door. It was opened for her by one of the bouncers and she offered a half smile; there was no response. She was hungry but she didn't want to see Myonghee so she walked a few blocks until she found an oden truck. She ate with night owls and said nothing. Soon she was back in her hotel room asking God to protect her.

For the next two weeks, she worked in the kitchen from 8pm until 4am and she ate with the kitchen staff during slower periods; most of the time it was eating on the run. She washed dishes most of the time but she did her share on the other stations when asked. Blue Park did not speak to her and the women in the kitchen didn't talk to her much although they laughed often with each other and Jinni listened to their banter. She smiled occasionally but she did not instigate conversation. Every now and then they asked her questions. They found out as much about her as she was prepared to give. It wasn't much although the release of information helped make her feel a trace of belonging. She was paid in cash at the end of each night and she used this money to pay for Room 33.

On the fourteenth evening, a bouncer entered the kitchen and ordered Jinni to follow him. She took off her gloves and apron and obeyed, a line of sweat ran down from her temple.

After they exited the kitchen, she trailed the bouncer to the end of the bar where Blue Park was sitting. Park nodded to the stool next to him and she sat as the bouncer returned to the shadows.

"Want a lemonade?" And Blue Park smiled at Jinni for the first time. His teeth were white and even.

"If you don't mind, I'd like a tonic water." Her smile was nervous.

The barman was standing nearby and he heard the order and moved off to prepare the drink, relieved that he didn't have to fake another lemonade.

Blue asked Jinni how the work was going and she reviewed her fortnight in the kitchen. Park told her that the ajummas thought she was adequate.

"They say you're not afraid to work. They also say that you've got a Business Degree from Ewha University."

They talked for a while before Blue told her to meet him at his office at 4pm the next day. And then, he stood up to leave; Jinni was dismissed. She stood and began heading toward the kitchen but Blue stopped her.

"No need to go back there."

But, Jinni did go back to the kitchen and she continued to wash dishes until the ajumma bustled her out. They said that she wasn't needed. For a while she kept working, ignoring the offer of an early night but the women squeezed her out and she was left standing in the kitchen looking at the backs of working women. Finally, she thanked the kitchen staff and withdrew; the ajumma did not watch her go.

She walked to the door and some of the girls nodded to her as did the bartenders. Once outside, hunger hit hard; she hadn't eaten anything in the kitchen. She felt a need to talk and she thought of the halmoni she'd met two weeks before. But, before turning and heading toward *MYONGHEE'S,* Jinni smiled at the two bouncers. The two men watched her go but they did not respond with more than a half smile. She did not look back; she was looking forward to talking to the halmoni and she was famished.

Jinni walked through the door of the restaurant and the sight of Myonghee at an empty table watching TV made her smile. "Halmoni, how has your night been?"

"Wow, look at ya girl, ya look good but ya shirts a bit stained. Ayego what have ya been doing? Ya really don't belong here but lookin' at ya face, I reckon I'm gonna see more of ya. Ya look good when ya smile ... do it more often will ya."

"Halmoni, I don't have any money; forgot to pick up my pay ..."

"Don't worry about it; sit yaself down with me and let's eat and ya can tell me about what ya been up to."

And with that, Jinni sat and the halmoni stood. She moved to the stove and lit the flame under a large pot of budae chigae. The smell of the rich stew made from spam, vegetables and chili filled the restaurant. There were half a dozen clients concentrating on their eating. There was not much talking but the sounds of eating demonstrated satisfaction with the food. "So, ya met Blue Park?" Jinni nodded. "Me and him go way back, like back before dinosaurs, back when Busan was just wakin' ... he's a good man. Sure, he looks rough, but he's as sharp as a pointy stick and, if he likes ya, he likes ya. Ya know what I mean? Ayego he's looked after me. He was thirteen when I first met him. Cheeky little blighter, he was."

Myonghee placed two plates filled with budae chigae over rice on the table and the two women ate noisily in silence. When the food was finished, Jinni spoke of her two weeks in the kitchen and about her appointment to see Blue Park the following afternoon.

"Still not sure about this but ya certainly seem determined

to do it your way."

"One day I will tell you but for now ..." Myonghee allowed the words to linger in the air and Jinni continued, "I might need a permanent residence ..."

The halmoni quickly cut Jinni off, "Hey, don't go gettin' ahead of yaself. Take the meetin' tomorrow and we'll talk again."

Jinni spoke a little about the *Love Always* Bar and the conversations with the kitchen ajumma. Myonghee spoke of her youth and of her relationship with Blue. It was easy to see that she had a maternal love for the man. The conversation was easy and an hour sped by. Customers had come and gone and now the little restaurant was empty except for Myonghee and Jinni. "I think I'll close up; ya wanna a beer?"

Jinni politely declined saying that she was tired and that she did not want to impose. Before adding, "But, thanks for the offer; I'll take it up soon."

The halmoni smiled and nodded her head.

And with that, Jinni stood and moved toward the door, "See you halmoni." And, the halmoni waved her goodbye and locked the door. She watched Jinni walk away before turning off most of the lights and moving to the fridge. She took out a cold beer and a cold glass and sat down at the table. As she opened the bottle, she smiled at old memories of Blue Park.

Jinni made her way through the streets and into Choi's Inn. She opened the door to room 33 and she wanted to just collapse on the bed, but her hair and clothes smelled of cooking and smoke. She needed a shower. And, she realized, she would need more clothes but, in the meantime, she washed her shirt in the sink and hung her jeans in front of the air-conditioner like she had been doing for the last few weeks. It was after two o'clock when she pulled the quilt up to her chin and it took less than five minutes for her to be lost in a dreamless sleep.

CHAPTER 19

The Pool Game

Stan arrives at Scrooge and there is no sign of Vince so he sits alone at the bar and orders a beer. He looks up at the blue fluorescent light spelling Scrooge and as he stares, it begins to change color and then it is a jumble of letters and shapes before it converts back to "Scrooge." He has a quick look around and no one is looking at him or the sign. He looks back and now it says, "YOU CAN BEAT MR. KIM." He calls over the barman and asks him to read the sign. The barman thinks he is joking and returns to his duties. Now the sign is flashing blues and reds, "YOU CAN BEAT MR. KIM."

Stan drags his eyes off the sign and looks over at the pool table; Mr. Kim, as always, is dominating. There are several US Soldiers mumbling into their beers that prove this point.

He looks back at the sign and it is still flashing, "*YOU CAN BEAT MR. KIM.*"

It takes a while but finally he stands up from his stool, walks over to the whiteboard and writes his name before drifting off to the bathroom. He splashes water on his face and looks into the mirror. Miji is behind him smiling. He spins around but the bathroom is empty. By the time he gets back, his name stands alone on the board.

"Where Stan?"

"That'll be me Mr. Kim."

"That your name. I see you often; I even talk to you sometimes but I never know your name."

"After this game, you will never forget it."

He can't believe he said those words. It's not his tone but he smiles and Mr. Kim wonders aloud, "Why?"

"Time and space, Mr. Kim, time and space."

As Stan busies himself with the racking of the balls, he puzzles over his words and manner. He pretends to be serious but he really does not care where each ball goes. While this is going on, a young man with a high-and-tight haircut walks to the white board and erases *Stan* and writes his own name in the space. Stan glances over and responds with, "So, you want to test your skills against mine?"

"I reckon I'll be playing Mr. Kim but your confidence is impressive."

Both men laugh and Stan places the triangle under the table and selects a cue from the rack. As he sights along its length to test its camber, Mr. Kim breaks and the balls fly hard but the white ball drops into the top right pocket.

The pool playing patrons stare in disbelief and the soldier breaks the silence, "Mr. Kim, what happened?"

"Don't know, never happen before, not for years anyway."

Stan takes the ball in hand and places it in line with the 7-ball. It is a simple shot and the 7-ball drops gently into the side pocket. He sinks three more balls before he misses a difficult bank shot. But, the white ball rolls in behind the black and Mr. Kim is snookered. A speculative shot sees the black ball drop into the right-side pocket and Stan wins on a foul. He almost moonwalks around the table but, out of respect for the old man, resists the temptation. Instead, he offers his hand and the two players shake.

"Well played Stan."

"A bit lucky but a win against the mighty Kim feels good."

Stan looks at the soldier and says, "You're up, mate."

"I don't think so. I'll sit this out. Mr. Kim and you can play a best of five. Ok Mr. Kim?"

"Sure, foul won't happen again."

"Rackem' up Mr. Kim." And Mr. Kim does his duty as the challenging player. Once the balls are neatly triangled, Stan breaks and the balls spread evenly around the table with two *smalls* down. Stan has never felt this kind of focus before. He is transcendental. And, soon the table is clear of the *smalls* and he is lining up the black. With no fanfare and no celebration, the black ball drops and Stan walks toward Mr. Kim and shakes his hand.

The whole bar is beginning to take notice and he speaks to no one in particular.

"I have never played like this before. Mr. Kim, rackem' up again."

Mr. Kim is not smiling but he does his challenger duty, again.

Stan breaks and the balls careen around the table but no balls drop. However, the white ball is awkwardly placed on the cushion and the black blocks its view of the other balls. Mr. Kim takes his cue to almost vertical as he attempts to screw the white ball around the black and onto the 2-ball. It is an impressive shot but the 2-ball comes to rest a centimeter short of the right center pocket. Stan shows no emotion; he does not look at Mr. Kim; he is not nervous. He takes aim at the 2-ball, sinks it and the rest of the game is a procession. Stan and Mr. Kim shake hands. "You owe me three beers. I'll take one for me, one for you and one for later. I'll be sitting in the corner; come sit with me."

As Stan sits at the table to wait for Mr. Kim and the beers, he looks back at the sign and it has taken over the whole wall and now it is flashing *"CONGRATULATIONS."*

Stan sits staring at the sign. He squints his eyes but it still reads *"CONGRATULATIONS."*

Mr. Kim arrives with three beers in hand, places them on the table and sits. The two men drink from their glasses while the other glass watches. The sound of pool balls colliding in the background is ignored.

"Good game Stan."

"Thanks"

Mr. Kim places his beer on the table. "No one ask me to drink before."

Behind the bar the sign is flashing again and this time it reads, *"ARE YOU MARRIED?"*

Stan looks at the old Korean man and asks, "Mr. Kim, are you married?"

Mr. Kim is puzzled by the question, but answers honestly, "Yes."

"How is she?"

"Ok, I guess."

For a while they drink beer in silence. In his mind, Stan knows he should slow down, don't rush things. But he is driven on by the flashing sign. Now it reads, *"DO YOU HAVE A DAUGHTER?"*

"Do you have a daughter?"

Mr. Kim looks at Stan, "Why you ask?"

Again, he knows he should back off and give Mr. Kim time to think and respond but he can't.

"Strange things have been happening of late. Do you have a daughter?"

At first, Mr. Kim does not react to Stan's question. He just looks into his beer. Finally, after what seems like minutes, he shakes his head and meets Stan's eyes. "Had a daughter." And Mr. Kim's voice cracks. "Died in Seongsu Bridge collapse, October 21, 1994."

Finally, Stan slows down. He drinks from his beer and looks back to the sign and it says, *"DON'T STOP."*

"Mr. Kim, is your daughter's name Miji?"

Mr. Kim just stares at Stan.

Stan looks into Mr. Kim's eyes, "She told me that I knew you and she told me to help *them*."

Mr. Kim's head falls onto his chest and tears run silently. He has nothing more to say. He stands up from the table and turns toward the door.

"Mr. Kim, before you go hear me out." Mr. Kim stands still but he remains facing the door. "Teach your wife to play pool. Bring her here on Tuesdays and Thursdays at 5pm and teach her to play." Mr. Kim does not even look at Stan. He just heads towards the door and is gone.

Stan looks at the closed door for a long time before he looks back at the beers on the table. Mr. Kim has left his glass half full; Stan's is three quarter full and the third glass is empty. And the sign behind the bar reads, *"Scrooge."*

CHAPTER 20

How did I get Here?

Stan orders a whiskey and sits alone drinking, wondering what had just happened. Eventually, he gets up and walks to the door. On the way down the stairs, he meets Vince coming up. The two talk for a few minutes before continuing their separate journeys. Vince, will drown his unsuccessful attempts at taking his love interest further, and Stan will head home to ponder the unreal. Stan doesn't have far to go and he is soon home. He turns on the TV, pours himself a whiskey, takes off his socks and lies down on the couch. Manchester United are playing Queens Park Rangers and Stan turns the Korean commentary down to a whisper. He takes a sip of his drink before placing the glass on the side table. He is not watching the TV; instead, he is staring at the bare light bulb trying to make sense of his new knowledge that his ghost vision is Mr. Kim's daughter. He doesn't know whether to feel pleased or afraid. He doesn't know how to help them and he can't work out why he made the suggestion that Mr. Kim teach his wife how to play pool. Eventually, his head comes to rest on the arm of the couch. His eyes close and he is soon dreaming.

Stan is in Central Australia just south of Alice Springs. He is in the back seat of an old Holden station wagon. He looks at the back of the necks of the two men in the front seat. They are wrinkled and the color of dingo shit and a few blackheads need attention. The driver has an eye patch covering his right eye. Stan can see it in the rearview mirror. And the eye patch asks him where he is going.

"I don't know."

The driver looks at the man beside him and says, "He don't know."

Both men laugh.

"He's fuckin' nowhere and where's he goin'? No fuckin' where."

Both men laugh again before the driver asks his mate to pull the top off another VB. He claims his throat is drier than the land beyond the open windows. He looks in the rearview mirror with his one good eye and says, "What ya say ya name was?"

"Stan"

Both men laugh again and. They have an expletive laden conversation about the feminine nature of Stan's name.

"Give poofta Stan a beer."

"I'm ok thanks. I'll pass on the beer."

"Ya hear that? Poofta Stan is gonna pass on the VB. Wanka. He's a poofta and a wanker."

Both men laugh again, and the driver gives the steering wheel a tug left and a tug right and the old Holden does a little fishtail and both men laugh. The driver finishes his beer with two long gulps and throws the can out of the open window. The passenger doesn't take much longer to finish his beer and he winds down his window and throws the empty can out. It bounces along the shoulder of the road before disappearing into the spinifex.

The passenger fishes around in the polystyrene Esky at his feet and pulls out two more VB cans dripping water. "Another?"

"Fuckin' oath. The drought, she ain't quenched."

Again, he looks into the rearview mirror.

"What ya think of the big word, poofta Stan? You know any

words starting with the letter Q..?

... let's play 'Eye Spy.' I'll go first. Are ya listening poofta Stan? Eye spy with my little eye something beginning with Q or is it P or is it W? What ya reckon poofta Stan? What about you Bill, get that big brain of yas working? I'll give you a hint. Look behind ya."

And the driver laughs again.

"Fuck me, mate, turn 'round and have a look will ya."

Bill turns around and looks at Stan. He sees a man on the wrong side of 40 dressed in a white linen Zara shirt with the sleeves buttoned at the wrist, blue Zara short pants with the bottoms folded up into cuffs, red Crock sandals on his feet and Rayban, Wayfarer sunglasses covering his eyes.

Bill starts to laugh, "Got it." but he can't speak further because he can't stop laughing. The two men laugh loud and long.

"Fuck mate, ya made me cry ya bastard."

And both men continue to laugh. The laughter goes on for several minutes before Bill is able to attempt to speak.

"Righto let's see ... it's in the back seat and it starts with a Q or a P or a W."

And both men start to laugh again.

"Na na, I'm gonna get this out before the laughter strangles me. In the back seat we have a Q for queen or is it a P for poofta or is it a W for wanka."

And laughter again fills the old Holden.

The driver claims that the crying has drained all his fluids and demands another beer. Bill hands over the can to the driver who uses his knee to hold the steering wheel steady while he pulls the ring-top off his can.

"Fuck mate, you've held onto this can for too long; it's now as warm as piss."

"Drink up and stop ya fuckin' winjin."

The beers are again polished off quickly and again the cans are thrown out of the windows.

Stan looks out at the harsh beauty. He watches as the blinding sun melts into the parched earth and it turns the sky into shades moving from orange to red. Clumps of spinifex grass sparsely populate the red desert. They survive off morning dew. The occasional scrubby gum tree fights for life in the dry land and their silhouettes turn the reality into a Heidelberg School landscape. As the sun disappears, the fauna starts moving. Goannas have spent the day in burrows shared with snakes and scorpions; all begin to stir. Giant red kangaroos have spent the day in the relative cool of the sparse shade in rocky outcrops. As the dusk takes over and the temperature begins to fall, these giants of the Red Center begin to prowl and to pick at the spinifex. They cross the road with not a sense of danger. The old Holden swerves; the men laugh and continue to open beer cans and swallow the contents. And, they continue to throw the cans out of the windows.

After a few close calls Stan says, "Hey guys, it might be a good idea to slow down a little now that dusk is on us, and how about not throwing the cans out the window. We can wait until we get to the next town and drop the cans into a rubbish bin."

"Ya hear that? Poofta Stan reckons 'dusk is on us.' Wanker. Ya're a wanker poofta Stan, a fuckin' wanker. Hey Bill, what ya reckon about poofta Stan?"

"Fuckin' QPW." And both men start laughing. But then, the driver turns serious and looks at Stan in the rearview mirror.

"Hey poofta Stan, Ya don't know where ya goin'. Ya know where ya is?"

Without attempting sarcasm, Stan says, "Well, it looks like Central Australia."

While the words hang in the stale air of the old Holden, the driver steps on the break and the car fishtails down the dirt road. He adjusts for a right drift and then a left drift and the car finally comes to a halt with the headlights staring off into the abyss of empty.

"You fuckin' wanker, get out. I'm done with ya poofta bullshit. Get the fuck out."

He even goes so far as to twist around in his seat. He turns his one good eye on Stan and it confirms no charity. The driver reaches for the door lever and pushes open the door. "Fuck off."

Stan starts to protest but quickly recognizes the futility of the protest. He picks up his daypack and steps out of the car. The driver revs the old Holden. Bill throws a couple of full beer cans at Stan hitting him in the shoulder with the first one and a glancing blow to the head with the second one.

"Don't waste good beer on the poofta."

"Sport mate. Like shootin' road signs."

The one-eyed driver drops the clutch; the old Holden's wheels spin furiously and the car speeds off leaving Stan in a cloud of red dust. The dust lingers. There is no wind to blow it anywhere, and Stan is alone.

The night closes quickly around him and his small pack. He is sitting on a rock by the side of a dirt road; his left foot rests on an ant nest and the ants begin to swarm around his Crocks. He is lost in his own confusion and he doesn't notice the activity around his feet. The land is flat, not a rise, not a ripple. The horizon is endless and the sky is infinite and stars pop into this infinity like gentle explosions as the sky moves through shades of ever deepening blue until it is blue-black. The stars continue to multiply and some streak across the sky. Stan notices none of this. There is no moon and the stars' light is an impressive display but not illuminating.

Stan looks up and down the road in desperation. He cannot see far but off in the distance he notices two bouncing lights. He has hope. He stands and pulls his pack over his shoulder and gets ready to wave down the approaching car. The lights tease him, appearing to be closer one moment and farther away the next. Sometimes they even rise into the sky and blend with the stars; sometimes they disappear only to return moments later. Stan's thoughts move from hope to despair and back to hope only to fall hopelessly into despair. And, despair swallows him and he begins to cry. He sits back onto his rock and allows his head to fall into his hands.

"Good evening Stanley."

Stan lifts his eyes and parked in the middle of the road is a new, white Range Rover. The interior light is muted and the passenger side window is open. Stan squints to make out the driver who knows his name. The driver's seat is reclined beyond 45 degrees. Lounging in the seat is an Asian woman. Her hands are cupped behind her head; her knees are spread and her feet rest lightly on the steering wheel. She is naked.

"I just wanted to thank you for making contact with my father. I enjoyed the pool game. Where were we ... yes that's right ..."

And, she is sitting in front of Stan with his foot in her hand.

"This little piggy went to market; this little piggy stayed home ..."

Stan forces his eyes open and sits upright in bed; he is shaking, unsettled and disorientated. He does not have an erection. The sun is sneaking over the eastern horizon and the greyness of his bedroom is disturbed by streaks of morning light. An agile breeze filtering in through the open window disturbs the curtains. There will be no more sleep for Stan this morning. He rises from the bed and looks back at the pillow; it is damp with tears. "Shit," and he pads off to the bathroom where he runs the shower, steps in and allows the water to massage his back and shoulders.

CHAPTER 21

From the Kitchen to the Books

Jinni's meeting with Blue Park ended with her being offered the job of bar manager. She almost declined the offer; however, Blue is a hard man to refuse. He had been putting off hiring someone thinking that the bar pretty much ran itself but Blue was a master at seizing opportunities. His business had thrived because he knew when to buy and when to sell. He knew it was time to buy.

Jinni was to balance the books, both of them, and she was not sure what complications this would present. And, she was to supervise the girls who were both waitresses and soft prostitutes. If a customer wanted them to sit and talk and drink, they did; the cost of drinks and food covered this service. If a customer wanted to take a girl out of the bar, it was the girl's choice to go or not to go. If the decision was to go, the customer paid the bar a fee, 50,000 won, and the girl negotiated her own fee for her services. Jinni was to aid in the negotiations and collect both fees. The girls' fees were banked for them. It was Blue's policy that helped protect the girls present and future. There were always big men in the shadows if a customer got nasty. They rarely did because Blue Park's reputation had been forged in violence. If Jinni wanted, she could make extra money by going with a customer but not until the bar closed and the takings securely locked in the safe. That was the deal and that was what Jinni shook hands on. She could choose her clothing but Blue Park made it quite clear that blue jeans and white T-shirt suited her just fine. But, he did suggest that she needed more than one pair of each. With that suggestion, Blue Park took a roll of notes from his pocket and gave Jinni 500,000 won.

"You start work at six tomorrow evening and the bar will close when there are no more customers. But, if there are people still around a 6am, my boys will remove them. The boys behind the bar look after themselves so don't worry too much about them. But, if they need your help, you help. That goes for anybody, if they need your help, you help and if you need their help, they'll help you. Got it."

She hesitated but she needed the job and the benefits. "I got it."

"And, in one month we'll sit down here together again and you'll tell me what you really want from me."

He gave Jinni a rare smile and stood up from his chair and ushered her toward the office door, "And, one more thing," Jinni turned, "Food and drinks are on me, but any sign of drunkenness, and you will be fired. No questions or explanations."

Jinni nodded and she started to walk out the door.

"By the way, I hear you've met Myonghee."

And, he smiled again. Jinni stopped and looked around at Blue but said nothing before walking out of the office toward the bar. She sat on a stool and spent some time digesting Blue Park's words. She thought about her former life in Australia, the Sampoong Department Store collapse and she thought about her family. Finally, she gestured with her eyes to the barman and he left his preparations for the evening and sauntered over.

"Nice to see you again; I'm Jinni and I'm moving from the kitchen to the front starting tomorrow at six."

He smiled, "I know."

Jinni returned his smile and asked, "Would you get me a tonic water please?"

"Yep, and call me Ho; actually, my name's Hochul but everyone calls me Ho."

With that, he moved back to his station and cut a slice of lemon and dropped it into a glass with a few cubes of ice before pouring in the tonic water. He returned to Jinni and placed a coaster on the bar and the glass on the coaster. Jinni put a 5,000 won note on the bar.

"Food and drinks are free for *Love Always* staff"

"I start tomorrow."

"You've been working in the kitchen and Blue told me to look after ya."

Jinni sat for a while sipping her tonic water and thinking. Two and half weeks ago she was drinking coffee in an expensive café in Seoul and now she was in the employ of a gangster in Busan. She tried to make sense of the vortex and she decided to follow the current. A half an hour later she stood up and said goodbye to Ho before heading out into the evening air. She did not go back to the hotel; instead, she hailed a taxi and was soon in the fashion and cultural district of Gwangbok-dong. It was time to buy some work clothes.

It was nine o'clock before she got back to Texas Street and she dropped into Myonghee's for dinner.

"Ya been shoppin' have ya?"

"Yeah, I got a promotion. You are looking at the new bar manager of *Love Always*."

"Ya gotta be jokin'. That was my job. Ayego ... ya look afta the girls and they'll look afta you. Have ya met em yet?"

"Not really. I plan on getting in early tomorrow to make myself known."

"How ya feelin'?"

"Don't really know. I don't know if I should be doing this and I don't know if I can do this."

"Ya qualified aren't ya?"

"Qualified for business but not for *the night.*"

"A few weeks ago, I was tellin' ya to go back to Seoul and now I'm encouragin' ya to do the job."

"Thanks Halmoni."

"We will see. Ya wanna eat? The Jaeuk bap is good if ya like spicy pork with rice."

"I'm Korean, of course I like Jaeuk bap, just ease back on the spicy will you."

And, the women laughed while the halmoni ladled the hot pork stew over rice.

"Halmoni, may I have a beer, please?"

"Of course, in fact, I'll have one with ya."

The food was placed on the table; the beer bottle was opened and two glasses were filled. "Cunbae."

"Yeah, cheers."

Jinni ate and the two women drank beer and Jinni told of her meeting with Blue Park and a little bit about her fears and hopes for the job but she still did not speak of her past. Myonghee did not push. That time would come but this was not that time. Myonghee spoke of her time in the job and gave suggestions and warned Jinni about the consequences of bad judgments. After a while, Jinni again broached the subject of an apartment or room to rent and Myonghee's reply was to give it a month.

"Ya got a good deal at Choi's. Like Blue said, give it a month."

Jinni wondered about the good deal, thinking 30,000 per night was pretty standard.

It was almost eleven when she left the restaurant. She walked toward her hotel and as she approached *Love Always,* she nodded to the doormen, "Evening Left, evening Right," and they nodded back and she sent a smile in their direction. Just a few minutes later she was about to enter Choi's Inn when a thunder-clap had her cowering against the wall of a building. She tried to calm herself as images of the collapsing department building flooded over her. It took some minutes for her to quell her emotions. She looked around; her brow was damp but no one was watching so she entered the inn and spoke to the window, her voice not quite her own, "I'll need three more nights, please."

"That'll be 30,000 won."

"No, three nights, not one."

"30,000 won, Blue Park said to look after ya so I'm lookin' after ya."

Jinni didn't know what to say, so she just slid 30,000 won under the window and thanked the voice before heading to the elevator.

As she waited for the elevator, the voice said, "Good luck with the job."

Jinni turned and looked at the frosted glass and wondered at the extent of Blue Park's influence. The elevator doors opened and she hesitated before entering the confined space. Sampoong regularly entered her thoughts and the unexpected thunder had rocked her. Finally, she stepped inside, the doors closed and she held her arms across her chest until the doors opened on the third floor. The moment she walked into her room, lightning and thunder danced in step and raindrops pounded on the window. She dropped her bags on the floor and held herself tight. Eventually, she removed her jeans and slipped into bed; she pulled the sheet up to her throat, rolled into a fetal position and prayed for sweet dreams.

CHAPTER 22

Meeting the Wife

Stan plans to keep quiet about his Central Australia dream. The Miji ghost really disturbs him. But not everything goes to plan. On the Thursday after the dream, after finishing his private classes, he heads to Scrooge at around 6pm. As he walks up the stairs to the third floor, he hears the familiar sound of colliding pool balls. The automatic door opens and there is Mr. Kim helping a middle-aged woman with her cue stroke. He looks up and half smiles at Stan.

"What's up?"

"Good to see you. I can only assume that this lovely woman is your wife. Nice to meet you Mrs. Kim."

He bows and offers his hand, which is taken by the ajumma.

"Not Kim, name Lee."

And Stan remembers that Korean women don't change their names after marriage. For such a chauvinistic society, it is a welcome bit of accidental feminism.

"Don't speak English." Mr. Kim's wife continues, but she has a firm grip and a smile on her face. "Nampyong tell me about you."

"Husband, yobo." Helps Mr. Kim.

"What?"

"Not Nampyong, English word 'husband.'"

Stan offers to buy them both a drink and he also suggests that Mr. Kim teach his wife English.

"Ajumma, beer? Mr. Kim a beer for you?"

Stan is already heading toward the bar before the replies are spoken. The words pass by him and are heard by the Pilipino barman who bends down to retrieve three cold glasses from the fridge.

"Saeng makju, segae chusaeo."

"I'm Pilipino not Korean. But sure, I'll get you three draft beers. ... Vince was in last night; he was asking after you."

"Did he say if he was coming in tonight?"

"Didn't ask, maybe. Go back to your table, I'll get Nancy to bring the beer to you."

"No, I'll have mine here and you can send the other two to the old pool players."

Stan takes his seat at the bar and looks around and counts six customers including himself. He twists a little on the stool so that he can watch the action at the pool table. Mr. Kim and his wife raise their glasses in thanks and he raises his in return. The ajumma looks like she will learn quickly; in fact, she looks like she has played before. Mr. Kim is pretty gruff with his advice but she takes it in good spirit and soon the two are smiling. Stan smiles as he watches. Mr. Kim puts his hand over his wife's hand as he teaches her how to steady her bridge. The touch lingers longer than necessary and the husband and wife turn their faces toward each other and their noses almost touch. They smile and the bridge breaks. They both move apart and pick up their beers and both drink deeply. Stan also drinks deeply and Miji is back in his vision. The image of her naked body reclining in the plush seat of the Range Rover with her hands clasped behind her head and her feet on the steering wheel disturbs and haunts him.

The barman's voice dissolves Stan's vision. "Mr. Kim brought the ajumma in last Tuesday too. She's learning quickly. They were at it for nearly two hours and they've been playing for over an hour tonight. And, this is their first drink."

"Impressive."

"Maybe, maybe not."

The door opens and Vince walks in.

"Stan, I heard about the pool game. Jaysus, you're a psychotherapist. Can I buy you a beer?"

He turns to the barman and orders a CASS for Stan and a San Miguel for himself and Stan downs the remainder of his beer in one gulp and accepts the fresh beer and asks Vince about the tango lessons.

"I danced with a chair last night."

"Well that must have been a thrill. You're that popular."

"Jaysus they have some pretty peculiar rules. Once in the studio, you are not allowed to have a partner, so even though I came with Jiyoung, I couldn't dance with her. Well I could but once in the blue moon."

"So, her name is Jiyoung. Nice name. But, there has to be other chicks to dance with, so what's with the chair?"

"Odd numbers, mate, odd numbers, and ... I guess I'm the worst dancer ... and the coach wouldn't let me sit down. He told me that I needed to practice and he forced me to pick up the chair. I tell you, it was a strange feeling ... maybe a little like you with the vacuum cleaner; at least I could keep my clothes on ... any news from the vacuum cleaner lady?"

"Nope."

"Mate you're scared. I can see it in your eyes ... you're scared."

"What about the tango girl?"

"The classic Stan topic change." Vince avoids answering because he doesn't want to mention that she only wants to dance. "Any dreams lately."

"Shit, I was hoping you wouldn't ask. I had a doozy a couple of nights ago, but I managed to wake myself up and get out of it. I was in Central Australia ..." And Stan retells the dream to Vince. And Vince listens sometimes, thinks about Jiyoung a little and watches the pool players. Stan gets as far as being kicked out of the car and stops.

"You want another beer?"

"Sure. You finished with the dream?"

Stan places the order and notices that the bar has filled and Mr. Kim and his wife have vacated the pool table and retired to a corner. They drink beer and watch two American GI's inexpert game. Mr. Kim explains things to his wife and she nods and the GI's miss shots and fluke others.

Stan explains how the dream freaked him out. It disturbed him so much that he pulled himself out of the dream. The beers are placed on the bar, and Stan picks his up and takes a good draught and starts in on the end of the dream.

At the end of the telling, Vince asks, "Mate, were you tempted to stay with the action, you know, like get in the car?"

"No, I just wanted out. It took me a week to recover from the last encounter."

"She was just trying to thank you. Maybe you could give her my address next time she visits."

"Drink up Vince. I'm going to have one more before getting out of here. Your shout."

Vince orders the beers and turns to Stan, "Can you describe this woman again?"

"Let it go Vince. Shit, she's a ghost; she can be anything she wants to be. I just hope that her mother and father get their act together so that she doesn't visit me again. Now tell me about your programming. Tell me about anything but change the topic. The dream has been related and I got out of it."

"Can I talk about my soccer team? The field opens up and I see where my team mates ought to be and I pass the ball into space and no one runs onto it ..."

Stan and Vince drink their final beer and they both nod to the old couple in the corner as they leave the bar.

CHAPTER 23

And, Another Dream Not Remembered

Stan sleeps and his dream takes him back to his mother's hospital ward.

Stan fills his glass with water and returns to the window to watch the dogs playing in the park. Some dogs are happy to explore on their own, sniffing at a tree one moment and rolling in shit the next; other dogs stay close to their owners and yet others hang in little canine gangs sniffing each other's bums over and over again.

He tries to explain what he sees out of the window but he is asked to continue with the story.

"Why can't I keep sailing with the wind?"

No one answers so Stan again returns the ward to Mulkila IV and his dream has him watch a movie of a known event.

Stan was peeing in the snow, making a little yellow hole in the ice and as he was peeing, he was looking around at the boundless panorama. A hundred meters or so down from his open-air toilet, a colored mass distracted him. Everything was white and yet there was a small mound of color in the white. It drew Stan to it and he probed the ice with his ice axe as he moved cau-

tiously downward; the fear of walking on the glacier un-roped unnerved him. The closer he got, the more the mass resembled clothing. He wanted to stop, to just turn around and forget what the mass resembled. The clothes cloaked a human corpse.

There is another pause as Stan fights his emotions.

"How did this influence you to leave Australia?"

His three companions responded to his call and they were soon standing next to each other looking at the body that appeared quite fresh. It was dressed in blue jeans, a checked shirt and a pale blue slicker. Beside him were a sleeping bag and a few cans of food. His eyes were empty sockets and his teeth shone white in a lipless smile but his skin was tanned and taught.

Stan stared out of the window remembering.

His mother prods him to continue but Stan stares out at the bright blue of the sky and marvels at the beauty of it, so much more welcoming than the navy blue of the high-altitude sky.

The four climbers discussed who the corpse could be and the consensus was a member of an Indian Army climbing group that had been on the mountain the year before. One of the guys had brought the two-way radio so they radioed Bobby Singh and he suggested it was a boy from a climb twelve years before. Stan disagreed but Bobby Singh spoke of a university boy who had been climbing with his two friends when he fell down a crevasse. He said that the other two had tried to get him out but they ended up leaving him and going for help to the nearest village, which was about three days fast hiking away. He spoke of glacial movement and global warming as a reason for the corpse's current position on the top of the ice. Stan still leaned toward the soldier theory so he opened up the dead man's shirt to look for dog tags. He opened three buttons but there were no tags, only flesh that was beginning to ooze. For some reason, he re-buttoned the shirt. They looked for other identifying features and Stan saw that he was wearing a watch. He was still

kneeling beside the corpse so he leaned across and undid the band and removed the watch from his wrist. It was not engraved but he thought that someone might recognize it. If not, it appeared to be a better watch than he could ever afford.

"You're kidding. You stole some dead guys watch."

"Kind of, I guess." And he looks at his mother with a weak smile.

This story ... this event ... really throws me. As you now know, it led to me walking away from Australia for ten years; maybe I'll be away longer"

"You spoke of an epiphany; are we close to this moment?"

"I'll speed it up a bit."

The four men walked back up to the campsite in silence and brewed a pot of tea. The sun was too high in the sky to get to the summit and back that day as was the plan, and motivation had leached into the snow. They sat around discussing who the corpse was and what should be done. They weren't geared up to take it down the mountain. They discussed dropping him down another crevasse but they didn't want to take that responsibility. What they did decide was not to attempt the summit. They decided to make use of the afternoon sun to get most of the way back to basecamp so they packed up and headed down the glacier taking more precautions than ever to keep the rope taut. But, they were going downhill and, going down is much quicker than going up. Within a few hours of basecamp, the light failed. They discussed the idea of continuing by torchlight but what they had seen that morning convinced them to make camp and push on in the morning. The campsite was just above the upper reaches of the moraine field. Bobby called on the two-way radio to tell them that he would send porters in the morning as far as he felt it safe to do so; they would take the loads for the final push. That night they prepared dinner and ate in silence, each man was at the mercy of his own thoughts. They were again inside their sleeping bags early and Stan dreamed

of sitting around a dining table as the host of a dinner party. His guests were his three climbing companions but their eye sockets were empty; body fluids were leaking from the empty sockets and they wore lipless grins. He served them roast pork with crackling and roast potatoes with Brussels sprouts.

"You don't like Brussels sprouts."

Stan wakes with the taste of Brussel sprouts on his tongue and as he brushes his teeth he

wonders where the taste came from.

CHAPTER 24

Not Again

After one month into the job, things had been sometimes good and sometimes difficult for Jinni. Some of the girls were pleased to have her style and negotiating skills around but others resented her outsider status; there was the occasional grumbling about her posh accent. And, some days she was confident of getting everyone onside and some days she just wanted to retreat to the kitchen. During the first week and a half, Blue Park spent more time in the bar than normal offering silent support. He was subtle when he made sure the girls did what she suggested, as subtle as Blue can be. Ho and his bar partner taught her to mix drinks and she enjoyed the banter with them and she taught them how to make lemonade. The bouncers were never far away and she felt that they had her back. At the beginning of each day, Blue and Jinni went over the books and she quickly got the hang of it; she was used to numbers and she enjoyed manipulating them. That was the easy part of the job.

The customers were a little intimidated by her touch of class and educated ways so they were pretty content to accept her compromises and suggestions. She stood out like a dolphin in a pack of sharks. She wore little to no make-up as opposed to her girls' excess. Most of the time she wore blue jeans and a white T-shirt although, once or twice a week, she wore black jeans with a white silk blouse buttoned low and occasionally she wore a navy-blue blazer. Her girls wore short skirts or tight dresses with too tight blouses and high-heeled shoes. The customers were a mix of respectable businessmen taking a walk on the wild side and dodgy characters whose earnings were unknown in quantity and legality. She treated them all with equal respect and equal distance. Most nights a customer or two would try some line or other but each were rebuffed with a controlled smile and a view of her departing back. Initially, the pick-up lines disgusted her and she always suffered the eyes as though they were Minho's hands. She was surrounded by desire; the potential sexual energy was a stretched bungee cord and for the first few weeks she felt unclean.

After those first few weeks Blue Park returned to his usual routine, which saw him sit at the corner of the bar for a few hours most nights. His wardrobe was impressive but there was never a color outside the spectrum of blue, not even white. He talked to customers who came his way. A few regulars were invited to sit but not for long. Jinni sat with him occasionally when things moved slowly. The two were building an easy connection forged from their Seoul education. Blue was not bitter toward the legal profession; he enjoyed the law and kept up with all aspects of criminal and business law. Both spoke little but both spoke intelligently. And, neither spoke of personal things. One was as closed as the other. On the night of the thirtieth day, the two sat together for a few minutes after midnight and Blue sipped his soda water and worried his coaster before saying, "It's been thirty days since you moved out of the kitchen. You've fitted in pretty well." He had been looking at the coaster when he said this but now he turned on his stool and looked at Jinni. She felt his eyes and returned his gaze.

"Thanks Blue."

"You have an appointment to see me at 4pm tomorrow."

Before she could respond, Blue had risen from his stool and was heading toward the door. On his way out, the barmen paid their respects with, "Goodnight boss," and Blue responded with a nod. He walked past various employees as he moved forward and he nodded to them and they also responded with, "Goodnight boss." Then, he was gone. The atmosphere in the bar did not change after his departure. His staff felt at ease and secure when he was around and they knew their jobs when he wasn't around.

Jinni gestured to Ho with her eyes and, in response, he took a bottle of tonic from the fridge, dropped a few ice cubes into a glass and began to pour the tonic over the ice. "Put a finger of gin in that tonic would you Ho."

The barman hesitated momentarily, "Tanqueray?"

"Tanqueray 10, I need a kick."

The barman looked at her with a hint of concern but he picked up the green bottle from the shelf and added a shot of gin to the tonic. He cut a slice of lime and dropped it into the glass and stirred the contents. He placed a single mint leaf on the top before picking up the glass and a coaster. Ho's movements were graceful and economical and the gin and tonic was soon on the bar in front of her. She thanked the barman and took a sip and then another. She did not want to think about Blue or about what she would have to tell him the next day. Over the last four weeks she had almost forgotten about her real motive for stepping into the shadows of Busan. She was just busy surviving the job. When she was at work, it was busy and when she was not at work she was tired. Park had given her a month to build the courage to tell her story but she was still not prepared for this exposure. She had only told her mother about Minho's abuse and her advice was to obey. How was a man going to understand her motives for faking her death? Blue does not accept half answers; it was going to have to be the whole story. She drained the glass before she headed to the kitchen to grab a snack. After a few minutes, she returned to her place at the bar with a plate of fruit and asked Ho for a tonic water. Ho went to work with a sense of relief.

While she was eating, one of the girls approached her with a request for assistance. She drained the remainder of her tonic, took a bite of watermelon and followed the girl to a booth where three men were drinking 18-year-old Blue Imperial Whiskey. She greeted the men with her trademark, controlled smile. The men were all around 35 years old. They were dressed in suits but all had removed their coats and loosened their ties. She looked from man to man and only one of them held her gaze. He was a foreigner with carefully groomed blond hair and he was broad shouldered, tall with a strong jawline and his half smile was self-assured. The self-assured smile and something in his eyes, his gaze, reminded Jinni of her ex-husband, something repulsive yet something magnetic. The girl sat beside the smallest man and Jinni remained standing. Even though she remained standing, she spread ease whilst remaining aloof. She outlined the bar charge and the girl's fee. The customer accepted without negotiation, handed the cash to Jinni, and soon man and girl were on their way out of the bar arm-in-arm. The remaining two men continued to drink and Jinni moved back to her stool wondering what a foreigner was doing in the bar and how could a foreigner look like her ex.

By the time it was 3am, the only customers left were the two men in their booth and they were putting on their suit coats and preparing to leave. They had settled their bill and they had said their goodbyes and one walked a little unsteadily toward the exit. The foreigner, the man who had held Jinni's gaze, turned and walked confidently toward the bar. He put his hand on the back of the stool next to Jinni.

"May I?"

A lighthearted chat might distract her from her thoughts so she shrugged her shoulders and the man sat.

"May I buy you a drink?" He asked in slightly accented Korean.

Jinni again shrugged so the man looked to the barman and pointing at Jinni's empty glass, "Gin-Tonic dugae chusaeyo." The barman looked at Jinni and she nodded.

The barman soon had two glasses sitting on coasters on the bar. Both said Cunbae and they sipped together. Jinni placed her drink back on its coaster and took a look around the bar. Two girls were cleaning the booth just vacated; two bouncers sat in the shadows drinking coke; the barman was organizing his bottles and one of the girls was assisting him with the cleaning. She spoke to the bouncers, "Think we're done for the night. May as well close up. Get the door will you boys."

One of the shadows moved quickly to oblige. The other sat and watched the action at the bar. He liked Jinni a little more than he should and he had never seen her allow a man to sit with her before.

"My friends call me Alexei."

Jinni looked into his confusing eyes.

"Look Jinni ..."

She jumped, "How do you know my name?"

"I've been watching you; I've noticed you around. I came into the bar last week, and I saw you at a restaurant down the road the other night. And, I've heard others mention your name. It's a nice name. I like it, and I'd like to know you better."

"You can't be serious."

And she stared at the man.

"It's not a pick-up line. I don't do this sort of thing. I'm a regular visitor to Busan for business and that's all I do."
Jinni got on the front foot, "What would your wife think about all this? I guess she's back in your home, wherever that is, looking after your kids and worrying about you." And, she stared at

Alexei before lifting her glass and taking a drink.

He smiled, "Not married, never been married; what about you." It was his turn to stir his gin and tonic and take a drink.

"Alexei, it's been nice meeting you but it's time to close this place so let's call it quits."

"I don't mind waiting. I'll meet you any place; let's say 4am."

She looked closely at the man sitting next to her. "No, this has gone far enough." And she called the boys to escort Alexei from the bar.

He placed 20,000 won on the bar.

Jinni spoke to the shadows, "Let him out boys."

Once the doors were locked, she asked the barman to add more tonic to her glass. She sipped on her drink while she tallied the cash and credit card receipts. As she was doing so, she asked the bouncer to open the door for the girls to leave and to turn the lights down. Soon there were only Ho, the two bouncers and Jinni left. Ho had finished cleaning up behind the bar and was ready to leave. One bouncer opened the door for him and he waved goodbye as he slipped into the night. The shadows were waiting for her to secure the cash in the safe before they could leave. They knew their job and they took it seriously. The takings were good if not spectacular and she collected everything into a leather satchel and headed to Blue's office. She turned on the light and knelt before the old safe in the corner. She deftly turned the tumblers and opened the door. She placed the takings amongst various documents and parcels and closed the door and gave the tumbler a spin.

It was 4:05 when the bouncers escorted Jinni out of the bar.

"You ok?" Asked Left. There was concern in his voice.

"Yeah, I'm good."

And she waved to the boys and walked away. The burly bouncers watched her go. They were tempted to follow. They had not seen her drink before and they had not seen her sit with a man before. They were concerned but they watched her walk away into the night. Eventually, the two bouncers looked at each other and shrugged. They both took a long look around the streets and saw nobody, nothing; their hands searched and found each other and their faces came close and they kissed gently and lovingly. And, they too walked off into the night.

Jinni walked into Choi's Inn, said hello to the frosted glass and slipped into the elevator and pressed the button for the third floor. As the doors closed, the fear of enclosed places tugged a little but it was easing. She opened the door to her room and walked straight to the bathroom to wash her face. Visions of Blue sitting behind his desk flowed around her; she wasn't ready to spill her guts. She dried her face and sat on the edge of the bath. She sat for a good two minutes with her head in her hands and then there was a knock on the door.

She was puzzled but she figured it must be someone from *Love Always.* Most knew she lived at Choi's Inn. She opened the door; she didn't think about the security chain and Alexei filled the doorframe. Before she could say anything, he gently pushed her back into the room and locked the door.

"I booked Room 42."

And then, he slapped her hard and she fell to the floor.

Her head spun as she tried to understand what had just happened. And then, she was lifted up by her armpits.

"How dare you say no."

He slapped her again and she fell back on the bed; a bubble of blood leaked out of the side of her mouth. He brought his elbow down onto her sternum and she gasped for breath but no breath came. As she struggled to breathe, he slapped her face with the back of his hand and a cut opened above her eye. He bent over her and licked the blood from her eye and lip. He lifted her up and she swayed on her feet. A short punch caught her on the jaw and she again fell back onto the bed. Her face was swelling and so too was his ego. He rolled her over and she had no strength to resist. He dragged her to the edge of the bed where her legs hung to the floor. Her body sagged and her soul fled, again. He forced his erection inside her and he thrust and pumped until he came and then he turned her over and punched her in the temple. Unconsciousness bathed her like a midnight swim.

When she regained consciousness, she looked around the room with blurred vision. She was neatly tucked into bed like a child. Alexei was nowhere to be seen but her clothes were neatly folded on the table next to the bed. Had they been ironed? Her face stung and her chest ached. It was 7am. She eased herself out of the bed and walked to the bathroom bent over. She kneeled down in front of the toilet and vomited. It hurt, but it cleansed and she vomited until there was nothing left but a single line of saliva tinged with bile hanging from her bruised chin. As she stood, she caught a glimpse of her reflection and she turned away, but not before she saw the Band-Aid covering the cut over her eye.

She scrubbed her skin for 30 minutes and during that time she wondered why and how. Why hadn't she seen this possibility; how had she, again, allowed herself to be the victim of abuse. She was angrier with herself than she was with her abuser. She continued to question the reality while she punished herself with a rough toweling. There was already a circular bruise on and just below her sternum. Her left eye was yellow deepening to purple and swollen, as was her chin. The cut above her eye probably needed a stitch or two. Her lower lip was cut and fat. In short, she was a mess.

Self-recriminations took over her mind as she sat in the armchair with the TV on. She tried to sleep but images of Minho, Alexei and Sampoong kept her awake. Finally, she dressed and packed her few belongings into her daypack and shopping bags. She stepped out of room 33 for the last time. She did not look back; in fact, she faced the back of the elevator as the doors closed and she did not turn around until the doors opened onto the ground floor. She slid the key under the frosted glass but did not say anything. She exited Choi's Inn and walked with increasing speed toward Myonghee's restaurant.

CHAPTER 25

LUUURRRve

Stan is sitting on the terrace of Jacque's restaurant drinking a long macchiato. Jacque is not around. The morning sun threatens a hot day and Stan is already grateful for the shade of the umbrella. He is thinking about his class with Wontae Oh when his cell phone rings.

"Stan speaking."

"Mr. Oh here. Sorry Stan, but no class today. Not sure when we can meet again. Take a brain-check?"

"Nice idiom Wontae. No worries, just call me when you have time."

Stan hangs-up before he says, "Idiot." He catches the waitress's eye.

"Insuk, I think I'll have breakfast. May I have bacon and eggs please, sunny side up and don't overcook the bacon."

"I don't cook; I just wait but I tell cook."

She turns quickly and heads back into the restaurant and Stan finds himself wondering if she is being sassy or just having a translation moment. He shrugs and smiles and goes back to his coffee and thoughts.

"Stan, well, well, well, long time no see."

He looks up and uses his hand to shade his eyes from the sun and he sucks in his breath before answering, "Bette, indeed it has been a while. I didn't get a chance to say goodbye the last time we met."

And Bette sits down opposite Stan before she is asked.

"You don't mind do you Stan?"

"I guess not."

In her good but not exact English, Bette says, "Stan, I been meaning to call you, but ... you know how things are."

Stan nods but he doesn't know. He has no idea. After the vacuum, cleaner affair, he doesn't have a clue what kind of life this woman leads.

"How are your friends?"

"Yeah, no problem." She pauses for a while and looks into Stan's eyes, "I missed you. Can we meet again?"

"The last time I met you, things got a bit weird for me. I'm not sure I can do that again."

"Stan" she stretched the 'a' "Come on, I always took you for the adventurous type. The do anything once type."

She smiles and the corners of her mouth show micro wrinkles and her eyes dance.

"Stan, I got appointment today, and I busy tomorrow but let's say we get together sometime for lunch, just the two of us? I'll send you a text and let you know time and place."

And she is up from the table and waving goodbye and she soon disappears into the Itaewon crowd.

"See you, I guess," Says Stan into the vacated space.

Insuk arrives with a swagger, "Eggs and bacon, eggs soft and bacon soft, hope you happy." And she spins on her heels, "Getting hot out here."

And, she is gone. Stan watches her go and thanks the empty

space, again. He is beginning to get on well with the space.

He picks up his knife and fork and attacks his breakfast. He is relieved that he does not have to meet Wontae Oh, but he is a little troubled by the prospect of being reacquainted with Bette. He eats the whites of the eggs leaving the yolks looking like stranded setting suns. He next eats the bacon before returning to the yolks, which he gently maneuvers onto his fork and puts them whole into his mouth, one at a time. He enjoys breaking the yolk in his mouth and the feeling of the warm fluid. It is both a taste and sensory experience.

"Monsieur Stan, Mon'Amie, Monsieur Stan." Jacque bounces along the pavement. "You are the only person I know who eats eggs like that." And he pulls up a chair and sits down. "Stan, I've been thinking about a new idea. I've been talking to a few people who want to invest money. You know Bernard, don't you?" He does not wait for a response. "Korean Woodstock, what do you think? It's a great idea; people camping out on farmland or, maybe a beach ... the water could be dangerous ... alcohol trucks, food trucks and bands playing on a giant stage; a full weekend happening. Do you have some money to invest?"

"Jacque, slow down. First, no I don't have any spare money. And second, are you sure the Woodstock concept is not a little dated? It was 1969, I think, when that happened"

"Time to bring it back. You know, the whole Lurve, Peace and Rock and Roll thing."

"The world has moved beyond Love, Peace and Rock and Roll. It is now Corporate, Credit and K-pop. There is no place for love, certainly no place for peace, and Rock and Roll only lives in the hearts of people over fifty."

"Nooo Stan, I don't believe it. Surely not." Jacque falls silent. His little upturned waxed moustache seems to wilt at the ends. "What is the world without lurve? What will us French men do without lurve."

"Don't worry Jacque, there will always be a place for luurrve, but love can be bought and sold."

Both men laugh and they enjoy the laughter. It stops for a while until one or the other says "LUUURRRve" and they start laughing again.

Insuk walks out shaking her head, "What wrong with you two?"

"It is all the fault of LUUURRRve."

And, the two men start laughing again. Insuk frowns and leaves the two middle-aged men to their laughter until two men in suits request Jacque's time and he heads inside the restaurant and leaves Stan alone. Stan's smile quickly fades and he closes his eyes and Jinni is projected onto the inside of his eyelids as he falls asleep for a few minutes and dreams that he is sitting in a café talking with her. The atmosphere is relaxed and familiar and the conversation is about shared experiences.

CHAPTER 26

More Running and Thinking

Stan finally leaves the restaurant and walks home. He longs for the gentle familiarity of being with Jinni but Bette and Miji compete for space. When he gets home, he changes into his running gear and is soon striding up toward the Hyatt. He turns right and runs over the footbridge into Namsan Botanical Gardens. He pushes up to the Namsan access road and turns right and runs down toward the outside gym. When he gets to the gym, he checks his watch and he smiles at the time.

"Pretty good time, Not a PB but pretty good, now for a few weights."

Stan pushes weights and daydreams distract him. After 30 minutes, he stands on the running track with his finger on the start button of his watch. He pushes the button and starts running.

"I've tried not to think, Thoughts won't stop, Just enjoy the surroundings and the run, Running as end in itself, doesn't have to be a means to an end. Jinni, Miji, Bette?"

The thoughts are persistent.

"Bloody milk ghost ... very disturbing, Alone in the Australian outback ... very disturbing, Two men in the car also very disturbing, Such a brazen chick, Man her nakedness but I don't want to touch her

again, I don't want her to touch me again, Jinni would be ok, I'd touch her."

Beep, signals another kilometer down and Stan is running under the gondola that takes paying customers who don't want to walk to the top of Namsan.

"'Ok laddy lets take the stairs straight to the top,' Granny you're back, good to have you along for the ride, But that's a good one and a half kilometers of straight up steps, No way, 'Up you go laddy, up you go,' Shit, here we go, Ten steps for Jinni and ten steps for Miji, ten steps for Jinni and ten steps for Miji, Let's see who finishes on top, I've lost count already ...

... Mr. Kim and his wife look ok, Hope Miji is happy, maybe she won't bother me again, The thank you has been said, Maybe that's it ...

... Shit this is tough, have to walk, 'Push it laddy, don't you dare walk,' Come on Granny give me a break, 'Distract yourself with your thoughts laddy, not Zen today think more,' I don't want to think, Vince seems pretty pissed with his soccer team, This is taking forever, may not be walking but wouldn't call it running, Actually, I think I am walking, Don't tell Granny."

Beep and he has 500 meters of steps to go. He is drenched in sweat. His face is red and his breathing is labored.

"This is the toughest run I've done, I'm puffing like the Puffing Billy, not been on that old steam engine since I was a kid, wonder if they still allow kids to sit half in and half out of the windows, Probably not, Australia's become a nanny state, Rules against this and rules against that ...

... The vision of the outback was so clear ... swear I was there, 'Come on laddy don't walk,' I'm not walking, Ok I'm moving slowly but not walking, Alright I'll push harder, The top there it is, almost there, Just a little further, Up up up you go you can do this, going to make it, One two three four five six seven eight nine ten and Jinni is the winner, She loves me."

Stan sucks the air in gulps as he walks slowly around the summit. The place is crowded with Chinese tourists. He can hear the Mandarin language everywhere. He tries to make eye contact, but these Chinese are not here looking for a middle-aged Australian. To them, Stan is invisible. Stan squeezes his invisibility and heads down the mountain. He takes the shortest route by turning left onto the Namsan access road and down to the turn-off into the Namsan Botanical Gardens.

"The sun feels good, like that run, might do it again, Then again might not, Toughy that's for sure, Garchys everywhere, catch that insect, Wonder what it's like to be swallowed alive, Does the insect scratch away inside the gut, How long does it live for, The Hyatt Hotel so two kilometers to go, Push up this final little rise and it's downhill all the way home."

CHAPTER 27

The Truth

Jinni got to the restaurant and opened the door. She stood just inside the door until the halmoni noticed her, and when the halmoni looked up, her reflex reaction was to smile at her friend; that is, until she noticed her face.

"Ayego, what happened to ya girl?"

Jinni began to tremble, "Poor judgment."

"Ayego, sit down. No stand up, we gotta get ya to hospital. Who did this?"

Jinni sat, "No halmoni, I can't go to the hospital.
"What do you mean ya can't go to hospital? Look at ya. That cut above ya eye needs stitches. I'll call a taxi."

"No, halmoni."

I'm not takin' no for an answer. You need checkin' out." And, she picked up the phone.

"Halmoni, I don't have an ID card. I can't go to the hospital."

"What ya mean no ID card? Everyone's got an ID card."

"I'll tell you everything, but for now I just want you to come with me to see Blue. I'll tell you both."

The halmoni looked at her two customers who were looking at Jinni.

"I need ya to finish up here, now."

"Yeah, we're done."

And, they got up out of their chairs and the halmoni escorted the two women to the door, "Not a word to anyone about what ya seen here, got it. Not a word." The two women were silent but they nodded.

"Leave ya shopping bags here, girl."

Myonghee pulled a broad brimmed sun visor off a hook and gave it to Jinni to wear to cover her face. She ushered her outside and locked the door. Jinni held onto the halmoni's arm and the two walked off in the direction of *Love Always*. As usual the bar was locked at this hour. The doors did not open for customers until 7pm. They went to the backdoor and Jinni fumbled in her backpack for the key. She opened the door and a light was visible in Blue Park's office.

The two women walked down the corridor toward the light and when they got to the door, Myonghee knocked softly. Blue looked up from his paper work and it took a while for him to comprehend what he saw. But, when he did, his lips twisted and he got up quickly and ushered the two women in. He took Jinni's arm and guided her to the comfortable armchair. Myonghee took a seat against the wall and Blue pulled a seat from the corner of the room and placed it across from Jinni. Nothing was said for several minutes.

Blue sat patiently until he said, "Jinni, you are safe here. You are safe with me."

Jinni's shoulders trembled and tears flowed but she held Blue Park's gaze. Myonghee, too, was crying quietly. Blue's calm face masked his anger; he felt a need for violence, violence like he hadn't felt for a long time.

"Poor judgment." Said Jinni.

Blue said nothing. A man does not rise to the top of a crime organization without violence and once upon a time, Blue breathed violence.

"Really, it's nothing much. My husband used to do worse. He just didn't leave visible marks. He was supposed to protect me. He was a bigger bastard."

Myonghee stood up, picked up her chair and moved it beside Jinni and sat down again.

"Jinni?" She said.

"I need some water, halmoni. This is a long story."

So, Myonghee hurried to the bar. While she was away, Jinni spoke to Blue, "I'm so sorry Blue. You trusted me and I've let you down."

"No you haven't. Poor judgment is nothing more than poor judgment."

And Blue thought about judgments he had made that had cost people their lives. He wanted to make such judgments again. He had seriously injured his own people to gain and maintain power and he had killed outsiders who had tried to muscle onto his turf. He looked at Jinni and puzzled at why he had become so soft and he realized that he had no need for violence anymore because he had eliminated the opposition and he had semi-legitimized his operations. And, there was something about Jinni that disarmed him.

Myonghee returned with a bottle of water and three glasses, and she poured water for all. Jinni took a sip, "No gin?" She smiled weakly but nobody in the room smiled with her.

"My name is not Jinni ... I mean, it wasn't Jinni ... it is now. My name is, was, Mejung Oh. I died in the Sampoong Department store collapse."

And, Jinni told her story, the whole story, everything. She started with the abusive marriage and she finished with that morning's rape.

The halmoni went from stroking Jinni's hand to wringing her own hands as the story unfolded. Blue sat quietly although he occasionally balled his fists. It was after 5pm when Jinni finished her story. But, she was not finished.

"One month ago, you asked me what I wanted from you. Here it is. I need a new identity. I can't go back to being Mejung Oh. I need a new ID card. I need a new university degree. I need a new life."

She unzipped her daypack and reached to the bottom and her fingers folded around what she was searching for. In her hand, she held her cell phone and Credit Card and she reached across to Blue Park and placed them in his hand.

"Help me, please."

Nobody spoke for several minutes. Jinni looked at her hands; Myonghee looked at Jinni and then at Blue. And, Blue stared at Jinni before he spoke, "I gather the boys can give me a description of this Alexei character. As for your husband, I want his address and his full name and his father's name."

"Blue, please ... it's ok. Nobody back in Seoul can know I'm still alive."

"Nobody will; I promise you that. And, it's not ok. Violence begets violence. Leave it with me." Jinni could not argue. "Myonghee, can Jinni stay with you for a while?"

"Of course."

"I'll send a doctor around to your apartment. She'll be there in 2 hours."

All three rose from their seats and the two women left the room. Blue Park moved to his seat behind his desk and began working the phone.

CHAPTER 28

Falling off the Wagon

Mr. Kim has been restless all day. He has been harboring dark thoughts and he finally gravitates towards his old haunt, Pagoda Park. He sits alone on a park bench and drinks two bottles of soju. He allows his depression to build and he fuels his anger with it. He can't quench his thirst. With the second bottle of soju finished, he looks around for someone to talk at. He pushes up off the bench and walks out of the park and into a silbijip not far away. He opens the door of the tavern that serves Korean traditional rice beer and traditional foods and as he opens the door, the stale smells of old budae chigae, kimchi chigae and soondae guk blow over him and mix with the outside air. He enters and stands still just inside the doorway. Unknown stains on a cold concrete floor feed on his dusty shoes and he breathes in cigarette smoke, sour fermentation and wasted lives. He strains his eyes to see through the shadows. The place is half empty and hollow arguments abound but he spots two ajeoshi he remembers from former days. The middle-aged men are sitting on stools around an upturned forty-four-gallon drum that is the table. A bored ajumma wipes a listless cloth across the top of the lonely drums. Life is moving too fast; change is hard to embrace. Mr. Kim sits on a stool beside the two ajeoshi. Nobody acknowledges anybody; they just occupy a common space.

"Yogiyo" Mr. Kim calls to the ajumma. "Give us a kettle of makoli will you."

And he looks at his companions who stare blankly back at him.

"Did I tell you that my daughter died in the Seongsu Bridge collapse?"

The two men stare at him but say nothing. They raise ceramic bowls to their lips and drain their rice beer.

"I was meant to drive her to school that day, but she caught the bus instead."

The ajumma arrives and places the kettle on the table between the three men and a ceramic bowl in front of Mr. Kim. He picks up the kettle and fills the two men's empty bowls and then he fills his own. The three men drain their bowls and Mr. Kim fills them again.

"She was my life."

He tilts his head back and empties his bowl and the other two men follow suit. Again, he fills the bowls and again he swallows his makoli in one gulp before reaching for the kettle again.

"We've all lost something," is a bored response. "You're not the only one who has an excuse to be drunk."

"Yogiyo, another kettle over here."

The three men sit in silence until the new kettle arrives. Mr. Kim fills his bowl again and drinks the contents before he fills the other bowls.

"Have you lost a daughter?"

"Lost plenty," replies an ajeoshi.

"But have you lost a daughter."

"Don't care what you've lost and you don't care what I've lost so just drink your makoli and shut up."

And that is what they do. The three men finish the second kettle and Mr. Kim calls for a third.

The third kettle is finished and a fourth is ordered and a drunkenness festering with anger begins to fill the silbijip.

"IRUN MANGHUL, what's your loss mean to me. Why do you think I care?"

"I've lost more than you."

"JENJANG, what have you lost?"

"Nothing ... everything."

Mr. Kim punches the top of the forty-four-gallon drum that serves as a table, which makes the makoli bowls jump and one ceramic bowl crashes to the floor and the milky brew splashes onto an ajeoshi's trousers and it mingles with other stains.

He rises drunkenly to his feet and lurches into the drum sending all the bowls toppling over.

"SIBAL!"

"Look what you've done."

The three ajeoshi are now pushing each other and the drum dances reluctantly with each man.

The ajumma calls out from the bar, "Get out you drunken fools. Take your petty squabbles outside. Get back to the park you pathetic old men."

"Show some respect to your elders."

"Respect you? Look at yourself. Yuksilhal, smell yourself."

"Give us a bottle of makoli to go."

"Show me your money and you can take as much makoli as you like. Just get out of here."

Mr. Kim hands over 30,000 won as payment for the four kettles and three bottles to take away. He hands a plastic bottle to each of his companions and the three men stagger out shouting at each other and shouting back at the ajumma. They spill out onto the road under the glare of the streetlights and they stumble through the gates of Pagoda Park like drunken cows returning to a familiar pasture. They keep pushing each other and shouting until Mr. Kim stops and squats on the ground. He removes the screw top off his makoli and drinks from the bottle; he didn't bother to shake the contents. The first mouthful is thin and watery so he replaces the screw top and upturns the bottle a few times to mix the sediment with the liquid before he gulps down another draught. The other two men keep walking deeper into the park. Mr. Kim is left alone with his makoli and anger and it doesn't take him long to finish his drink. He sits alone, his anger turning to misery and turning back to anger.

Eventually he rises and makes his way out of the park. His drunken footsteps have him swaying along the pavement. Men and women vacate his space as best they can and, somehow, he finds the bus stop and waits for the 425-bus that will take him back to his apartment in Bokwang-dong. The bus arrives and he rides it in an alcoholic fog and his anger squeezes his balls.

By the time he gets to Bokwang-dong, 30 minutes later, the fog has lessened to a mist and his anger has loosened its grip. He climbs the hill and fumbles with the key to his apartment and before he can open it, it opens from the inside. His wife is standing in the doorway.

"Don't talk."

"Are you ok?"

"No, drunk ... angry."

"I can see that. Go to bed and we'll talk tomorrow."

"Don't tell me what to do."

The wife moves aside and allows her husband to enter the apartment. He goes first to the bathroom before he falls onto his bed fully clothed. She goes back to the lounge and sits on the sofa in the dark. Her mind is busy with thoughts of Miji and fear that her husband has fallen back into a malaise that he may not rise from. It is a fitful sleep that takes her, and Mr. Kim's snores vibrate the sadness that hangs in the house.

The following morning sees the old couple sitting around the well-worn kitchen table eating the breakfast that the wife has prepared. It is a quiet meal.

The wife asks, "You ok?"

"No I'm not but yes I am ... sorry yobo. I couldn't stop it."

"Eat your breakfast ... you're ok."

"I guess I am."

They finish their breakfast in silence and the wife washes up while Mr. Kim sits at the table looking at his hands. After cleaning up and putting the dishes away, the wife tells her husband that she is going shopping and she won't be back until the evening. Mr. Kim does not acknowledge his wife's words and she closes the door on a silent house.

Mr. Kim spends the day cleaning out the cupboards and draws of the apartment; it is a safer distraction than drinking makoli. He ends up with a bundle of old clothes that he takes down to the unwanted-clothing bin at the intersection to the main road. Each item of clothing speaks memories as they drop into the bin and Mr. Kim tries not to listen.

That night, Mr. Kim and his wife sit at home together around the kitchen table. It is a harsh fluorescent light that shines on the couple. The walls have a lifetime of sadness baked into the bareness. The floor is yellow linoleum that the wife keeps polished. A portable burner sits in the middle of the table and a pot of kimchi chigae simmers on it; steam and the sour smell of boiling fermented cabbage drift through the space above the table. A pair of steel chopsticks, a spoon, a glass of water, a bowl of rice and an empty plate sit in front of each person. The wife picks up her husband's plate and begins ladling the stew onto it. She places it in front of Mr. Kim and then she fills her own plate. When she is finished with the stew, she picks up her glass of water and raises it to Mr. Kim who does the same.

The old couple smile, "Cunbae." They sip on their water and attack the kimchi chigae.

"Sorry about last night yobo. I couldn't control it."

She remains silent but she looks at her husband and his eyes meet hers. He shrugs his shoulders and she returns the shrug. She allows a small smile to crease her face. "No harm done. No harm, no foul."

Mr. Kim looks at his wife and smiles and speaks in English, "Great food, honey."

His wife smiles and responds in English, "Thank you." And they return to their food.

Fifteen minutes later the stew pot is almost empty and Mr. Kim rises from his chair and starts to clean up. The wife also gets up from the table and takes some bowls to the sink where she runs hot water and begins to wash-up. Mr. Kim puts away the burner in the cupboard under the kitchen bench and he takes the almost empty pot over to his wife. He retrieves a plastic container from a cupboard overhead and ladles the remaining stew into it. He then walks to the fridge, opens the door and places the plastic container on a shelf. He looks at the soju bottle on the inside of the door while his wife starts cleaning the pot.

"Would you like a nightcap yobo?"

The wife continues to wash the remaining dirty dishes and turns her head to look at her husband, "Soju? You sure you're up to it after last night?"

"Yeah, I'm a tough old ajeoshi. If you drink with me, it'll be good. In fact, my hand is closing on the bottle right now."

"I'll just finish these dishes; be ready in 10 minutes. Take the bottle and glasses to the living room and I'll be with you soon."

She turns back to the sink and smiles to herself.

Mr. Kim removes the bottle of soju from the fridge. He closes the door and then picks up two shot glasses from the shelf.

"I'll get a head start if you don't mind."

"I'll join you for the second glass."

Mr. Kim sits on the floor at the coffee table in the lounge room. He pours himself a glass of soju and calls out to the wife, "Cunbae." He thinks to himself that last night was an aberration, a minor back-step. He takes a sip of his soju, just a sip, just a taste to make sure that he can handle it. Once upon a time he would have thrown it back in one gulp and quickly poured another (as he did with the makoli last night) but life has changed since the last anniversary of his daughter's death and things have changed even more since his pool game with Stan. He leaves the almost full glass sitting on the table for a while as he looks around the room. Like the kitchen, the lounge is dull and shabby, neglected would be the best word. He returns to his soju but his thoughts remain on the room and how it reflects the past decade of his life. He sips his soju and enjoys the flavor but he can't shake the sense of life led wastefully, and he looks forward to his wife joining him, which she does just as he finishes his first glass.

As his wife sits across from Mr. Kim, he pours her a glass of soju and slides it across the table.

"Yobo, I can't promise that nights like last night won't happen again."

"I know."

"So, what do we do about it?"

"Nothing, it's a bridge not arrived at."

Mr. Kim ponders this comment for a while before he nods.

"It's time we redecorated. This shabbiness, this greyness is something I want to leave behind. Got to add color."

The wife looks around the room.

"I've lived so long in this greyness that I almost feel comfortable in it ... I agree; let's add colour."

"Yobo, thanks for making me talk the other month."

"Thanks for talking. Yobo, I'm enjoying our pool games. Thanks for teaching me." And she raises her glass to her husband.

"I'm enjoying the games too. Playing pool with you was the last thing I would have thought of doing. That Stan man is strange, good strange but strange."

"Have you been having any more dreams about Miji?"

"Weekly, or that's what it seems. She grows older with each dream; in fact, she's almost as old as she would be if she were alive today. I'm not afraid anymore; I'm still sad, but I'm not ... I don't know how to describe my emotions ... I'm not really sad, like devastated sad. I finish these dreams smiling where as I used to wake up sobbing. It's during the day when anger sometimes builds."

Silence fills the space around the couple. They occasionally catch each other's eye and share a weak but sincere smile.

"The last few dreams I've had, Miji was dating a foreigner. I have these pleasant little mother-daughter conversations with her and she spoke about this Australian man. You know, these contacts are more real than dream but I know that Miji is not alive."

Mr. Kim refills his wife's glass and then his own, and he shrugs his shoulders toward his wife.

"This whole thing, you know, you and me and, well everything started with the last anniversary of the bridge collapse, of Miji's death and it went really crazy with that pool game against Stan. He made me look like an amateur." He stops talking and stares at the ceiling trying to put ideas in order. "He bought me a beer and told me that he knew Miji ..."

Mr. Kim leaves his thoughts hanging in the air and gets up and walks into the bedroom to get the bedding just like he has done every night since the anniversary, every night except for last night of course. He comes back with his arms full.

"Let's go to bed."

He drops everything on the floor before heading to the bathroom to brush his teeth. When he returns, the bedding is arranged and his pajamas are neatly folded on his pillow. The wife picks up the empty soju bottle and the glasses and takes them to the kitchen. Mr. Kim removes his clothes and throws them on the back of the chair before pulling on his pajamas. He lies on the thin mattress and listens to his wife brush her teeth. When she returns, she turns out the lights, removes her clothes, folds them neatly and puts on her pajamas. Mr. Kim is on his side facing the wall. She lies down and faces his back. She reaches out and lets her hand rest on his shoulder.

"Yobo, we're ok, aren't we? Are we going crazy?"

Mr. Kim rolls over and looks at his wife in the semi-darkness. He cannot make out her features clearly but he knows where her face is. He leans toward her and kisses her. For the first time in over twenty years, Mr. Kim kisses his wife. It is clumsy but it is honest and the wife's clumsy reciprocation is also honest. Husband and wife are silent as they fumble in the dark. The wife strokes her husband through the cloth and she feels him rise. Mr. Kim reaches for her pajama cord and unties it and helps her out of her pants. He pulls down his own pajama pants and places himself gently between her spread legs. She desires him and she receives him in silence.

Thirty minutes later they are both asleep and dreaming.

"Mum, dad you're looking good laying there like spoons in a cutlery draw. It feels good to be able to talk to you like this. In the past I could only contact you one at a time; I owe Stan."

They both smile in their sleep and nestle in a little closer.

"This may be the last time I visit ... you don't need me anymore. Just look at you. It's been a long journey and I've hated feeling your struggle. Your pains were my chains, and your connection is my liberation. And dad, don't worry too much about last night. It's going to be tough but I have faith in you. I trust you; I always did and I still do. I'm going to miss you two."

And, Miji is gone.

The husband and wife stir a little but they do not wake. They don't wake until late the next morning. They wake feeling refreshed and neither can remember having slept this soundly, ever, and the morning sun is streaming in through the cracks in the blinds. While Mr. Kim showers, the wife prepares a simple breakfast from last night's leftovers along with a few leftovers from other nights plus rice, and when Mr. Kim walks into the kitchen, the dishes are arranged on the table. They sit down together feeling at ease.

Mr. Kim asks, "Have you ever been to Starbucks?"

"I thought it was for the youngsters."

"Why don't you have your shower while I clean up these dishes, and when you are dressed, let's go to Itaewon and give Starbucks a try. I've heard some girls in the bar talk about a *caramel macchiato.*" He smiles broadly, "I want one."

CHAPTER 29

The Ocean Restores

Jinni was surprised by the size of Myonghee's apartment. It was on the eighth floor of a twelve-story apartment block about one kilometer from Love Always. The block was about ten years old and the apartment had three bedrooms and a large kitchen-dining-living space and the windows looked over the Busan Railway Yard and beyond to the sea. The halmoni directed Jinni to one of the bedrooms. "I'll put the kettle on. Join me when ya ready."

Jinni hung her few clothes in the wardrobe and placed her underwear in one of the draws. The room smelled clean, neutral as though it was waiting for human habitation, waiting for the right person to give it a smell. She sat on the edge of the bed and allowed her chin to fall almost to her chest. She remembered her parents' apartment; she remembered her old room, its sense of safety, its sanctuary and she hoped ... and the tears began again.

The halmoni was standing silently at the doorway of the bedroom watching and when she saw Jinni crying, she quietly moved to the bed and sat beside her. Their hips lightly touched; their shoulders touched; each held her hands clasped together in her lap, and they cried together. They sat this way for several minutes until the shrill scream of the kettle broke through the sadness. Myonghee kissed Jinni on the side of the head.

"Come on, tea's ready."

"Yeah, give me a minute will you."

With that, Myonghee rose to her feet and walked out of the room. Jinni also got up but she walked into the attached bathroom where she gently splashed water onto her face and looked at herself in the mirror. She ran her fingers through her hair, pulled out a hairband from her pocket and pulled her hair back into a ponytail. She looked again at the damage to her face, and the cut above her swollen left eye began to bleed again. It was deeper and bigger than she first thought.

The women sat on stools at the kitchen bench sipping green tea. Jinni held a bag of frozen peas that she moved between her left eye and chin. They sat this way for a good hour, few words passed between the two until the silence was broken by a knock on the door. Myonghee got up and went to the door and opened it to a woman in her late forties. She carried a doctor's bag and the greeting was a familiar one.

It didn't take long for the doctor to examine Jinni and deftly insert four stitches in the cut above her eye. She was efficient and gentle and her questions were neutral, just deep enough to understand the force and direction of the blows, but not deep enough to intrude on privacy. She was soon packing her tools back into her bag and heading toward the door. But, before leaving, she looked into Jinni's eyes, "I'm sorry this happened to you, but you can trust Blue, you know that, don't you?" Jinni smiled, and the doctor placed her card on the bench before saying, "If you need anything, call me." With that, she said her goodbyes to Myonghee like the old friends they were.

Jinni rested at Myonghee's apartment for two days before boredom inspired her to get out and explore. Blue had told her not to come in until the following week so she caught a bus to Haeundae Beach. The first thing she did was buy a pair of Ray Ban Aviator sunglasses. She ignored the salesgirl's open stares and she handed over the cash and strolled out with her shoulders straight and her new sunglasses covering her eyes.

For a while she sat on a bench overlooking the ocean and watched school children playing in the small waves. They shrieked and laughed even though the waves were no more than 20 centimeters high and Jinni tried to rejoice with them. It wasn't easy because her emotions were battered. She sat thinking what it was about her that made men want to abuse her. Was it something within her that craved to be beaten? Did she collude in this violence? She was wondering about what she had escaped and what she had gotten herself into and the old English saying from her days in Australia, *out of the frying pan and into the fire,* came to mind. She almost laughed. And then she did laugh. It started as a smile but it gradually grew until her bruised sternum hurt and her swollen lip ached. She almost enjoyed the pain as if she was laughing at Alexei. An image of Blue's shadows inflicting pain flashed through her mind. She almost felt sorry for Alexei but she was not in a forgiving mood. She wanted Blue and his boys to do some damage.

She rose from the bench and strolled along the street with a shallow smile on her face until she found a surf shop. Inside the shop, she tried on a number of bikinis. The sales assistant barely batted an eyelid at Jinni's cuts and bruises. "Men" was all she murmured, and Jinni nodded and the two of them shared a knowing look and got on with business. The girl was in her mid to late 20's and she flattered without gushing. She genuinely liked Jinni's body. She assisted Jinni with the bra clips. She encouraged Jinni to let out her hair and she helped her tie it up again. They looked in the mirror together and each smile reflected back at the other. The girl assisted Jinni to test the bikinis at hip level and she pulled the sides up a little higher over Jinni's hips to check for the positioning that best suited her slim but bruised body. Jinni was enjoying the gentle attention. Finally, they found a bikini that she and the shop assistant agreed best showed off her sleek body. It was azure (Blue would appreciate that) and a yellow band rimmed the top and the bottom. The yellow bands of the bottom sat best on her hips and the yellow straps of the top tied in a bow at the nape of her neck and between her shoulder blades. Jinni also selected a pair of board shorts, knee length, a white T-shirt with a breaking wave printed on the front and a pair of blue flip-flops. She finished off the purchases with a green sarong and a beach bag. The shop assistant snipped off the labels with a pair of scissors and Jinni put her old clothes into the beach bag, paid with cash and strolled out of the shop and headed to the beach, but not before exchanging names with the sales assistant, who turned out to be the proprietor, and promising Annie that she would return.

Jinni stood on the sand and allowed the water to caress her feet. She enjoyed the cool embrace. After standing in the shallows for 10 minutes, she dived in and swam a few strokes before swiveling around and standing in the waist deep ocean. The cold water soothed her bruised body and the sun warmed her soul. There would be no more skin whiteners. She wanted a tan and by the end of the week, she was the color of wild honey. Her bruises had almost disappeared into the tan, her lip and jaw were no longer swollen and the cut above her eye had healed well and on the Friday, she visited the doctor's surgery to have the stitches removed.

Each day of that week off work, Jinni caught the bus to Haeundae Beach, and she sometimes had lunch with Annie before or after swimming and sunning herself. Annie, like Jinni, had a degree in Business; she had graduated from Busan National University and had worked for a few years in an office before deciding to throw it in to open the surf shop. The conversation was easy; the smiles also came easily. At the end of the week, Jinni promised to visit as often as she could.

CHAPTER 30

Payback

Blue's enquiries quickly located Alexei's office. His business was a small scale importing and exporting affair with offices in Vladivostok and Busan. The Busan office was on the third floor of a non-descript office building not far from Jungang Subway Station. He originally made good money by importing Choco Pies into Russia. The hockey puck sized, chocolate-coated cakes were a great hit for a while but the Russians were making their own version now so Alexei diversified into filling containers with second hand clothes and the occasional secondhand car and shipping it off to Vladivostok. He made a decent living and he supplemented that income by bringing small quantities of drugs from Russia to Busan, just large scale enough to give him spending money but not large enough to give him trouble with the local gangs. Each month he sold the drugs to a US Soldier stationed in Daegu and he didn't care what happened after that. He always thought himself better than what he was and better than others who had achieved more. He talked bigger than what he was.

Once this information filtered back to Blue Park, he devised a plan. Blue's connections in the Busan Police Force handed over a police car. There were no questions asked. Left and Right, dressed as plain-clothed police officers, approached Alexei on the street outside his office. Storm clouds were gathering and it had just begun to rain. Without fanfare, they handcuffed him and shoved him into the back of the police car. They drove to the docks and through the entrance to a shipbuilding yard. After they drove through the entrance, the guard closed and locked the gate and walked back to his guard post. The police car pulled up to a ship under construction as thunder rumbled closer. A ramp ran up to the second level of the ship and the boys sped the car up it. The deck and walls were unpainted metal and the car stopped in the middle of the vast space. One of the boys opened the back door of the car and pulled Alexei out. He had not yet realized the trouble he was in and he tried to bluff confidence. Left opened the trunk of the police car and removed a large duffle bag while Right escorted Alexei deeper into the hulk of the ship. It is funny the way nicknames stick and ever since Jinni had called the boys Left and Right on the first night she met them, these names have stuck to them. Blue Park was seated in an armchair about 20 meters away. He, of course, was wearing variations on blue. Even his soft leather gloves were blue.

"Been waitin' long boss?"

"I've not been to the docks in a long time. I got here early to look around and reacquaint myself. I feel like a national soccer player who has been injured for a long time. I'm enjoying the little shots of adrenaline, the little jangle of nerves. I'm looking forward to this"

"Jeez boss, we're just gonna hurt him. No national pride or anythin' like that."

"Tie him good," And Alexei was led toward a bare metal ladder that led to an upper floor. He still thought it was a bluff and he went without too much resistance. Left unzipped the duffle bag and pulled out seven leather belts with super strength Velcro on the ends. Alexei was backed up and the cuffs were unlocked and relocked with his hands behind his back and around the ladder. The first belt was wrapped around his upper chest, under his armpits and the Velcro was secured. Then, the shortest of the straps was used to secure his ankles to the pole. Now that Alexei was secured at his chest and ankles, the boys could go about their work with a degree of pleasure. Alexei still did not resist or complain. Left and Right talked about what they would like to eat that night, and what they would do once this business was all over; they smiled often and occasionally laughed. The third strap was used to secure Alexei's hips and the fourth was used to bind his thighs to the pole. A fifth belt held him just under his chest and the sixth belt strapped him tightly just below the knees. The final belt was used around his neck; it was left a little loose. Blue watched without smiling.

"I feel like singing. Did you bring the noraebung box?"

"Always, boss," and Right moved toward the car. He came back with a boom box and microphone. Blue held the microphone to his lips and looked toward Alexei and he began by testing the sound with a few squeals and groans, "That'll be the sounds you'll make soon," before crooning to Bing Crosby's, White Christmas. Bing and Blue crooned a duet. Blue's voice was just a bit lower than tenor and it made a sweet harmony with Bing Crosby's baritone.

While Blue sang, Left walked back to the duffle bag and rustled around inside and he brought out what looked like a small fishing net about 50 centimeters in diameter. It had a 1.5-meter length of fishing line hanging from it. He held it up toward Blue and Blue nodded.

"But gag the bitch first. Use the special gag."

Left threw the small net device to Right and again bent down over the duffle bag. He quickly found what he was looking for and held it aloft. It was a hard rubber dildo with strong cord exiting each end. As he approached, Alexei began to struggle but he could only move his head and he began to beg and ask what he had done. No one answered his questions or pleadings. Left tried to get the rubber penis in Alexei's mouth but he clenched his teeth shut and twisted his head from side to side.

Blue reclined in the comfort of his armchair back in the shadows, singing. He watched the struggle for a while before pausing the sound track. He spoke into the microphone and the sound reverberated around the empty, silent ship.

"Break his fuckin' teeth."

Right moved toward the duffle bag and retrieved a plumber's wrench and walked back toward the struggling Alexei. Blue resumed his singing.

"It's ok, I've got it in," and Left began securing the cords behind Alexei's neck.

Again, Blue paused the sound track, "Break a tooth anyway."

"Which tooth boss?"

"Your choice my boy, your choice."

Left stood behind Alexei and held his head in a tight grip. Right gently tapped a few of Alexei's teeth with the end of the plumber's wrench and Alexei tried to move his head away. A short backswing like a taekwondo snap and there was blood in Alexei's mouth and two teeth were on the ground.

"Sorry boss, I got two of'em."

Blue smiled and the two boys laughed and Alexei began whimpering like a beaten cur, his head hanging on the belt around his neck.

Blue resumed his singing as Right bent down and picked up the net he had dropped and placed it over Alexei's head and secured it under his chin. The fishing line dangled from between his eyes. Alexei's confidence had fled and he dripped fear as he dripped sweat.

Blue stood from his armchair, placed the microphone gently on the padded armrest and pulled a knife from his pocket and walked up to where he could face Alexei; a meter separated their faces. He held the knife up to Alexei's eye line.

"You hurt a friend of mine, very stupid. You hurt an innocent, unforgivable. But I am a man of the law so I followed a legal process. I have listened to the evidence from the prosecution. It was compelling. Eyewitnesses to the events preceding the crime confirmed your identity. I have found you guilty of rape and assault with grievous bodily harm."

Alexei's eyes pleaded, and Blue continued, "Your evidence was not required. In fact, it was deemed that if you spoke, you would only incriminate yourself further. So, we showed you mercy."

Blue stepped back and handed the knife to Right who approached Alexei and cut off his trousers. He cut through the waistband on the right side and sliced down the leg. He walked around to the left side and did the same. The top of Alexei's trousers fell over the belt securing his thighs and his underpants were exposed. The boys stood back and admired their handy work until Blue asked them to continue. Right handed Left the knife and he tossed it lightly from hand to hand before he cut off Alexei's underpants; they fell to the ground like an abandoned jellyfish. Alexei's genitals were exposed and shrinking.

Both boys went back to the duffle bag where they retrieved surgical gloves and they stretched them over their hands as they walked back to Alexei. Left grabbed Alexei's penis and stretched it up while Right pulled the line down. Blue Park assisted by pushing Alexei's head forward. Right tied a neat loop into the end of the line and placed it just under the circumcised knob of Alexei's penis and pulled it tight. Alexei tried to straighten his head but the noose tightened and the pain forced him to keep his head down.

Blue watched Alexei struggle with his situation for a while.

"I don't like you; I don't like your type. You like to watch others and their pain. This time you are going to watch your own pain."

And Blue stood at military attention and spoke again.

"Under the rights and privileges given to me by my legal and illegal status, I sentence you to witnessing your own pain. Let us proceed."

Left picked up the plumber's wrench and handed it to Blue who twisted open the mouth. With Alexei's penis pulled up tight, his testes were unprotected and Right held the right one at a stretch. Blue placed the mouth of the plumber's wrench around the testis and twisted until the wrench held firmly but not crushingly.

"Open your eyes bitch. Your sentence is to watch your pain. Open your eyes."

Alexei did as he was told and he looked down at his right testis inside the mouth of the plumber's wrench and Blue's thumb was on the winder. He watched as Blue twisted the mouth closed just a little and he tried to scream but the hard rubber dildo pushed into the corners of his mouth. He tried to pull his head away but that only caused the loop around his penis to tighten. There was pain everywhere. Blue twisted again and continued to twist. Alexei's right testis burst in a small explosion of blood, flesh and pain.

Blue placed his hand on Alexei's head and gently caressed his hair through the net. Alexei groaned and tried to move his head but the noose around his penis tightened again.

"I want to thank you bitch."

He took two steps back to better admire his work before stepping forward again. He brought his face close to Alexei's ear and he spoke confidentially as if talking to a close friend.

"I was getting soft. You know, it's been five years since I've been hands-on. My boys here do all that is needed, not that there is much to be done in this line these days. Things have been running smoothly; people pay their dues and we protect and support." Blue took off one glove and held his hand up to Alexei's eyes, "Look how soft my hands have become, not a callus to be seen. And then you come along. Thank you bitch ... and we are not finished."

Fifteen minutes later, Alexei was semiconscious and in shock. The boys worked quickly to untie him and lay him almost gently on the cold metal deck of the ship. They removed his sweat-drenched clothes and put them into a plastic shopping bag. They wiped him with a damp cool towel before they dressed him in plastic baby's diapers and blue pajamas. They returned the boom box to the trunk of the car. Then, they loaded Alexei into the back seat and threw the plastic shopping bag and duffle bag in after him. Blue stood in the opening of the ship's hull as the boys drove down the ramp and on toward the gate. The storm clouds had passed and the sun was setting in reds and oranges. The guard came out of his guard post and unlocked the gate to allow the boys to drive out. Before doing so, Left got out of the car and opened the trunk; he gave the guard the noraebung boom box.

Blue walked down the ramp and up to the gate as the police car was driving away and the gate was being relocked. The guard faced Blue and bowed low before inviting him in for a cup of tea and a blueberry muffin. Blue followed him into the guardhouse where they drank tea, ate muffins and sang together.

Alexei was driven to the hospital where two plain-clothed policemen admitted him to the emergency ward. No explanations were asked for and none were given. The police car was driven back to the police station and parked outside. The keys were left under the seat. A large duffle bag and a plastic shopping bag were removed from the back seat. Two men hailed a taxi and were driven away.

CHAPTER 31

Nothing Like a Good Scrub

When Jinni returned to Love Always, the comments were about her tan and not about the scar above her eye. Blue Park did not speak of the past. Jinni and he sat at the bar in their usual position talking about business and general things but not about Alexei. The bartenders and the girls were natural and normal. Only the shadows made mention of Alexei, and their words were brief.

"He won't bother you again. Won't bother any girl again." She did not ask for details; she was content enough.

Jinni continued to work for Blue at *Love Always* and live with Myonghee. She had no identification and Blue continued to pay her in cash. She never again allowed a customer to get close. Her relationship with the girls began to prosper and she helped them with investments and matters financial. But she did not make friends. She was their boss. Myonghee and Jinni developed a surrogate mother/daughter relationship with a heavy dose of friendship thrown in. Myonghee was usually in bed when Jinni returned from work in the early hours and she was gone when Jinni woke up. They often had lunch together at the restaurant, but their time to talk was in the evening of Jinni's day off. Myonghee never had a day off but she closed the restaurant when she wanted. Anyone who walked by the little restaurant on a Thursday night, and many people did, would see the two women sitting in the locked restaurant with the lights dimmed. Depending on the time or the mood, passers-by would see a young woman and an old woman absorbed in eating, deep in conversation, drinking beer, crying quietly or laughing like school children. Like the waves at Haeundae Beach, the events came one after the other and sometimes one wave rode the back of another. Jinni talked and Myonghee listened and as words were spoken and listened to, the events the words described could be filed away. Myonghee's attention was like a salve that healed, a massage that relieved. Sometimes the two women would drink too much and catch a taxi back to the apartment, but most of the time they walked home arm-in-arm, sometimes silently and other times deep in animated conversation, but always arm-in-arm.

Before having dinner with Myonghee at the restaurant on Thursdays, regardless of the weather, Jinni spent time at Haeundae Beach. And, regardless of the weather, she swam. After her swim, if it was cold, she would wrap herself in her beach towel or, if it was hot, her sarong and walk 300 meters to the nearest mokyoktang. A few hours at the local sauna is a regular weekly recreational cleansing program for most Koreans. The mokyoktang has separate sections for men and women and the resting areas are segregated. The jjimjilbang is also a sauna but they have a mixed resting area and restaurant that caters for both genders, and families and couples often reunite in this area for a meal after cleansing. Jinni preferred the mokyoktang; she didn't want to see men in anything close to undress. The women's space at this mokyoktang had shower heads a meter off the floor arranged in T's along 20 meters of wall. Women squatted on low plastic stools and cleansed their bodies. It is common for family members to assist each other when washing. Even strangers are happy to wash another's back. After washing, patrons enter one of the baths ranging through mild, medium and hot plus an icy plunge pool. There was also a jade kiln-sauna and a salt one. And, there was the ever-present seshin corner where the scrub mistress dressed in black underwear scrubbed women with an abrasive cloth. The mokyoktang had always been a part of Jinni's life and she missed it when she was in Australia. On her first visit to the Haeundae mokyoktang, the women stared at her tan but after a few visits, she became a familiar sight and she was often greeted with a good-humoured barb about having a peasant's tan although her bikini marks illustrated something else.

On that first visit, she laid down on the scrub table and the typically grumpy ddemiri went to work with her coarse cloth. The ddemiri's massage was not gentle; in fact, it was predictably painful. Dead skin was scraped off and 30 minutes later Jinni's skin burned red and she watched soapsuds, dead skin and some of the shame of her poor judgement wash down the drain.

After the sauna, Jinni often stopped for a chat with Annie. If the surf shop was quiet, Annie closed it and the two would sit at a local coffee shop. They weren't friends but they had become comfortable with each other and Jinni liked the contact outside of Texas Street.

CHAPTER 32

Miji's Milk

Stan has spent the last month working little, reading little and drinking lots. He has not run for weeks. He is now wandering the streets of Itaewon. For a change, he enters a new bar. It is a modern bar, and the bar staff wear hearing devices attached to curled wire. He doesn't want to be recognized so he sits on a stool at the corner of the bar and drinks beer while striking up an intermittent conversation with the barmaid, a conversation that fills in time but does not expand the intellect. The girl is tall with pale skin. When she smiles, dimples crease her cheeks, and she smiles often. She greets every customer who enters with a bright, "Anyang husaeyo."

Stan is soon onto his third beer and he feels comfortable enough to ask the girl if she knows anything about the Seongsu Bridge collapse. Her face doesn't register the event and when Stan tries to give her a history lesson, her eyes glaze over. He finishes his beer and says his goodnights and he is soon out on the streets again. He walks past Jacque's restaurant and looks in the window but he does not see anyone he knows; he keeps walking. Eventually, he stops at a kebab truck and orders a kebab, extra hot. He watches individual faces in the crowd walking by and he recognizes no one; he feels deeply alone. Now, he wants to be recognized because he has become bored with his own thoughts. He decides to take the kebab home. There is nothing worse than feeling alone in a crowd.

Stan opens the door of his small apartment and the first thing he does is turn on the TV. He flicks through the channels until he finds Liverpool playing Stoke City. He is not that interested but what else does he have to do. He gets a plate from the cupboard over the sink and a beer from the fridge before returning to the living room where his kebab waits. He sits on the couch, chows down and watches the soccer.

By the time he goes to bed, he has drunk more than he should have. His sleep is instant but shallow and he hopes for Jinni, but Miji is waiting for him.

"Stanley, you are looking haggard my friend. You are drinking too much and you are not talking to anyone. Stanley, you haven't seen Vince in weeks. You can't continue to do this 'alone with your thoughts' thing; it's not good for you."

"Miji, I don't feel like sex."

"Stanley, you don't feel like anything lately but you've got to find some motivation for something."

Miji is wearing a tight black dress that fits snugly over her form. It is cut low and her whiteness contrasts with the blackness of the dress. Her hair is free and it hangs across her face. Her feet are bare and she is sitting on the side of the bed.

"Mum and dad are doing well. I don't need to see them anymore." She pulls back the blankets. "I'm cold." She rolls her dress off her body like a stocking; she is not wearing underwear, and she slips in between the sheets. She maneuvers her hand behind Stan's head and draws him to her. His head fits into the nook of her shoulder, just above her breast.

Stan and Miji remain in this position long enough for Stan's body to begin to relax. Miji gently caresses his ear, a light touch.

"Stanley, drink from me."

"What?"

She is gentle, quiet, her voice soothing.

"Suckle on my breast." And, she eases his face toward her nipple. "Don't think Stanley, just drink." And, she sings ever so softly,

"Hush little baby do not cry.

Miji's gonna send you through the sky.

Please don't think about how to fly.

Miji will help you by and by."

Like a newborn baby, Stan's lips search for her nipple. His movements are not sexual; they are hungry. When he first takes her nipple into his mouth, he sucks hesitantly. Miji sings,

"Drink little baby don't be shy;

Miji's gonna send you high and wide."

Stan sucks and the first drop of milk rests on his tongue. It doesn't taste like any milk he has ever tasted. He holds it there, savors it. He doesn't need to suck again because the milk drips into his mouth like water from a drip irrigation unit, slowly but regularly. He swallows the essence. Miji arches her back and her nipple attaches to Stan's lips like a baby kangaroo attaches to its mother nipple. Her body is liquid and it follows Stan's form, and the milk drips and Stan swallows. Miji moves onto her right hip and reaches under Stan's hip with her left hand. She draws him forward and he is absorbed into her before he realizes what has happened. It is almost as though the two bodies have merged. And she continues with the lullabies.

"Stanley, Stanley give me your body do.

I'm so crazy all for the love of you."

Stan does not move; he cannot move but Miji's liquidness flows all over him; she consumes his body but enriches his spirit with her milk. And, they lift off the bed: drip, drip.

Miji holds Stan lightly around his head and hip. She holds him gently but securely, like a mother holds a child, and they evaporate through the ceiling of Stan's small Itaewon apartment. He is not afraid. He is able to see in a full 360-degree panorama but he cannot move his head and his lips cannot release Miji's nipple.

The bizarre Madonna and child rise above the rooftops. Stan looks at his neighborhood, his haunts and Miji croons,

"Look little Stanley see down there,

It is a place where souls are bare.

Itaewon is not for you,

Move away or you'll be blue."

And, they rise higher into the air, higher than the pollution, and the stars fill the sky and Miji's chi drips into Stan's very being.

Stan reaches for Miji with his thoughts, "Where can I go? Itaewon is where I am known and it is what I know." And, Miji sings,

"Wait little Stanley wait and see,

Miji's gonna make all things appear.

Look little Stanely see down there.

It is lonely no hope there."

And they sail on the winds of the stars. She has them sliding along the Big Dipper. She drinks from the Milky Way and feeds the fuel to Stan: drip, drip.

They hover, for a period, over Chuncheon in the lakes district of Korea. The city sits at the bottom of a bowl of mountains and Stan's mind is filled with the reality of cycling and running. He can feel the sweat of exercise, the joy of exercise and the beauty of the natural environment. Miji sings,

"Here little Stanley this is nice,

But it will come at a price.

Let's fly on to somewhere new,

Somewhere you'll never be blue."

"But I like Chuncheon." Thinks Stan

"Not tonight Stanley."

And, they soar higher into the sky. Miji does a loop-to-loop and laughs out loud. Stan's mind returns the laughter. Miji speaks again, "I have two places in mind for you, Stanley."

And, they are soon swooping over Busan. The ocean is filled with the reflection of stars. And Miji flies along Haeundae Beach.

"Someone is waiting for you here, but if you miss her," And, at the speed of light they are hovering over the cityscape of Melbourne and he can see Prahran Market, "You will find her here." Drip, drip.

Stan has drunk his fill and Miji soon has them floating above the small Itaewon apartment. The roof melts and the liquid couple drift down and onto the bed. Stan is still merged with Miji and her liquidness begins to slide over him, ever so tenderly. Stan has never felt gentleness like it and she hums softly and soothingly,

"Miji can't come back again,

She has done all she can.

It's now up to you,

Take your life and do for you."

Her body remains in liquid form and Stan feels his orgasm building. She reaches for Stan's foot and she caresses the middle toe; her touch is like warm, running water, and she speaks tenderly, "This little piggy had roast beef."

She then takes his second to last toe in her liquid grip, "And this little piggy had none."

Ever so lightly she takes his little toe, "And this little piggy ran all the way home. You need to find a new home Stanley, my friend."

Miji's unhurried touch is extreme and Stan has no control. He cannot hurry to a climax. His lips are still around Miji's nipple but the milk has stopped dripping. Without warning, his body tenses and he comes in an explosion of emotion. His body shudders and his semen is absorbed into Miji; it becomes part her liquidness and Miji's milk fills his mouth in a burst. He swallows her and polished milk fades to black.

CHAPTER 33

You are Jinni

Five years after Jinni was raped by Alexei, she was sitting at the bar of Love Always drinking tonic water. She was still not completely comfortable in this environment; she still found the open sexuality of it threatening but, for the most part, this unease was not obvious to others. Only Blue and the two bodyguards and, of course, Myonghee were aware of her internal conflict. She always had her eye on her environment. She was definitely the boss but her leadership was subdued; the girls, for the most part, followed her direction. They now dressed like confident college girls out for the night, but only Jinni wore blue jeans and a white T-shirt or black jeans and a white blouse or, occasionally, white jeans and a black blouse. Jinni had stopped wearing make-up altogether, not even a hint of eye shadow. The five years had flowed like a river; at its origins, it was small and unsure before gaining strength and turbulence and now it was flat and predictable. And, her body was toned from weekly swims that were often supplemented with swims in the mornings at the local swimming pool before work. Her skin was the color of wild honey all year around although, in the summer, it deepened even more. The barman, Ho, continued to do his thing behind the bar and his number two had learned most of his tricks. Jinni enjoyed their company at work but she never met them outside of work. She knew the two bodyguards had her back; in fact, she often sensed them in the shadows as she walked home early in the morning. Sometimes she sensed them when she was in Haeundae; their covert presence was a comfort. She was content but she was not happy. Laughter did not come easily. Myonghee and Blue were rewarded with full smiles, but they never witnessed the eruption of a full laugh.

Blue interrupted her reverie. "I need to see you in my office at 4pm tomorrow."

And, as he often did with these kinds of announcements, he stood from his stool and walked out of the bar nodding to the "Night Boss" salutations.

Jinni did not think much about the meeting with Blue, she often had private meetings with him where they discussed business and legal affairs. They talked a little about private matters but both had built strong emotional fences so, the following afternoon, Jinni walked into Blue's office with thoughts about the bar's finances and some possibilities for investment.

Blue motioned toward the old armchair. It absorbed her but it did not comfort her. A memory of sitting in the office after being raped tore into her soul and she winced. Blue picked up a large envelope from his desk, got up from his chair and walked around to stand in front of Jinni.

"You are Jinni."

Jinni accepted the envelope and Blue went back to his chair behind his desk. She just looked at the envelope until Blue said, "Aren't you going to open it?" And, she did.

The envelope contained a Korean ID Card, a Korean Passport, a Certificate of Birth, a Bachelors Degree and a Master Degree from Korea University with a major in English Language and Literature, a Credit Card and bankbook from the Korea Exchange Bank and all these items were in the name of Jin Hee, Lee. Jinni just looked. She opened the passport and saw that there were stamps from several countries she had never visited. She had only been to Australia for two years as a middle school student. She opened the bankbook and saw that it contained the Korean Won equivalent of $150,000. She looked at Blue, "How?"

"It took a while ... documents needed to be real. I could have got you forged documents in a month but real documents take time, chance and coincidence. Remember, I'm a lawyer. These documents will pass any scrutiny; you are Jin Hee, Lee."

"What about the money?"

"That took time too. Your ex-husband gambles in dark places and I can see in the dark. Or should I say, 'I have eyes in the dark.' You know how you have helped my staff prosper with your business knowledge; well, my legal knowledge has helped many of my shadowy allies." He paused and smiled before continuing, "The law and organized crime is a heady mix. We all work on the edge of society and I have helped most. We have built alliances. My old boss was a hard man but he looked after good people. Not many worked within the law but they were good. He looked after me even though I was not particularly good at the time but he saw something in me. I see something in you. We only take money from those who deserve to lose their money and your ex-husband was one of those losers. My group is not into gambling but many of my allies are. Let's just say their games are not straight. We milked your ex-husband for five years, $30,000 a year over five years equals $150,000. It's your money."

Jinni continued to sit in silence. She looked from one item to another and on to another and back again. And, Blue spoke again, "There's a few things you need to do. You need to exercise these cards. I want you to go to the hospital for a check-up; use your ID Card. I want you to use your Credit Card and withdraw some money from your account. From now on, I'll have your pay deposited into your account. Also, I want you to go to Japan on the ferry to exercise your Passport and finally, you need to get a job that matches your qualifications. You need to build references outside of this work. You have an interview with *Miss Moon's Hagwon* next week. You will work here three nights a week and at the English language institute three afternoons a week."

"Thought you said I had an interview."

"You know the way things work around here."

Indeed, she did know how things worked. "Blue, I don't know what to say."

He replied in pretty good but accented English, "You'll be great. I look forward to your tales."

This was the first time Jinni had heard Blue speak English and she replied in English, "You are full of surprises."

And, she stood and walked from the room. Blue smiled as he watched her leave.

Jinni sat down at the bar and Ho interrupted his preparation to pour her a glass of tonic water. He put a slice of lemon on the rim of the glass and picked up a coaster. Jinni accepted the drink with a distracted smile and Ho returned to his preparations. He glanced regularly at Jinni but he did not intrude on her thoughts. The two bouncers arrived and greeted her. They too noticed her distracted persona. They looked at each other, made a mental note, but they did not enquire. By the time the girls arrived, Jinni was back into work mode. Ho relaxed but Left and Right did not. It was their job to remain alert and when it came to Jinni, they were beyond diligent.

CHAPTER 34

The Search Begins

After Stan's last encounter with Miji, he has begun spending weekends in Busan. He gets to Seoul Station before 9am each Saturday and catches the KTX to Busan and returns on Sunday afternoons. He reads and he looks out the window of the train as it accelerates beyond 300kpm. He watches the season change. When he arrives in Busan, he flags a taxi and asks, in shaky Korean, to be taken to a region he has not explored before. Often, the taxi drivers make suggestions and other times Stan points to a place on a map. He doesn't know what he is looking for but his dreams tell him that there is something out there and he is compelled to investigate; flashes of Jinni are a bright flames and he willingly falls into the fire.

Love hotels are cheap and plentiful so when searching different regions, he uses them for accommodation. But, being alone in a love hotel is the height of loneliness and, as he has found out on a few occasions, empty sex with a stranger who looks like Jinni is just another lonely peak.

Stan had not met with Vince for more than a month because he had tried to fight Miji's orders but now he has slipped into meeting him on Sunday evenings. He gives Vince a call when his train is nearing Seoul Station and they decide on a meeting place. They begin to move beyond Itaewon with meetings occurring in the university district of Hongik or the art and drama district Haehwa-dong. Sometimes they end up back in one of their old haunts for a nightcap and sometimes they bump into Mr. Kim and his wife. The old couple has become a powerful doubles team and the wife holds her own in singles. If they are not playing pool, they can be seen talking and smiling together over a couple of beers. They drink slowly and bar patrons often interrupt them for a friendly chat. They often buy Stan a beer but his retreat into the task of unearthing Jinni, and his unwillingness to talk of his last meeting with Miji, means that he rarely sits with them for more than one beer.

Stan has lost weight; his hair is unkempt; bags hang like storm clouds under his eyes and his obsession with finding Jinni makes him unapproachable at best. Most of his days are spent in a battle with himself. However, Vince feels an obligation as a friend to listen but it is a strain. The discourse struggles through politics, philosophy, soccer, literature, tango (even though Vince has not been for months) until, inevitably, it returns to dreams. They are sitting in a bar in Haehwa-dong drinking slowly.

"How much did I tell you about my last encounter with Miji?"

Vince doesn't need to think before answering, "You told me about drinking from her. You talked about the taste without actually describing the taste. You told me a bit about the sex, not much, but you did tell me that it differed from the hardcore stuff of her previous visits. You told me that you doubted whether she would fill your dreams again."

"You know why I'm visiting Busan on the weekends don't you?"

"Something there for you. Something you needed to find."

"Someone, actually. Did I tell you that she told me to keep meeting you?"

"Jaysus, that's all I need." And the two men drink from their beers.

"Miji is or was Mr. Kim's daughter."

"Jaysus mate, pull it together ... you're an idiot. She's a dream. Pretty coincidental I must admit but don't lose everything chasing a fucking ghost, a ghost in a dream at that. Mate, be careful; that's all I'm saying, be careful."

They go back to sipping slowly from their beers and the barman gives them an impatient look. They have been sitting at the bar for 30 minutes and they are only halfway through their first beer. The bar is full and people are being turned away.

"Do you two want another beer?"

Vince is quick to bristle, "Glasses are half full. I'll let you know when I'm ready for a refill."

The barman's sarcasm drips from his lips, "Tomorrow probably."

Stan and Vince look at each other and begin to laugh and they enjoy the therapy. The barman does not enjoy their laughter and he moves to the far end of the bar and begins chatting with a waitress.

"So, what did you find?"

"Don't know; I never know what I find because I don't know what I'm looking for."

"Maybe you should stop searching and just start being. You know, a little less desperation and a little more Stanleyness ... you've been awfully tight for months now. Quite frankly, you're not fun to be around. I talk with you because you're my friend. I've known you for a long time ... but I can't imagine a stranger wanting to talk with you."

"But I've hooked-up with strangers and had sex with them."

"And I bet they're still strangers in the morning."

Stan just stares into his beer.

"When you're not with me, how often do you laugh? Whom do you talk to?"

Stan picks up his beer and takes a drink. He puts the glass on the bar and picks up the coaster and tears at the edges. He looks around and, for the first time, he notices that the place is full of couples and groups smiling, laughing and talking loudly. There is great energy and Stan looks into the mirror behind the bar. His mouth is drawn down; his brow is wrinkled; his eyes are empty and he doesn't want to be with his reflection.

"Maybe I should go and live in Busan. Maybe I need to immerse myself in life down there."
"Pathetic. That's not what you need to do. It's not the town or the country; it's the space inside that needs to be embraced."

The noise of the tavern encloses the two men sitting at the corner of the bar. They have stopped talking. Vince is thinking about the loss of tango and just how bored he is with Stan. Stan keeps thinking about Miji's milk and its power. He hears what Vince is saying but it is easier to rely on a medicine than self-enlightenment.

"Shit, Vince."

"Yes indeed, shit it is and shit it will remain until you start to believe in yourself... Jaysus Stan, forget the milk and start living."

"I watched some of the soccer game last night in the love hotel. Did you watch it?"

"Yeah right, nice change of direction. Think about what's been said tonight. Miji told you to keep meeting me. So, listen to me and think about what I've said."

Vince picks up his beer and drains it. "It's time for me to get moving ... Stan, mate, embrace your inner self and do it soon before it's too late ... I've got a class the day after tomorrow at 11am that needs a break from programming. I want you to give a talk to the class."

"In two days? What about?"

"Jaysus Stan, it doesn't matter. You just need to do something different. You know how to get to the university. I'll call you on the morning of the day after to confirm."

And, he stands up from the barstool and walks out of the bar without looking back. Stan sits for a few minutes before he too drains the last of his beer. The barman tells him it is time to leave because he has paying customers waiting. Stan tells him to 'fuck off' as he leaves. The barman cleans up the two glasses and hopes that the two men will not return. His wish will be granted.

CHAPTER 35

That's Uncomfortable

Vince hails a taxi outside of the pub and asks to be taken to Gyeongnidan, which is down the hill from Itaewon along the road that runs from the US Military Base up to the Hyatt Hotel. In fact, the locale has taken its name from the road itself, Gyeongnidan-gil. The place has become a Western enclave with many bars and cafés owned by, or co-owned by foreigners but hipster Koreans are beginning to search out its craft beer taverns, Mexican restaurants and other foreign inspired delights. Vince is looking for a little social interaction as a salve against Stan's discontent and a distraction from his unrequited desires for Jiyoung. When not meeting Stan and not dancing, he has been drinking in a number of bars. He has become a familiar figure and his drunken humor is tolerated by some and laughed at by others.

Vince lives in the area so he knows quite a few drinking holes and he knows many foreigners and Koreans who visit them. He walks into the *Sound Bite* with a smile on his face and immediately starts up a conversation with a group of foreigners he knows from the soccer competition he plays in. Some are teammates and some are members of competing teams. In the group are also a few women he has not met before. He quickly introduces himself to the unknown women before ordering a beer. He disdains the craft beers and orders a HITE Max. The conversation revolves around soccer, both the local and the European competitions. Vince is a major Manchester United fan and he enters into a lively discussion on Ryan Giggs and how long he can continue to play. While talking soccer with the guys, he flirts with the women. His flirting is speculative rather than determined; he throws out his charm and waits for a bite.

Halfway through his third beer he orders two Jameson's Irish Whisky, one for him and one for an Irish woman in the group.

Her eyes are hazel, edged in green and her hair is black, edged in grey. She is not tall and she is not slim and her smile is sisterly kind. And, for the most part, she holds a small, bug-eyed Boston terrier in her arms. She has warmed to Vince and she laughs at his flirtatious affectations. She finds him funny. Vince finds her sexy but as he drinks more, clouds cloak his senses.

Within an hour his attention is solely on Grace and the others in the group have faded away into a variety of other groupings and other bars. Vince and Grace continue to drink Jameson's and the flirtations become physical; the Boston terrier sulks on the floor under Grace's chair. And, the whisky falls like water.

Vince remembers getting into a taxi with Grace but not much more. Now he is waking in an unfamiliar apartment. He is prone on an unfamiliar bed. His legs are spread wide and his face is buried in the unfamiliar scent of an unfamiliar pillow. His left hand is entangled in someone's hair. A sensual touch on his balls has him stretch his legs but last night's shots of Jameson preclude any other reaction. He just remains motionless; he cannot respond to the touch. Grace's snoring is a rhythmic whistle and the contradiction between the touch and the snoring drags him out of his drunken inertness. He twists his head around and he is looking into the bug-eyes of Grace's Boston terrier as it enthusiastically licks his balls.

CHAPTER 36

An Australian Homestay

For the most part, Jinni enjoyed her work at the hagwon. She didn't have any administrative duties although she occasionally acted as a translator for the foreign faculty. She enjoyed the fact that she only had to teach the young students; in fact, she found their youth and energy motivating. She was a little envious of their carefree ways because her husband had taken that from her too early. Ms. Moon was pleasant enough although her demands had begun to increase and she was tired of saying no. The other teachers did not bother her and she did not bother them. They chatted well enough in the teachers' room, but she was reluctant to meet them after work. She told no one about her work at Love Always. Ms. Moon, of course, knew but no one else had any idea of her second life. There were always two foreign teachers in the hagwon but they were not always the same. Every six months or so, one would leave and another was soon occupying the recently vacated chair. Every now and then, one would ask her out but she always declined. She never actually said no but her controlled smile and retreating back was answer enough.

She slipped into a routine. On Friday, Saturday and Sunday she was the manager at *Love Always;* and on Monday, Tuesday and Wednesday she was a teacher at Moon's English Hagwon.

Thursdays remained the same; she swam and spent time at the mokyoktang and drank the occasional coffee with Annie during the day and she spent time with Myonghee in the evenings. Mondays were tough; the other days had their moments and Thursdays made any hardship during those other days worthwhile and she was happy enough. She didn't think much about Seoul although her discussions with Myonghee kept the memories alive.

Five years of juggling two jobs has started to wear thin. Jinni is tired, really tired. Thursdays have been her only free days in 10 years. At the bar, she starts work at 5pm and finishes between 3 and 4am. At the hagwon she starts work at 3pm and finishes at 10pm. She needs a holiday. And, this Wednesday she is in bed before midnight and sound asleep soon after. Her dreams start slowly with family images, almost like old sepia 8-millimeter film. She is part of the show but she is also a spectator to the show. Her mind feels the sensations of the past images. She feels a childhood love for her mother and father, an antipathy for her brother. Yet, her spectator mind feels anger toward her father and disappointment toward her mother. The images pass and are replaced by scenes of Melbourne.

It has been twenty years since she was a middle school student at Penleigh Girls Grammar School. She has not felt that sense of freedom before or since. She boarded with a host family whose only child, Bill, had died at the age of 18 during the final stages of the Vietnam War. His father, Walter, had encouraged him to go to war, suggesting that it would, "Make a man of you." Walter had lived his life between wars and had never experienced conflict outside of the school ground. He would struggle with that flawed advice until the day he died. Bill's mother, Mary, struggled to live with her silence. She opposed the war as she opposed all violence but she said nothing at the time. She allowed Walter his words.

Mary and Walter lived in Essendon, in a three-bedroom Federation style house built before WWII. Mary and Walter's bedroom held a double bed with an oak Edwardian bedhead and wardrobe. The windows were draped with heavy cotton cloth of faded green and a faded brown Edwardian lounge chair occupied the space between the window and the bed. The walls were covered in faded yellow wallpaper with a floral motif. There was only one picture on the walls. It was a picture of a smiling Bill in his army uniform and it hung behind the bedhead. The other two bedrooms were empty, not a bed, not a wardrobe, not a chair. The floral wallpaper on one wall had uninterrupted views of the floral wallpaper on the opposite wall. There were no pictures in frames, nothing and the polished wood floor was a playground for dancing dust motes.

At the center of the dining room stood a solid oak table surrounded by six uncomfortable oak chairs. This room was rarely used as the couple had taken to eating in front of the television in the lounge room. If they sat at the table, they would have had to talk; they preferred to let the television do the talking.

The living room was sparsely decorated with a coffee table and a faded crimson velour lounge suite that included a two-seat sofa and two lounge chairs. Mary and Walter had arranged the coffee table in front of the sofa with a lounge chair on either side. A television squatted on a low stool next to a neglected fireplace framed by a busy oak surround. The wallpaper was beige and the window was covered by a venetian blind. When Walter arrived home from his work as an accountant for Ford Motor Company, he would sit in the lounge chair on the left and read a newspaper and watch television. Mary would make dinner and serve it on trays and she would sit in the lounge chair on the right. The couple ate their meals and watched television until one or the other went to bed. The remaining spouse would go to bed once the other was asleep.

This collective loneliness ate away at the couple and in 1985, Mary saw an advertisement in the local paper asking for volunteer host families for international students attending Essendon Boys Grammar or Penleigh Girls Grammar schools. Bill had been a student at Essendon Grammar before he was conscripted to fight in someone else's war and Mary remembered Bill's sporting achievements, strong grades and smiling face. She called the phone number before discussing the prospect with Walter. Mary and Walter attended an interview and were accepted as a host family. One month later they were at the airport picking up Mejung.

Before Mejung arrived, Walter wallpapered one of the empty bedrooms in sky blue. Mary bought a single bed and decorated it with lively colored sheets and quilt. She bought a lime-green wardrobe and study desk and she bought a navy-blue lamp for the desk. The impending arrival of Mejung gave the couple a reason to talk again, a reason for living again.

The house initially intimidated Mejung. She had always lived in her parents' modern apartment. This house smelled of old lives and stale dreams. The small windows created beams that spotlighted random emptiness and it had a garden of concrete and neglected lawn. She found her host family a strange delight. Unlike her parents, they included her in their lives and they surrounded her with an unaccustomed affection. The dining room became a place of discussions where bums deadened, backs ached and hopes were aired. Mary bought and displayed flowers once a week and the house shed its mustiness. Walter, now, shied away from giving advice but his years of silence had made him a good listener and Mary was an easy conversationalist once she had rekindled the art.

Mejung thrived in the school and home environment. But, after two years, her father demanded that she return to Korea. Of course, her mother acquiesced. Mejung, Mary and Walter shared a tearful goodbye and this is what Jinni is experiencing in her dream.

She is crying. She watches the lively home fade to grey. She watches Walter turn the key on her bedroom. She watches the flowers wither.

And then, her dream moves forward to an event she did not experience; she is experiencing it for the first time, in a dream, but she knows the truth of the event.

Walter and Mary are sitting in their much loved, old Mercedes Benz. The car is in the garage and the roller door is down. There is a tube running from the exhaust pipe through the rear window. The end of the tube rests in the center of the back seat pointing at the ceiling above the old couple who are staring straight ahead. Cello music is playing on the tape deck.

The loss of a second child was too much. Walter turns his face to his wife; tears stain his cheeks. Mary acknowledges her husband with a weak smile and a slight nod of the head. Walter returns the smile before he reaches toward the ignition. He twists the key to the right and the reliable old Mercedes starts immediately, just like it always has.

Jinni twists in her sleep as she tries to avoid the image but she cannot.

The old couple's eyes close and their chins drop to their chests. Their breathing slows and then stops. They are held in a sitting position by the seatbelts and this is the way neighbors would find them two weeks later.

Jinni rolls over in her sleep and the bar of *The Cullen Hotel* in Prahran replaces a fading image of the Coburg Pine Ridge Cemetery. She has never been to the cemetery and she has no memory of *The Cullen Hotel.* She never saw her Australian mother and father buried and she was too young to drink when she lived in Australia and she cannot remember ever hearing of this hotel but the image is real enough.

It is "Wet Hour" on a Friday night and the drinks are half price. She is surrounded by English conversations in a multiethnic guise. There are men in suits and men in short pants and T-shirts, women in business attire and women in gym tights and tank tops. The crowd is predominantly White but there is a smattering of Asian. She is sitting alone at the bar drinking a glass of pinot noir. The barman strikes up a disinterested conversation.

"I haven't seen you in here before."

"I just arrived in town last night. I think I'm staying in this hotel."

The barman isn't really listening, "Can I get you another drink?"

"When I finish this drink, I'll let you know."

And she steps off the stool and takes her drink to an outside table where she sits down and sips from her half full glass of wine. The windows are wide open and she can watch the action both inside and out. The barman goes back to his bottles and glasses.

Jinni is enjoying the dream.

She is admiring the paintings on the walls of the hotel. The subject matter drips into the canvas; strange paintings, she thinks. She smiles at her dream's cast and feels a wonderful lack of history or malice. She is smiling to herself when she notices a man about 45 years old sitting alone at a neighboring table. He mistakes her smile as being directed at him and he shyly returns the smile. She realizes the miscommunication and holds up her hand.

"Sorry, just smiling to myself."

"No worries but, I must say, you have a beautiful smile."

Jinni squirms in her sleep.

"Thanks."

And she returns her attention to her pinot noir and the stranger returns to his beer.

The images fade to black and Jinni's sleep continues dreamless and she wakes up refreshed.

CHAPTER 37

Jinni Makes a Plan

It is Thursday morning and Jinni wears her bikini under her clothes and packs her underwear, wetsuit and sarong into her small pack. While on the bus to Haeundae Beach, she thinks about her dream. She misses the freedom of her time in Melbourne. She misses Mary and Walter. She didn't attend their funeral; in fact, she didn't hear about their death until a letter she had written was returned unopened. She spoke to her homeroom teacher about her concern and she helped her contact Penleigh Grammar. She took the deaths hard. The strain of studying for university entrance exams coupled with this news left her emotions raw. Her parents were dismissive of the deaths. They never did understand her life in Australia and they complained about her changed attitudes. They fought hard to bring her back to subservience and the death of Walter and Mary was the broken connection they needed. They took the opportunity to begin collecting her mail and disposing of any with Australian stamps. Mejung was soon reabsorbed in preparing for the entrance exams with no time to think beyond them. She attended an English hagwon, a mathematics hagwon and an accounting hagwon. And soon, the only thing she had left from her time in Australia was her command of the English language. Now, while riding the bus toward Haeundae Beach, she allows herself to remember the past and the recent dream.

When Jinni arrives at the beach, the temperature is hovering around 20, but the water is closer to 13 degrees. She removes her clothes and stuffs them into her pack and slips into the 2-millimeter triathlon wetsuit that Myonghee had given her for the anniversary of their first meeting. Before plunging into the water, she looks across to the surf shop. Annie is standing outside and the two women wave to each other. Jinni turns back to the water and dives in and begins stroking easily toward the buoy 300 meters out to sea. As she swims, she remembers her swimming lessons at Penleigh Grammar and she draws a powerful stroke along the midline of her body. The ocean is cold but flat and she allows her mind to drift to last night's dream. Her strokes are clean and automatic and Mary and Walter's watery image absorbs her salty tears. She is soon back on the beach and she stand with her legs apart and her hands on her hips as she looks out to sea. Water drips from her hair and rolls off the shiny black neoprene that embraces her muscled shoulders. She pulls the top of her wetsuit down to her hips and sits on the sand enjoying the sun's warmth. As the sun warms her skin, she thinks more about Melbourne and her dream. She tries not to think about Mary and Walter although a desire to visit their grave won't go away. She tries to focus on the *Cullen Hotel*. She needs to do a little research about this hotel. In the meantime, she soaks up the sun.

After a 15-minute rest, Jinni pulls up her wetsuit and takes to the ocean and again she swims to the buoy and back. Her routine sees her do this circuit three times before she removes her wetsuit completely so that she can recline on her sarong to rest and worship the sun. After 15 minutes on her back and 15 minutes on her front, Jinni stands up, wraps the sarong lightly around her waist, puts on a t-shirt and walks across the road with her pack swinging from her shoulder. Annie is busy with a customer when Jinni enters the surf shop but she steps out of the negotiation for a moment.

Jinni asks, "Feel like lunch? I'll have a sauna later."

"Sounds like a plan. I'll close up as soon as I finish here."

Jinni browses for ten minutes before Annie finalizes a credit card transaction. The young pale-skinned couple thank Annie and they hold a large bag each. Jinni smiles at them. After the couple leave the shop, Annie places a "Back Soon" sign in the window and locks the door.

"Where are we going?"

"I had a dream last night about Australia so let's have a sandwich."

"Paris Baguette?"

"Reminds me of my first few days in Busan, a lifetime ago."

It is a short walk to the cafe and they are soon settled at a table sipping café lattes and biting into sandwiches. Jinni is telling Annie about her middle school years in Australia and selected bits of last night's dream. At a table, across from the two women, a middle-aged Western man is deep in a book and coffee and when Jinni gets to the part of the dream about the *Cullen Hotel*, she notices the man.

"See that man to your right? I think I know him."

"From Seoul?"

"I don't know; he could have been in my dream last night but I need to get out."

The two women drink the last of their coffees and pack up their sandwiches and leave. Stan looks up from his book and watches them go. He gets a sense of recognition but it is too fleeting and the moment passes. He goes back to his book and coffee.

Outside, Jinni and Annie walk back to the beach and sit down at a bench in the shade of a canvas sail and continue eating and talking. The question of the man's identity is left open and they soon get back to discussing Australia and other countries neither have been to. The discussion quickly moves from the almost possible to the remotely fantastic. Eventually the list progresses to the ridiculous and the two women are laughing and trying to outdo each other.

"Let's canoe the full length of the Amazon."

"You couldn't ride a motor boat across the Han River in Seoul."

"How about climbing Everest."

"You couldn't climb Namsan."

Finally, Annie stands up and says that she has to get back to the shop and earn some money. They say their goodbyes and head off in opposite directions.

CHAPTER 38

Breaking Habits

Stan is sitting at his little kitchen table drinking coffee and eating toast when the phone rings. He picks it up and it is Vince.

"You right for this morning? You need a welcoming committee?"

Stan thinks for a moment before responding, "I'll be there. And, you said I need to meet more people so sure, send the welcoming committee."

"Eleven remember?"

"Yep, done deal, see you at eleven."

Stan finishes up his morning ritual of coffee and shower before dressing in his familiar and what he calls, "casual but cool" clothes. His colors don't get far beyond blue, black and white and this morning he laces up a new pair of running shoes. With his feet sheltered, he opens the door to a beautiful autumn day.

The wind is teasing the leaves that remain on the trees and Stan begins walking to the university campus, which nestles into the side of Namsan. It is a walk of about four kilometers that follows one of his running routes and he is soon into Namsan Park and on the Namsan peak access road. He turns to the right and heads downhill. At a curve in the road, he pauses and looks out over Southern Seoul. From this vantage point he can see over the Han River, over Gangnam and beyond into Kyongi-do. The new rich with their freshly minted money live south of the river. Behind Stan is Northern Seoul where the money is older and soaked in power and intrigue. Early industrial Europe saw the owner's mansions on a hill above a river and beyond the river stood the factory and the workers hovels. The river was the barrier between the means of production and the owners of production. It was one thing to own a factory and employ factory workers; it was another to associate with the same workers who made it possible for the owners to live lives of luxury. Korea's industrial development occurred without consultation, without an industrial revolution, without unionization. Industrialization was constructed on top of a feudal plan. The Military Dictator, Park Chung-he had coaxed the laborers off the farms and put them to work in the new factories. They exchanged hard work in the fields, in the elements and fresh air for the hard labor of the factories that poisoned their lungs and the Seoul air. Park Chung-he guaranteed profits to the family owned Chaebol like Samsung and Hyundai and these families' wealth and power expanded while the laborers struggled without unions and without support. The powerful live north of the river and the workers live south of the river but the modern wealth of Korea means that prosperity has expanded and south of the river has become a place of trends and bright lights.

With a quick glance at his watch, Stan spins around and strides away leaving unfinished thoughts in the midmorning breeze. Down to the rubberized running track that snakes its way across and around Namsan, he builds his energy. The exercise is helping him feel better about himself. He increases his pace. His confidence is a display and he deliberately swings his arms in a reproduction of cool. He hasn't used his soft leather briefcase for some time and it hangs from his shoulder looking like it belongs to someone else.

As he walks, he takes in his surroundings. Ajumma crouch

on the side of the track to talk and he sees them as flocks of middle-aged women gaggled in squats like a gift pack of chopsticks. They are wearing hiking boots, *North Face* hiking jackets, black hiking pants, oversized sun visors and their hair is curled and dyed-black.

About a kilometer further along, to the right of the running track, not far from where he thought he saw Jinni before nearly killing the little kid, is the unpaved path that leads to Donggook University. Stan approaches the turnoff and there are three students waiting for him. The two girls are freshmen. The boy is also a freshman but he has recently returned from compulsory military service and his face displays his insecurities. He is here to captain the girls, to protect them. He is sure of his role but unsure of its execution so most of the time he looks lost. Stan sees the girls as unmatched canaries. One is slim and tall and the other is short and stocky. As Stan approaches, the girls smile, "Are you Stan?"

Stan straightens his shoulders and says, "Are you the welcoming committee?"

"Welcoming committee? What is welcoming committee?"

"Did Vince send you?"

"Yes, Professor Vince is your friend?"

The boy stands uneasily to the side with a smile trying to break his mask. It does not succeed.

The shorter girl is wearing pink Chuck Taylor's on her feet and blue jeans that stretch over her healthy curves. She is shapely; cuddly comes to Stan's mind. Her white sweatshirt has the words "Nice Claup" stretched across its front. Her breasts distort the shape of the letters.

Stan tries to be funny, "What is a Claup?"

"What?"

"A Claup. Your sweat-shirt says Nice Claup."

"Claup? Boyfriend gave me"

"Oh dear?" Another attempt at humor falls flat.

Stan looks into the girl's cherubic, lineless face and allows a smile to develop. Her questioning expression breaks into a matching smile and they shake hands. As they do so, she bows a little and her bobbed, black hair falls across her face.

The taller girl is wearing pale-blue Nike runners and a fresh-green mini skirt that finishes more than a ruler length above her knees. She is wearing black leggings and her calf muscles are well defined and the muscles of the quadriceps are well defined. She looks as though she would shine on a sports field. Her hair has been pulled back into a ponytail and her exposed ears attract Stan's attention. He cannot stop looking at her ears.

"And good morning to you; you're tall."

With almost perfect English, she says, "Does my height concern you?"

Stan pushes away the comment. "Where did you learn English; you're great."

"I spent a few years in Canada. Why are you interested in my height?"

"Well you're not short."

"*Bul sang han*, pitiful." And she scratches her left ear.

Stan drags his eyes away from her ears and meets her eyes. They are black, not deep brown but black. And now her eyes mesmerize him. They are like almonds viewed from the side and they are black. And when she smiles, they almost close shut.

He holds out his hand.

"Good morning."

And they shake hands. She does not bow her head and her eyes remain locked on his.

"Good morning *Middle-Aged Man*."

"What?"

"Well you're not young."

Her smile erupts across her face and her eyes disappear behind their epicanthic folds.

"Fair enough." And Stan's voice betrays the sting of the verbal slap. He turns to meet the young ex-soldier.

Stan holds out his hand, "Are you still in the army?"

"Not soldier. Finished one month. Now I student." This is said without a hint of a smile.

"Well, good morning to you."

"Good morning Vince's friend."

"Call me Stan."

Stan's practiced cool has taken a battering and his shoulders droop as he walks off surrounded, but not supported, by youth.

CHAPTER 39

Catharsis

The classroom is filled with students when Stan arrives and he attempts to pull his shoulders back. The three student guides head to their respective seats and Stan pushes on to the front of the classroom where Vince is waiting for him with an outstretched hand and a mischievous smile.

"Vince ... thanks mate. The walk and the company ... you're right, I need this ... I think."

He smiles, "How was the walk?"

"Autumn is hanging on. Only just but it won't give in to winter easily."

"Indeed, and short skirts and tight shirts have not yet disappeared."

"And, exposed ears."

The taller girl finds herself unconsciously reaching to scratch her reddening ears.

A hand has risen in the front. It is insistent so Vince acknowledges it with a, "Yes, Minnie?"

"I don't understand what you said. My English is good. I understand your words, but I don't understand what you said to each other. Please explain."

Vince speaks for a while about the power of the unspoken, the unconscious connections of old friends and how communication goes beyond words and into a realm of knowing. "Does your father need to explain his every need to your mother? Does your mother arrive at your father's side with a bottle of Soju just at the right time? Does your father need to ask when dinner will be ready? Are there long periods of silence between your mother and father, between your family members?"

Minnie thinks for a while before replying, "Yes, my father often grunts rather than speaks. He has different looks for different needs. I know when he is angry; I know when he is happy; I know when he wants me out of the way."

"Ok, let's move on. Maybe we can discuss this in more depth later. My office is always open."

Minnie looks as though she wants to continue but then she recognizes the opening Vince has left. She smiles broadly, "I'd like that."

Vince looks at Stan with a face that pleads for understanding; a face that hopes the *Lost in Translation* moment has been understood, and he motions for Stan to take the floor.

Stan moves to center stage and begins to address the class. He has decided to talk about his experience during the Tsunami of 2004. He was traveling in Sri Lanka at the time. After an unsteady beginning, he warms to his task. He doesn't know how much of his words are being understood; it is not important.

"The tsunami of 2004 killed more than 200,000 people. Its epicenter was off the coast of Sumatra, and it swallowed life from Indonesia, Malaysia, Thailand, India, Sri Lanka and even as far as the East African coast. It was a monster. I was traveling through Sri Lanka for the first time and I thought I would spend some time in the hills of Kandy before heading to the East coast to scuba dive. I was a day's bus ride out of Kandy when the Tsunami hit; I missed the wave by 30 kilometers.

I woke late the day after Christmas because I'd been reading until late at night and I'd had a few too many drinks. I stood at the office of the guesthouse ready to pay and asked the receptionist where the bus terminal was. The receptionist told me to take a look at the TV. I sat and watched. The television showed scenes of desolation. Coastal villages were flattened.

I'm sure you've seen the images ... but ... I want you to close your eyes and picture a sand castle, let's say a castle of compressed sand that is one meter in diameter and half a meter high. Have your mind place this castle on a sandy beach. Now, picture the tide coming in and a wave, not a very big one, let's say twenty centimeters high but one with greater force because it is being pushed by the incoming tide. Can you see what it does to the sand castle? The wave wraps around the castle like a jealous lover's arms, breaking and suffocating. It then spurns its lover and leaves it in tatters before heading off in search of another lover.

The wave hit Batticaloa, Trincomalee and Kalmunai on the east coast and wrapped its arms around Jaffna in the north and Matara and Galle in the south before swallowing the west coast and the capital city Colombo, destroying life and property as it went. And, it kept on going all the way to the East Coast of Africa.

I caught a bus back to Kandy in an attempt to regroup. The town was filled with foreigners either trying to get back to Colombo to fly out or discussing pretty naïve plans to help. I watched the images on TV and the scenes kept getting worse. It took two days before I could connect to the outside world. I called my parents in Australia and found out that my father had already reported me as missing. They were surprised but delighted to hear my voice and I found myself choking back tears as I talked to my mother.

When I finally got back to Colombo, I hired a motorcycle taxi to take me to the coast. I never got there because the wreckage of homes and lives had been washed kilometers inshore. It was like a deconstruction site. As far as the eye could see, there was a deconstructed reality ... chaos. The vision was hard to comprehend. There were square kilometers of destruction, square kilometers of broken timbers, broken bricks, broken concrete, broken cars, broken motorcycles, broken bicycles; there were broken toys and lost dolls lying lonely amongst the debris; there were fishing boats high and dry in the street, and there was the smell of death. I did not see human death, but there were dead dogs and dead livestock bloating in the sun. There was the recently homeless sifting through rubble that was once home, pulling at broken timber and throwing bricks aside. It was hard to know what they were looking for. Men and women, and boys and girls, and grandfathers and grandmothers squatted in the mud. Some were crying quietly; some were sobbing and others were staring with empty eyes. I was emotionally shot. There was too much death, too much sorrow. I needed to get to the airport."

Stan finishes his talk by saying that living through the tsunami of 2004 both saddened and enriched his life and he will never take life for granted.

"I make, and plan to continue to make, every moment of life a memorable one, a treasured one, a positive one. Thank you. Any questions?"

There is a pause as the students look to Vince for directions.

Vince stands up from his chair in the corner and guides the students to ask questions.

"Is there anything you miss from Australia?"

He talks about the football but explains that he can watch it via the computer.

"What about food?" Comes another question.

He says that he loves the unique flavors of Korean food but does crave a good meat pie.

Stan is puzzled by the lack of questions about the tsunami experience, but he figures that near-death experiences are difficult to empathize with. The language barrier and the experiential barrier make true empathy difficult. *So be it.*

Polite applause ripples through the room as Vince thanks Stan. And as Vince walks Stan to the door, they make a plan for meeting later that evening at around 7pm.

As Stan walks out of the classroom, his legs weaken and he chokes-up. He gets himself to an empty bench and sits down, surprised by the rawness of it all. He struggles to shore up his exposed emotions and he is only partially successful. He sits for a long time. Sometimes with his hands covering his reddened eyes, sometimes with his head tilted back to the sky and the students who walk by don't notice his pain.

And, he doesn't know where he belongs but he is beginning to get the feeling that he needs to belong somewhere. He just doesn't know where or with whom. Jinni is a dream and Miji is a ghost and he is removing himself from reality more and more.

CHAPTER 40

Miji's Invitation

After being scrubbed at the mokyoktang, Jinni walks the streets of the Haeundae district. It has become Busan's equivalent of Seoul's Gangnam which translates to "South of the river" or Melbourne's South Yarra. She ponders this linguistic coincidence for a while. Haeundae is a district of new money, stylish apartments, fashionable shops and body conscious people. Gangnam was her district when she lived in Seoul and it houses the new money of Seoul. She chastises herself for the vacuous life she had led. She had allowed her parents to control her and her husband to abuse her. How did it get to that? How had the vibrant, athletic Penleigh Grammar School student give up her freedom so easily? She had allowed her father's constant talk of money to break her sense of charity and she had been seduced by the idea of a business degree and the accumulation of more money. She had even allowed herself to be married off to a rich family.

Jinni walks the streets of Haeundae trying to shake off this past. She gets her mind off the horrors of Seoul and back to her middle school years in Melbourne. She remembers venturing south of the Yarra River one adventurous night. As a 16-year-old, she and a few of her school friends sat in an outside café and drank café latte. Jinni didn't like the taste but she told her friends how good it was and how she often drank "latte" in Seoul. Her friends laughed at her claims of enjoyment contrasted with her grimaces and it was not long before she joined in the laughter and confessed that it was her first experience with coffee. It took her several months to acquire a taste for it. She is leavened by these memories and she is soon sitting in a café drinking a café latte and smiling to herself. It feels good to smile.

At 6pm, Jinni walks into MYONGHEE'S. She is smiling and Myonghee notices and keeps the mood high.

"So, what's happenin' girl. Good to see ya smilin'."

"I've been dreaming and thinking about Australia. Remember, I told you that I did a couple of years of middle school in Melbourne? I just might go back for a holiday. I'm worn out."

"Good idea. You wanna beer?"

"Yeah, why not." The bottle is placed on the table and Jinni fills the two glasses. "I feel a need to visit my host parents' graves."

Myonghee lets this statement pass. She's not sure what to say. She just nods. The two women settle in for an evening of speculation, planning and simple conversation. Myonghee does not close the restaurant and soon regulars are joining in the conversation. Some express a desire to see Australia; some express a desire to see anything outside of Busan and one man had spent a week in Sydney that coincided with the Gay Mardi Gras. He describes it as life altering or was it life affirming. Jinni leaves MYONGHEE'S at midnight and walks back to the apartment. She is in bed by 1am and she is soon dreaming.

She is again in the Cullen Hotel and sitting across from her is an Asian woman with skin as white as chalk but as smooth as silk. Her age is difficult to determine as her body is lithe and her skin translucent.

"Let me buy you a drink, Jinni. I believe you are a pinot noir kind

of girl."

"Actually, I'd like a Riesling."

Jinni is puzzled but not afraid. She knows it is a dream and she feels open to its direction.

"Easy enough."

With a sexy move of her head, she summons a waiter. He has no choice but to attend to her desires. She orders two Rieslings and a bowl of nuts.

The waiter begins to say, "We don't provide nuts," but before he can finish, Miji fixes him with a look that promises everything. And, he finishes with, "I'll find some."

"Jinni, I'm having a party here on February 7. I want you to come and feel free to invite Myonghee and if you can get Blue Park out of the Love Always, it would be good to have him here too. Actually, you can invite anyone you like or come alone; that would be fine too. I do like those protective boys who hide in shadows and kiss in private."

"What are you talking about?"

"You can book into this hotel."

The wine and peanuts arrive and Jinni sips and Miji drinks her wine in one swallow. The waiter watches.

"Nice, I'll have another."

"Who are you?"

"Jinni, Jinni, Jinni, I am your best dream. By the way, I like the new name. It has a more musical sound to it than Mejung Oh."

When the waiter returns with the second Riesling, Jinni is alone. The waiter places the wine on the table and says, "She will be back, won't she?"

"I don't know who she is; I don't know where she went. But, leave the wine, I'll drink it."

The waiter's face drips disappointment and he slowly returns to his station. Jinni drains the remainder of her first wine and does the same to the second one. She is very conscious of this being a dream but she is reluctant to leave. Her dreaming mind keeps repeating, February 7, February 7.

She rolls over and the dream is gone. For a while she struggles to relocate it. She creates an image of Miji in her mind but she does not return. She rolls over again and attempts to re-enter the dream from a different direction but her subconscious is not cooperating. Miji is gone; the waiter is gone and the Cullen Hotel is gone. Jinni's sleep is empty but not relaxed. She sleeps and her mind won't go where she wants it to go; she just sees billboards advertising February 7 and the Cullen Hotel. She wakes and her mind won't slow down. It is 9am and she is tired.

CHAPTER 41

Jaysus

Stan and Vince are drinking at Scrooge Tavern and the conversation is traveling in known circles until it moves to the day's lecture.

"Why did you choose to talk about your tsunami experience? You'd told me you were there but you'd never spoken about the details before."

"Don't know. Guess I felt a need to offload some luggage. You know, just following old Vince's advice."

"You're older than me." And they share a smile and Vince takes a swallow of his beer and Stan does the same. "How much did it really affect you, Stan?"

"Not really sure; I'm not good at dealing with emotions. I tend to compartmentalize a bit but when I told the story today, especially the bit about calling my mum, well ... let's just say there was a rather large cockroach crawling around inside my throat."

"Do you want to talk about it now?"

"Not really. Didn't like the taste or the feel of the cockroach. The telling of the story was useful, I think, but ... yeah, let's leave it at that. But, thanks for pushing me to give the talk."

Vince reinforces his comments of the other night about drawing on his self and forgetting about Miji's potion. He tells him to get on with life and then there is silence between the two men and the bar hums a lonely tune.

"Stan, did I tell you about the dream I had about a month ago?"

"Did Miji visit?"

"No Miji ... look, let me get another beer and I'll tell you the gist of it."

Vince and Stan drain their beers and order two more.

After more than a few swallows and more than a few minutes of silence, Stan speaks, "Ok, I'm ready for the gist."

"Right, here we go. Strap yourself in ..." And Vince begins to retell his dream.

"In the dream, I was trying to get home, the childhood home in the outer suburbs of London. I could see the post WWII built council flat ... it was within reach. It was a three-bedroom place and when I was a kid, there were Ma and Da and seven kids living in it. It was cramped and noisy. There always seemed to be a squabble going on in some corner or other and my Ma went from patting one kid on the head, cleaning the snot from another and slapping the backside of yet another. I couldn't say that the house was filled with love. I don't think it was. It was filled with nine people surviving.

I was trying to get home but between my old house and where I stood there was a soccer pitch. I'd played a lot of football on that pitch. I spent hours alone kicking goals and practicing trick shots. I used to string up a bicycle tire from the crossbar; I'd move it up or down or across and I'd kick the ball at it from the penalty spot and from longer distances. I got really good at drilling that bicycle tire. And, I played center forward with the local team and I was pretty good. There weren't any scouts looking at me but I was better than solid. But, I would freeze with penalties. Not actually freeze but overcomplicate the matter, over think it. If only I could have hung a bicycle tire from the crossbar."

"Jaysus Stan, I came from an Irish factory-working family but my mind never slowed down. As a kid, I was always wondering why the world spun as it did ... why some lived on the streets and others lived in mansions. My Da worked his whole life in a factory and never questioned the rightness or wrongness of it. He just provided for his expanding Catholic family."

Vince stops the monologue and picks up his beer.

"Shit Vince, this is pretty deep stuff."

"Na it's not. Not deep at all. Just life. The struggle may be different but all life is the same. It is a struggle to get from one end of it to the other ... for some, the end comes soon after the beginning and for others it goes on too long. But, no matter how long the life is, it is a continuous struggle to survive, and I say 'survival' in a physical and a metaphysical sense."

"Yeah, as I said deep. So, what happened in the dream?"

"Unlike your dreams Stan, there is no sex in this one. I'm not saying that I haven't dreamed of sex in the past but this dream was sex free."

"I was trying to get across the soccer pitch but it was a quagmire. I was sinking up to my mid shins in mud and there was a weight on my back that just kept getting heavier. I wasn't wearing a pack nor was I carrying a bag ... but this weight on my back was sinking me into the mud of my childhood soccer pitch. I ended up on all fours, crawling toward the family home and all it held. Funny thing was, all this happened without emotion. I wasn't angry; I wasn't sad. I felt nothing; I was just struggling to get to where I thought I needed to get. And then it got a bit strange."

And Vince lapses into thoughtful silence.

"Ok, go on."

"Na, you can think about it for a while, while I go for a pee." And Vince gets off his stool and heads to the bathroom.

Stan goes back to his beer and thinks about his childhood, very different from Vince's. No cricket team of siblings, no Catholicism and not working class.

Vince returns and picks up his beer. He doesn't sit down but he does look around the bar as though he is saying hello or goodbye to it. Finally, he sits and continues recounting the dream.

"Ok Stan this is what happened."

"I wallowed in the swamp of a pitch for quite a while, not being able to go forward or backwards. Muddy pitches have a sour smell of fertilizer that bubbles up from the depths. After a short while, I was covered in this sweating earth and then, I felt the weight on my back shift and lighten slightly and a memory from my childhood landed in the mud beside me. It squirmed and tried to return to my back. For a while, I just looked at it as it struggled before it sunk into the sludge. A teenage experience landed beside me and the weight lightened again. Memories and experiences started to fall in a chaotic memoir that struggled to return to my back, but the quicksand of my childhood soccer pitch swallowed my history. As the memories sank, the pitch dried and I found myself standing on the penalty spot, light and unencumbered."

Vince paused and drank from his beer and Stan followed his lead.

"Is that the end?"

"Almost mate, almost."

Vince replaced his empty glass on the bar top and ordered another, as did Stan.

"For a while I stood on the penalty spot thinking, 'Do I go right top or left top, or right bottom or left bottom, or should I go straight at the keeper and anticipate him going one way or the other.' I froze on the penalty spot ... and then the insight hit me like a bar of soap. There was no mud holding me to the spot; the filth had slipped from my body. I was clean and there was no weight on my back; I was free to move toward my childhood home and I was free to walk away. I left the ball on the penalty spot; I didn't need to take the shot. I walked away."

"Shit and you say that's not deep. Man, that's Marianas Trench deep. You surprise me Vince; you drink with me and you listen to me and my stories of dreams yet we rarely talk of what matters to you."

"It's just a dream. No big deal. As I said before, life is a continuous struggle. Decisions have to be made; do we go back or do we go forward? And, in some cases, back is forward."

"Ok, enough, how goes the tango, mate." And the conversation meanders through Vince's lost tango love and soccer woes, and it picks its way through Stan's teaching assignments and travels to Busan. Both are drunk by the time they stand to leave. They wave their farewells to Mr. Kim and his wife who are watching a pool game.

"One last drink Stan?" Asks the wife in pretty good English.

"Yeah, why not," and Stan moves toward the couple.

"What about you Vince?"

"No, I'm done. I'll catch you next time." With that, Vince heads to the door and down the stairs while Stan orders another beer and sits opposite the old couple.

Vince continues down the stairs and is soon out in the cool night air. He too does not feel like going home. His apartment is to the right so he turns left and walks the streets. The first bar he comes to, he enters and orders a beer. He drinks it quickly and moves back out into the night. Four bars and four beers later he climbs the stairs to the *Hollywood Bar* and it is showing the English Premier League, so he settles in and strikes up a conversation with the stranger sitting next to him. Vince cheers loudly for Manchester United and the stranger cheers loudly for Chelsea. By the end of the game the score is 0-0 and the two are drunk and ready to fight. They spill down the stairs and out onto the street and throw a few drunken half blows but soon strangers join the fracas. Just when the fight looks like dissolving, Vince is hit from behind. He is unconscious before his head hits the curb and he is dead before anybody checks his vital signs.

Stan is home in bed when ambulance sirens and police sirens wake him. He thinks nothing of it and returns to sleep. The sleep is drunken and unsatisfactory. Vince's face drifts across his vision; it's a contorted mask. The eyes are open and the pupils dilated and the frozen mouth communicates pain. Stan shakes off the image and raises his consciousness but does not fully waken. His drunkenness keeps him asleep. Stan rolls over and the image returns; blood is trickling from Vince's eyes. His cheeks are streaked in crimson but now his mouth is smiling.

"Go home Stan."

Stan is bolt upright in bed. The sheets are askew. Alcohol still pulses through his veins but he is as sober as he has ever been. He reaches across to the nightstand and picks up his watch. It is 6am. He is crying but he is unaware of the tears. He pushes himself to the side of the bed and sits with his head in his hands. He stifles a few sobs. Five minutes later Stan is dressed in jeans and T-shirt. His tears have dried and his emotions are frozen. He doesn't bother brushing his teeth before leaving his apartment. He walks down the steps to the lane that runs in front of his apartment and turns toward the departing sirens. He increases his pace. He is almost running but when he gets close to the *Hollywood Bar*, he slows; he doesn't want to see what he knows he will see. There is a bloodstain the size and shape of a pillow on the curb and seeping into the gutter, but there is no comfort in this pillow. There are a few people milling around, not many, and a lone policeman is interviewing a Westerner in good English. Stan listens to the conversation and waits for the policeman to be free.

"Where did they take the body?"

The policeman looks at Stan, "How do you know there has been a death?"

Looking toward the bloodstain, Stan says, "That's a lot of blood."

"Do you know the deceased?"

"I think so."

The policeman thinks for a while before responding, "That's a pretty strange answer. What do you know about this?"

"I don't know anything. I just woke from a dream and I think my friend is dead. Please, tell me where they took the body."

"I'll do better than that, I'll drive you."

The policeman opens the back door of the police car and Stan struggles in and stares back at the stain on the curb. He sees a vision of two men sitting at a bar drinking and laughing but it soon dissolves and the reality of the blood pool hits and he slumps back into the seat.

The siren has been turned on but Stan doesn't hear it and five minutes later the police car is pulling into a *No Standing* zone at the entrance to *Soonchunhyang Hospital.*

"Follow me."

Stan lets himself out of the back of the car and follows the voice into the hospital where he watches distractedly as the policeman talks to a woman behind the counter. They both look at Stan before the woman points to the elevator. In the elevator, the policeman asks, "Are you up to this."

"Of course not, but I'm here."

The elevator stops at B2 and the policeman and Stan step out and turn left. They stop outside a door marked, MORTUARY. Both enter the office and the policeman talks in Korean to the mortuary attendant before turning to Stan, "This way."

Double doors swing open and a burst of cold air escapes. There is a stainless-steel table in the center of the room and a white sheet shows the outline of a human body. The attendant points to a square painted on the floor next to the head of the table and Stan steps on it. The policeman stands beside him. The attendant walks around to the other side of the table and grasps the end of the sheet. Without hesitation, he pulls the sheet off the dead man's face. Vince's dead eyes are closed. Stan has seen many a TV show where people say that the dead look like they are sleeping. Stan can't believe how dead Vince looks. His skin is grey. His cheeks are hollow. He is definitely dead and it is definitely Vince.

"Do you know this man?"

"He is Vincent Patrick O'Manus. He was my friend."

Back at the Itaewon Police Station, Stan gives as many details as he knows about Vince. He tells the name of the university where he worked. He doesn't know any details about his family's address in England. He doesn't even know his birthday. It is a pretty short statement that covers a long friendship.

Stan walks out of the police station, alone and helpless. There is nothing he can do to help Vince; he is dead. He doesn't know anyone to contact. His family in England will receive a phone call from an unknown Korean voice. That's all it will be, an unknown voice that delivers unspeakable news.

A short while later, Stan finds himself outside Jacque's restaurant. He cannot remember walking across the road from the police station. He sits down at an outside table; all the other tables are empty. It is a cold day and the wind blows dead leaves around Stan's feet. He doesn't notice them; he doesn't notice the cold.

"Mon'Ami, why don't you sit inside?"

"No."

Jacque stands opposite Stan, "You ok?"

Stan does not look up, "No."

"Stan?"

"One black coffee and no conversation."

Jacque begins to pull out a chair to sit down and Stan lifts his pale face and dull blue eyes.

"Please Jacque, don't sit, just black coffee."

Jacque hesitates before retreating into the restaurant. Ten minutes later he returns with a scarf wrapped around his neck and a tray filled with two black coffees and two plates of bacon and eggs. He places one coffee and one plate in front of Stan. He places the other coffee and plate on the adjacent table and sits down. The two men eat in silence. Jacque occasionally stops eating and tries to say something but nothing seems appropriate. Stan does not acknowledge his presence. He does not look up at those who pass by. He does not feel the cold that has others rugged up in coats and scarfs. His eating is robotic and he has soon finished his food and coffee. He stands up from the table and walks away. Jacque watches him go.

Stan walks to Namsan Park with his hands deep in his pockets. Vince's crimson streaked face hovers in front of his eyes. He cannot shake it off. He can hear Vince's voice, "Go home." It is clear, but he doesn't want to go home. He tries to tell himself that he doesn't know where home is anymore. He tries to pretend that home is his little apartment in Itaewan. He recognizes the lie but he walks a long way trying to turn the lie into truth. Five hours later, Stan is opening the door to his apartment. He is shivering and finding it difficult to get the key into the keyhole. The apartment is not much warmer than the outside air so he turns the heating on and sits down on the sofa. He cannot stop shivering.

"Bejaysus mate, have a hot shower."

"Good idea, Vince."

And Stan drops his clothes on the lounge room floor and

walks naked to the bathroom. His hands are shaking as he fumbles with the shower controls. The water is almost scolding as it slams into his shoulders and back and it takes a long time for his skin to thaw but the steam quickly clouds the full-length mirror so he does not have to look at himself.

CHAPTER 42

The Smile Returns

Christmas in Busan arrives with snowflakes brightening a grey sky. Moon's Hagwon is closed for ten days including Christmas and New Year. Annie's Surf shop is closed for a similar period as Annie visits family in Jeju. Jinni still swims each day. The bracing cold of the water and air is a tonic to her troubled mind. Love Always is never closed and Jinni continues with her management duties. Myonghee's routine stays much the same although she is beginning to worry about Jinni's growing unease. She can feel a heaviness in Jinni; she can sense a dark place growing darker and deeper. Myonghee's laughter is met with half smiles. Her questions are met with empty eyes. She worries that Jinni is in need of her mother but Jinni has grown to love Myonghee more than her own mother. Her mother is an itch that does not need to be scratched, a faded scar, a deep cut long healed. And, her little group of confidantes is more supportive and more valued than any group from her past. But, her emptiness grows. Her life is not her own and when she realizes that truth, she begins to float to the surface of her malaise.

The realization that protection does not equal freedom hits hard. For ten years, Jinni's life has been lived inside a protective unreality. Ever since her run in with Alexei, she has not moved beyond the known. Apart from one day in Japan to test her new passport, she has not left Busan. And now, she is considering Australia. Since her dream, the idea keeps growing and this is an itch that needs scratching. And, she keeps having visions of kneeling by a grave.

She feels a need to keep her plan to herself until the last minute. She goes to the bank to make sure that her cash card can be used internationally. She speaks with a travel agent and has her book a ticket to Melbourne flying via Singapore with a return date 30 days later. She has the travel agent research the *The Cullen Hotel* in South Yarra and reserve her a room for two weeks from February 3. She organizes a visa from the Australian Consulate office in Busan and she plans to spend a month thinking and planning her departure.

On New Year's Eve, she sits down at Myonghee's restaurant and eats with her friend. It takes an hour of small talk for her to mention her plan to fly to Australia in late January and she asks Myonghee to keep it to herself, "Ayego girl, whaddabout Blue, he deserves to be told. He's been good to ya and ya can't leave him without a manager, not without givin' him time to find someone to help out."

"Suppose you're right. I just don't do goodbyes well."

"Rubbish, that sounds like Mejung talkin'. Where's the Jinni I've grown to love. She's better than that. Ya're better than that."

The two agree to go together to speak with Blue Park. It takes 15 minutes for the few customers to finish their meals and in that time Myonghee speaks of the pride she feels for Jinni and how excited she is for her. At *Love Always,* Blue's support is passive. He advocates Myonghee return as manager to cover the hole Jinni will leave. He soon returns to his corner of the bar while Myonghee and Jinni talk and laugh together. At midnight, the bar erupts with cheers and the girls throw streamers and shout nothings into the air. The streamers rise and fall rapidly and the nothings hover hopefully, briefly near the ceiling before drifting back to their owners. Jinni turns to Myonghee and hugs her. The two rock together and tears flow from two sets of eyes. They split and Jinni walks over to Blue; his smile does not betray any emotions. She ignores his facade and wraps her arms around him for a short embrace. Blue steps back from the embrace and his hands, with their star tattoos, hang by his side. "Are we married?"

Jinni laughs and replies with, "Yeah, why not."

"I'm serious. We may as well be married."

"What, I don't think so. I don't know ... no Blue, I don't think so."

No one else has heard this little interplay and Blue breaks into a baritone laugh that shocks Jinni. No one has ever heard Blue laugh and it does not last long but all eyes turn to the couple and Jinni is crying and Blue's face has returned to poker. He turns toward the door and heads out. He does not respond to the salutations.

Myonghee looks at Jinni and at Blue's withdrawal; she knows him too well to question his departure. Instead, she looks toward Jinni, "Happy New Year ... Happy New Year."

"Halmoni ... friend, thanks for all you have done for me."

"No, thank ya for what ya've brought to our little world," And they are soon surrounded by several girls who are not engaged with customers; the two barmen are busy but they call out their wishes as they mix drinks; the two bouncers desire inclusion but they know their jobs. Hugs are given and received and laughter and smiles brighten the little bar.

The bouncers have agreed to secure the takings in the safe for Jinni's assessment the following day so, at 1am, Jinni and Myonghee walk arm-in-arm to their apartment. Once inside, the two continue to talk.

For the next four weeks, Jinni continues her routine, almost. When she tells Ms. Moon of her intentions, she is embraced and is told that she always has a job, if she wants one. Jinni is surprised by the response and a little embarrassed by the hug but Ms. Moon hangs on to the clinch but Jinni does not yield easily. "You are loved and you belong, you know that, don't you?"

When Jinni talks to Annie, she squeals with delight and starts jumping around like a teenager, "Bring me back a koala bear. No, no bring me the latest bikini style. Hell, bring me both ... bring me the sun in a bottle."

The time leading up to departure passes easily. Her smile returns and she begins to laugh again. She bounces into both her workplaces and she lights up gloomy rooms. Her soul is light and she is ready to travel, ready to experience. Maybe not completely ready for a visit to a cemetery but she is building strength.

On the evening of January 30, Jinni and Myonghee talk together while Jinni packs. She doesn't pack much because she plans to buy new clothes in Singapore and Australia. After all, thanks to Blue Park, her bank account is healthy. At 1am Jinni hugs Myonghee and the two say their goodnights. Jinni's flight from Gimhae Airport is in 11 hours' time.

CHAPTER 43

Moriath and the Poem

Stan has had a tough few days. He has drunk heavily and slept little. The image of Vince's dead face keeps appearing night and day. "Go home." Finally, Stan walks into Unique Travel and books a ticket to Melbourne leaving in ten days and returning 30 days later. He works the phone to give his clients the news that he will be out of town for a month. He makes these calls while sitting in Paris Baguette; he still can't go back to Jacque's. He gets halfway through dialing his mother's number when he stops himself and decides to surprise her as he has done in the past; besides, he really doesn't feel like talking to her right now. She'll ask questions that have no answers. He has finished his calls and he is trying to put his mind in order as he sips on a long black coffee when his cell phone rings. He picks it up and sees that the caller's name is Vince. He is about to draw on Miji's power but Vince's name flashing in front of his eyes stops him. He lets it almost ring out before answering the call. "Hello."

A woman's voice asks, "Am I talking to Stan?"

"Yes."

"My name is Moriath, I'm Vince's sister."

Stan almost breaks and he finds it difficult to talk. Moriath tells him that she has just picked up Vince's belongings from the police station and his name was the most dialed number on the phone so she dialed it. Stan listens to her talk before offering his assistance. She is looking for support to go to Vince's apartment and Stan agrees to accompany her although he has never been there before. She is at the Itaewon police station so he arranges to meet her in five minutes.

The phones are closed and Stan sits for a few minutes trying to work out how to play this situation. What would Vince advise? He'd tell me to be myself. He'd say: 'just be Stan.' He leaves his half-finished coffee and rises from the chair.

As he walks across the road, he sees a woman in her thirties standing outside the police station. She is dressed in grey with a green scarf around her neck and a small plastic bag in her hand. He approaches and offers his hand. Moriath takes it but then she wraps her arms around him in a strong embrace. He holds on and waits for it to break. She is crying into his shoulder and the embrace continues before she finally pulls away and wipes her eyes while looking up at Stan. Nothing is said. They just look at each other. Stan tries to say something but no words seem appropriate. Eventually he says, "Come" and he leads her to a taxi waiting for a fare.

As they get into the taxi, Moriath hands him a piece of paper with Korean writing typed on it. He takes it and looks at it before passing it to the taxi driver. The driver punches the address into the GPS and turns on the meter.

The taxi is a few hundred meters along the road and Stan is looking straight ahead while Moriath looks out the window at nothing.

"So where are you staying?"

"Hamilton Hotel."

"How is it?"

"You know, ok."

"And the flight."

"Alright, I suppose."

Stan returns to his thoughts and Moriath begins to talk.

"He didn't say much. Even with his family. Always seemed only partially with us when he came home. He would bounce in all smiles and back slaps and within a few days, he was out of the house early and not back until late."

Stan looks in her direction but says nothing.

"Loved him more than my other siblings. He protected me ... he was the second youngest and I was the youngest and we had a bond ... he took some beatings from our eldest brother in my name. Jaysus, he could scrap."

Stan bursts out laughing and Moriath looks at him, "What?"

But, Stan just keeps laughing.

"What?"

"Jaysus, you said Jaysus. That was Vince's word." And he starts laughing again and Moriath begins laughing too.

"Everyone in the family says it. Probably comes from the Irish in me Da."

The taxi driver looks into his mirror and he smiles at the two laughing passengers. He has no idea of the pain behind the laughter.

The taxi driver drops them at a small apartment block. The Koreans call it a villa but the English would call it a block of flats. Moriath takes the key out of the plastic bag and looks at the number engraved into the head of the key. Number 3 is on the second floor and they climb the stairs in silence. They stand outside the door of the flat and Moriath hands the key to Stan. "You do it please."

The key slides in easily and the door opens without effort. He reaches around the door and turns on the light. The fluorescent tube sends its incandescence to all corners and Stan steps inside and Moriath follows.

"Shit, it's tiny."

They have entered directly into the living-kitchen area, which also has a desk sitting under the only window. There is no dining table and the sink holds some unwashed dishes. To the right is a door that leads to a bedroom and they enter to see a double mattress on the floor and a battered black wardrobe with mother-of-pearl inlay. Moriath walks over and opens the doors. It is as good as empty; one coat and a few shirts dangle from hangers and the shelves contain some T-shirts, a couple of sweaters, a pair of jeans, underwear and socks.

"He was living like a student."

Moriath stays in the bedroom. The austere scene has her thinking about childhood poverty. She pulls stuff out of the wardrobe and piles it on the floor; it is a small pile. Stan moves back to the living room and rifles through the contents of the desk like a thief in broad daylight. He can hear Moriath crying in the other room but he does not interfere with her grief. The desk draw holds a few pens and a stapler but not much more. There is no computer and Stan figures that it must be at the university, but a thick spiral bound A-3 notebook rests on the desktop. He opens it and begins to read and he is still reading when Moriath walks back in with her arms half full.

"What can I do with these? ... Stan, any ideas?"

"Sorry, what did you say?"

"These clothes, any ideas?"

"I'm sorry, yeah, there's usually a secondhand clothing bin on a corner somewhere. But, put them down for a bit and look at this."

She does and joins Stan at the desk where they stand together with their heads bent over the yellow notebook. It is filled with poetry.

"I had no idea."

All His Belongings

It was no surprise that he dreamt

The field that he played on as a child:

Waterlogged and humped with molehills,

A slow traversal of frangible Earth,

The old world moved beneath him;

The sky, rolling in its azure socket,

Clouds granular like powdered snow.

What did puzzle him, though,

Was the weight of books on his back;

The pile of cherished vinyl

Playing endlessly on the mind's turntable.

These burdens, ones he couldn't offload,

Made the journey slower than before.

As he reached the football pitch,

Site of many own goals, Anna Karenina

Fell across his train of thought

Like a tarot card tossed onto wet cement.

This was followed by Bringing It All Back Home,

Spiralling djinn-like in the air:

Dylan's dada stare pulling him into the vortex

Of a puddle forming on the penalty spot.

What lay ahead was a decision deferred,

Home winked its lights across the way;

But the wind-startled trees bore down,

Wagged their fingers in admonition –

Stay or flee, they seemed to whisper,

You are still rooted to the same old place:

Same smack against a young boy's face.

He shifted the weight of his belongings

And eyed the firmer ground, the bricks

Of home breathing as though near death;

The roof sinking, falling off the edge of the world.

And the oak tree, that stalwart friend

Of yesteryear, those healing arms

Around his childhood, was stunted now.

So he turned again - this time did not look back:

All his belongings, one by one, falling from the sack.

CHAPTER 44

I Remember When You Were a Funny Man

Stan just wants to be alone but he knows that Moriath needs his help. He lies to her. He tells her that he has a lot of important classes with businessmen who don't accept excuses but he promises to help get some things done. Clothes are dumped into a Salvation Army bin. A secondhand furniture store collects the desk and wardrobe. The landlord hands Moriath the five million won key money; he seems genuinely saddened. Vince's computer and a few other effects are collected from the university and sad salutations are accepted with worn smiles. On the third day Vince is cremated and on the fourth day Moriath is on a plane with an urn filled with her brother's ashes in her wheelie bag. Stan doesn't see her to the airport; he says goodbye on the phone.

Stan is again alone and the decision to return to Australia has been made and the ticket booked. He still feels unsure about any decision and it is getting more and more difficult to get out of bed. He doesn't want to dream anymore so most of his time in bed is spent staring at the ceiling. Today, it is midday when he gets up. He doesn't shower and he dresses in clothes that he wore yesterday. As he closes the door behind him and stands on the balcony, he looks up at the sky; the sun is bright. He doesn't have a destination in mind; he just heads down the steps and out onto the laneway. Everything reminds him of Vince. He walks past bars that he drank at with Vince. He walks by the Hollywood Club and thinks he sees a fading blood stain in the gutter. His aimlessness has him approaching Jacque's restaurant; he steps inside. Jacque is talking in French to three men.

"Mon'Amie, give me ten minutes. Take a seat. 'Capitaine get Stan his usual please.'"

Stan takes a seat by the window and he is bathed in the weak winter sun. He is half asleep; half dreaming that he is running through the streets of Melbourne. Jinni is running in front of him but he cannot close the gap; the gap is widening. Behind him, a dead Vince is gaining without his legs moving and before long they are side-by-side. Stan is running and Vince is gliding and a dead mouth speaks without moving, "I remember when you were a funny man." Then, he puts his fingers into his eyes and pulls off his skin and it is Jinni's face smiling back. She runs ahead and her face slides to the back of her head. She is running away and smiling back. And then, the sound of a coffee cup being placed on the table brings him to the present. He is surprised by his location and an involuntary laugh escapes as reality returns.

"You are a strange man. Look at you; you look like you slept in your clothes and yet you laugh. Are you mad?"

"Maybe Insuk, maybe." And Vince's words prod him. "I must say Insuk, you are looking particularly beautiful today. Your hair shines like black gossamer and your skin has the clarity of an autumn morning."

"You are mad," And she turns on her heels and strides toward the kitchen.

Vince's voice asks if that's as good as he can do.

Jacque finishes his conversation and the three men walk out of the restaurant leaving him free to approach Stan's table, "Before I sit down, would you like eggs?"

"Yeah, why not? Thank you," and he gives Jacque a cracked smile. Jacque looks around and finds the Captain and places the order and then he sits and faces Stan.

The two men sit for a few minutes and Stan tries another smile, also cracked, before he starts talking, "Sorry about the other day ... has it been weeks? In any case, sorry."

"Mon'Amie, that's ok. How are you now?"

"I'm flying to Melbourne in a few days' time."

For once, Jacque says nothing. He smiles warmly and his eyes encourage Stan to continue. And Stan tells the story of Vince's death and the story grows and he does not stop the tears. His words go beyond the story of Vince's death and into the realm of aloneness and loss; he even talks a little about the aloneness and loss he feels for Melbourne, friends and family. He briefly mentions his father dying of cancer. He speaks of his mother and her weakening body. Jacque's comments are few. He listens and Stan's words that started as a trickle become much more. By the time he has finished talking, he begins to feel a little less burdened but ashamed from the exposure.

Two hours after sitting down, Stan thanks Jacque for the coffee and eggs and stands to leave.

"So, what's your plan for the next few days?"

"Think I'll take a trip to Busan tomorrow to have a look around. You know, a farewell sojourn and then it is some packing and out."

"So, see you for a final breakfast?"

"Don't think so but nobody knows what nobody knows."

"Mon'Amie, this seat is always yours."

"Thanks Jacque, I'll see you in a month."

CHAPTER 45

Do You want to be my Caddy?

That night Stan drinks alone in his apartment. He starts with wine and finishes with whiskey. He is hoping alcohol will facilitate a dreamless sleep. But, his sleep is fractured and, out of boredom and frustration, he pulls himself out of bed early and takes a shower. He is out of the door at 6:30 and he arrives at Seoul Station at 7:00. He plans to go to Busan but, at the ticket counter, he changes his plan. He buys a ticket to Chuncheon. Several years ago, he did some relief teaching at the local university and enjoyed the recreational lifestyle and he feels a need to test Miji's words; what can she mean by saying that it will, "come at a price."

From Seoul Station, he catches the subway to Yongsan Station and from there, the semi-fast ITX train to Chuncheon. As usual, he reads and watches the scenery go by. The winter scenery makes for a vision in grays.

Stan has decided to check out his old stomping ground at the back gate of Kangwon National University. He catches a taxi from the station and has the driver drop him at a love hotel. The place is typically seedy but typically clean. He chooses his room from a vending machine. He slides his credit card into the slot and presses the picture of a room on the third floor and a key attached to a plastic stick drops into the tray. It is room 33.

Stan retrieves his credit card and picks up the key and wonders about the significance of the number. He has seen the number in dreams but the details are not clear. He shrugs his shoulders and catches the lift to the third floor. He drops his bag on the floor and throws his Polatek jacket on the bed before heading to the bathroom to wash his face and clean his teeth. One of the great things about love hotels is the bathrooms and Stan can't help smiling at the size of the bath, the array of moisturizers and the complimentary condoms in Room 33. He studies his face in the mirror and he is determined to follow Vince's advice and he vows to present an impression of a happy tourist.

He pulls on his jacket and heads outside into the cold winter's day. He decides to take a walk through the grounds of the university and he ambles for a good hour remembering the past and avoiding the future. He keeps his hands deep in his pockets and his blue beanie is pulled over his ears. He nods to students as if he knows them and they nod back wondering if they know him. The sun is feeble but pleasant enough and he appreciates its anemic rays. After an hour, he finds himself walking out of the university grounds and through the streets of Chuncheon toward Uiam Lake. As he walks, he continues to smile at and nod to strangers. The nodding and smiling started as a pretense, as a lonely game but it is beginning to feel real enough. The nods become sincere and his eyes sparkle their blue invitation and he thanks Vince.

At the lake, he thinks about hiring a bicycle before opting for a casual walk. He stops for a while at a railing and is looking out over the water when a black Hyundai Grandeur pulls up to the curb. The tinted window slides down, "Stan, is that you Stan?" The 'a' is stretched.

Stan turns and squints in an attempt to focus his eyes and then he sees the driver. "Bette, what are you doing here?"

"I'm not stalking you if that's what you're asking. I'm here for a golf tournament tomorrow."

"Oh."

"Hey Stan, do you want to caddy for me?"

"Caddy? Me?"

"Come on, get in the car." And he does.

Bette is wearing a golfing outfit of greens, whites and yellows. Her visor advertises Titleist, and her skirt is too short for a woman of her age although Stan does look at and admire her legs. As she drives, her skirt rides further up her stockinged thighs and Stan finds his gaze wandering.

Bette drives toward Doosan Golf Resort and as she does she talks. Stan isn't really listening; he is wondering what he is doing in the car with Bette.

"Got to get some practice. You know enough about golf to be a caddy?"

"Yeah, I guess so."

"Where are you staying? Stay with me. I've got a suite at the resort. It'll be fun. No vacuum cleaners, I promise. What color are your underpants?"

She laughs and Stan is gripped with panic because he realizes that he is wearing peach colored Calvin Klein's.

She reaches across and pats Stan on the knee. "What do you say Stan? The two of us will make a great team on and off the course." Stan doesn't answer. He stares at Bette and tries to smile. "That's the boy, Stan." And, she slides the zip of her tight top down so that her cleavage shows. "Now, that's more comfortable. What do you think Stan?" And the 'a' is again stretched.

The Grandeur glides into the Doosan Resort and Bette parks it neatly.

"Well, here we are young Stan, here we are." And, she reaches across and strokes his cheek. "Let's go. The clubs are in the trunk. Get them for me like a good boy. I'll be in the pro-shop." She flips the trunk latch and opens her door. Stan opens his door and climbs out. He closes the door and leans on the roof watching Bette straighten up on her side of the car. He can see the black lace of her bra that cups her ample breasts. “Come on now Stan don’t just stand there ... do as you’re told and get the clubs.”

Stan turns and starts running like a mad man across the car park. His running shoes kick up gravel as he heads for the open road.

“Staaaaan, come back Staaaan.”

But, he doesn’t. He runs until his jacket is soaked in sweat and his lungs are burning. He finally slows to a walk about halfway between Doosan Resort and his love hotel. He flags down an approaching taxi and is soon dropped off outside his hotel. He takes the elevator to the third floor, enters his room and picks up his bag and is soon heading for the railway station.

CHAPTER 46

Jinni Returns

Jinni's plan is to spend a few days in Singapore before flying on to Melbourne. She has booked into the 5 Star Orchard Hotel on Orchard Road, and her days are spent eating, shopping and swimming in the hotel pool. Because she wants to avoid unwelcome attention, one of her first purchases is a wedding ring. At night, she sits in the hotel bar drinking gin and tonic and watching the pick-up moves. She keeps her wedding ring prominently displayed and no one bothers her. After three days, she is still uncertain and unsure about her Australian plans. She boards the plane to Melbourne with more trepidation than anticipation. She reclines in her seat and the seat beside her remains empty. She watches a movie, reads a Murakami book and twists the wedding ring around until the habit annoys her. She removes it from her finger and puts it in her purse and goes back to Murakami.

At Melbourne airport, the long line to the immigration counter has Jinni concerned. She is still not fully comfortable with the passport but the process goes smoothly and she watches with a smile as the immigration officer stamps her passport and wishes her a pleasant stay in Australia. Out through customs and into the crowd of people waiting for loved ones, Jinni stands and looks around her. Walter and Mary's welcome is a lifetime ago. The airport has changed but it remains the same. It is small, crowded and alive with the English language. There is no welcome but she knows where the taxi stand is. She drags her wheelie bag and tired body out through the doors and is struck by the heat of the Melbourne summer. The wind is from the north and it blows loose rubbish and dead leaves through the air. Women hold down their skirts and men hold onto their caps. The smell of smoke hangs in the air.

The taxi driver opens the rear door and helps Jinni with her bag. She tells the driver the address, "*The Cullen Hotel*, South Yarra," and she settles in.

"Where are you coming from?"

"Singapore."

"Have you heard about the fires?"

"I noticed the smoke. Is it bad?"

The taxi driver gives a lengthy monologue on fires, past and present. He predicts that this one will be one of the worst on record. The country has been in drought for seven years. Jinni's experiences make it difficult for her to imagine a one-year drought let alone a seven-year one but she does notice how brown and dry the fields are. They look like they have already been burned.

She sits in silence with her thoughts split between kneeling at a grave, the Australian fires and the Sampoong Department Store collapse: disasters past and impending.

After a 30-minute drive, the taxi driver pulls up outside *The Cullen Hotel* and Jinni hands over $65 and climbs out. She stands on the footpath to get accustomed to the heat after the air-conditioned car. Beads of sweat appear on her forehead and the wind dries them almost immediately. She looks up and down Commercial Road and strangers brush past without touching her. Finally, she walks into the reception area and back into more air-conditioning. Before she can address the woman behind the reception desk, she stands looking up at a large painting above and behind the receptionist's head. The painting is of a blue rat on a pink background. Saliva and paint drip into the pink. She looks and thinks that it is somewhat crude, even adolescent in its execution but it sure is striking. And, she can't help staring at it. The receptionist is practiced polite and allows Jinni time to comprehend what she is looking at.

"You're not the first person to stare above my head. It takes the breath away, doesn't it?"

Jinni lowers her eyes from the painting and she returns the receptionist's smile, "Sorry about that, but I've not seen art quite like it before. Well I did in a dream, but ... I don't know if it has been painted by a child or a professional ... or a professional with a child's eye."

"Definitely professional, Adam Cullen is certainly famous. But, between you and me, his stuff scares me. I wish they'd hang that painting somewhere else."

"So that's the origin of the hotel's name. I thought the owner must have been Mr. Cullen ... I have a reservation; my name is Lee."

The receptionist taps a few keys on her computer.

"Here we are, Ms. Jin Hee, Lee. You're on the third floor. Welcome and enjoy your stay and if there is anything I can do to make your stay even better, just let me know," And she hands over the electronic key. Jinni first saw one of these keys in Singapore so she knows what to do. She looks for the room number on the envelope and she winces when she sees that her room is #33.

Room 33 has a modern airy feel to it and more Adam Cullen paintings hang on the walls. There is a border-collie dog dripping paint and a horse in orange and browns. Jinni drops her bag onto the queen-sized bed and looks out of the large window that opens onto a small balcony. She slides open the window and walks outside. The heat slaps her face. The immediate view is of Commercial Road and the Prahran Market and the distant view to the northeast is of smoke from the bushfires. She watches the action down on Commercial Road for a while. She needs to reacquaint with Melbourne but her confidence is shaky. She puts off the activity with the decision to take a shower. In contrast to the ostentatious bathroom of *Choi's Inn*, this bathroom is a small efficient affair without a bathtub. Room 33 at *Choi's Inn* encouraged her to soak in a bath; room 33 at *The Cullen Hotel* has her washed and dried in no time and she is soon mixing with the summer crowds. She is surprised at how well her English stands up. She understands when people talk to her although she sometimes finds it difficult to follow the conversations of groups of strangers. She allows the foreign language to wash over her and she walks through the market and marvels at the friendly bustle, the high quality of the produce and the outrageous prices. Back on Commercial Road she turns left onto Chapel Street and continues to walk and watch until a café beckons. Cafés are personal places. Why one person chooses to sit at one café but reject another is a mystical process. Sometimes it is the quality of the coffee and other times it is the ephemeral nature of light and shadow or smell and sound or something else as indefinable yet just as important. Cafés tend to choose the person rather than the person choosing the café and Jinni sits at an outside table and immediately feels her apprehensions fade, just a little. A waitress breezes out with a menu and a smile.

"She's a hot old day, you sure you want to sit outside?"

"The umbrella is good enough, thanks."

And she orders an iced café latte and allows herself to remember the latte with her school friends and she smiles. But then, her thoughts return to a vision of a cemetery and a forest of gravestones.

CHAPTER 47

Jinni Attracts a Crowd

Jinni spends a few days wandering the streets, sunning herself and swimming in the hotel pool. In the evenings, she puts on her ring and walks around Chapel Street. If she finds a bar she likes, she sits in a chair on the street and drinks tonic water. She avoids eye contact. Sometimes she has the bartender add gin but usually she drinks tonic. Before retiring to her room, she drinks a glass or two of Riesling or Pinot Noir at the hotel bar and the bartender talks her through the wine list. While she drinks, the bartender and her talk about the fires as they watch the horror on the TV, and an Adam Cullen painting drips dry color and observes without emotion.

On February 6, Jinni asks the receptionist directions to the beach. The receptionist writes down the tram numbers and Jinni returns to her room to pack her bikini and sarong. She wears a pair of blue shorts that she bought in Singapore and a white tank top that she brought with her from Busan and a hat she bought the day before and a pair of running shoes. As she walks out of the door, the receptionist reminds her not to leave her bag unattended and tells her to, "Have a great day."

The tram is not crowded but the smell of old sweat lingers in the conditioned air that struggles to fight the outside heat. The number 16 tram drops her off across from St. Kilda Beach.

It is crowded but not as crowded as Haeundae Beach in summer. The wind has the sand spitting and bathers hold onto their towels. Jinni spends a short time lying in the sun but it is fierce, much stronger than the sun of Busan and the biting sand stings her skin and eyes. She cannot spend much time in the water to cool off like she does at the hotel pool because she is afraid to leave her belongings for long so, eventually, she packs up her things and heads back to South Yarra.

Even though the heat and wind are oppressive, she decides to walk back to the hotel. She walks along Fitzroy Street, stepping around the homeless and admiring the expensive restaurants and bars. The wind continues to build and dust and dirt cling to her sweaty skin. She detours around Albert Park Lake where, for the second time in her life, she is surprised to see that the swans are black. She walks around the Albert Park Golf Course and then into the Albert Cricket Ground. Nobody is playing, but the antique buildings and manicured grass speak gently to her. She sits in the shade of a tree, in the lee of the grandstand, surrounded by a foreign history and her current anxieties. Tomorrow will be February 7 and flakes of soot swirl in the sky like black snow.

Back at the hotel she swims a few slow laps and visions of her birth family, Busan protectors and Australian family crowd her mind. They all stand around the pool and talk to each other and compare their understandings of whom Jinni is. They can't agree and they begin to bicker. The Busan crowd is loud in its support; the Australian family speaks in whispers and her birth parents are stubborn in their criticisms. Jinni shouts into the water for them to all go away and when she gets to the end of the pool, she stands and looks around but nobody is looking at her. She sprints two fast laps and leaves her antagonists in her wake.

After showering and dressing, she heads out to a dumpling restaurant on the corner of Commercial Road and Chapel Street and it is here that she sits alone at a table for four. She was hoping to eat Korean mandu but she settles for spicy Sichuan momo and she eats the steamed delights in silence surrounded by conversations she is not part of. After eating, she walks along Chapel Street for a while looking in the shops and watching the people. She enjoys the contrasting features and varied fashion of the pedestrians; they cut an individualistic style. The diversity has her thinking about the mono-fashioned nature of Korea. Finally, she returns to *The Cullen Hotel* bar and orders a Riesling. She sits and begins a debate with a vision of her parents; finally, they tell her that she has lost her way and they turn and disappear into the recesses of her memory; she tries to lock the door but the key won't turn. She has a consciousness of an impending something. She has been on the periphery of life for some time now and she feels reality shifting. As she sips on her wine, she asks the bartender if there are any parties planned for tomorrow night.

"Not that I know of although Friday nights can be pretty busy. You know, last day of the week and all that."

Before going up to her room, she asks the receptionist for directions and tram numbers to the Coburg Cemetery

CHAPTER 48

A Homecoming

Stan gets himself to Incheon Airport three hours before his designated departure time. He likes to head the line so that he can get an emergency exit seat. Once this is achieved, he heads toward immigration. From the moment his boarding pass is checked and his passport is stamped, a sense of freedom washes over him. He has always found goodbyes difficult, even when there is nobody to say goodbye to. Airports represent freedom to him. He enjoys the anonymity of the crowds. He enjoys the energy of departure, the thrill of potential new discoveries. He does not see the fences and walls as barriers of exclusion; he sees them as protection from the mundane, from the ordinariness of ordinary life. Even though he is returning to an unsure reality, he is enjoying this space. He will worry about the reality of Australia when he gets there.

The flight is uneventful and Stan watches movies and reads and the time passes quickly enough. Twelve hours after departure, the plane is descending over a parched land. He is on the left of the plane and he can see smoke from fires in the northeast of Melbourne.

Immigration is now electronic for Australian citizens so Stan moves through quickly but he has to wait more than 15 minutes for his bag to be offloaded. The arrival foyer is a small crush and he buys an Australian SIM card for his phone before stepping outside and into a furnace fueled by a northerly wind. He pays $18 for the Airport-City bus and climbs aboard for the 20-minute ride to Southern Cross Station on Spencer Street. On the plane, he kept himself occupied and did not think much about Melbourne and his life within it. He is now confronted by his past because he sees it flashing by the window of the bus. He had friends and a secure job. His father died 12 years ago and his mother's mind is quick and flexible but her body is slow and brittle, and she relies on home care for her important needs. He is not sure whether she will happy to see him or regard him as another burden.

From Spencer Street, he catches a tram up Bourke Street to Elizabeth Street where he changes to tram number 35 that takes him up past the hospitals on Flemington Road and finally into his childhood of Moonee Ponds and Essendon. By the time he gets off at the corner of Pascoe Vale Road and Buckley Street, his apprehension is prickly. He feels ashamed that he has not visited his mother for so long, and not calling her to tell her of his pending arrival compounds his shame.

He hoists his backpack onto his shoulders and exits the tram. As he walks along Buckley Street, he passes the *suicide house*. He wasn't living at home at the time but he remembers the story. His father came home one day complaining of the smell coming from the garage of the house he is now passing. His mother suggested calling the police, which he did, and then, the two of them returned to the house to wait and see. When the police arrived, they knocked on doors and windows before forcing open the garage. They found a vintage couple dead in the front seat of a vintage Mercedes and his mother still struggles with her sense of smell. Stan knew the couple in passing and he knew that their son had been a student at his old school. He must have seen his name, although he does not remember it, on the honor board commemorating ex-students who had died in wars.

He walks by that memory and more come to greet him.

Eventually he arrives at the gate of the double-fronted Victorian weatherboard that was his childhood home. He observes that the lawn is kept much better than when the task was his source of pocket money. He knocks on the door and waits, but the house is silent. He is troubled as he knocks again. He sniffs at the keyhole. Finally, he cups his hands on the windowpanes and emptiness looks back. He walks around to the side of the house and bends down at the base of the drainpipe and feels for the spare key suspended behind it, and he wonders how long the tarnished key has hung undisturbed.

Sliding the key into the lock reminds him of Vince's flat but the inside is as different as a light year to an hour. He leaves his bag at the entrance and walks down the hallway; he calls for his mother and he sounds like a child in pain. He searches the empty house. Most things are as he remembers them. The three porcelain ducks tacked to the wall of the living room continue their journey nowhere. His mother's smell has aged but is familiar and his father's scent has long seeped through the walls although framed photographs tell his story. Stan, as a young boy, holds a young man's hand and harmonizing faces smile for the camera.

After looking in all the rooms, he retrieves his bag and dumps it onto the single bed that occupies his old room. He reclines with his head on his bag and the mattress sags as it always has. Sleep is swift and unexpected and the tears on his cheeks dry as he dreams.

He is in a bar and the walls are decorated with large colorful paintings of dogs, rats and horses that drip into their frames. The place is filled with familiar people. His mother and father are dancing a tango; they are 18 years old. His grandparents are sitting at the bar in deep conversation with Mr. Kim. His old-school friend, Robert, is talking to Vince and the suicide couple's son. A group of his primary school friends are lifting beer glasses to their childlike lips. Jinni is part of a group that includes every woman he has ever dated; most are faceless and they are drinking a variety of drinks and they laugh often. The two hostile blokes from Central Australia are drinking VB from cans and laughing at the dancing couple. The suicide couple sits at one end of the bar in silence and Stan sits alone at the other end staring at life reflections that do not include him. Miji is the bartender and she pours Stan a glass of champagne.

When he wakes, it is late afternoon and his mother has not returned. He goes to the fridge but before he opens the door, he sees a paper stuck to it by a magnetized map of Korea. It is the address and phone number of the homecare head office and he immediately calls the number.

The voice on the other end of the phone tells him that his mother fell and broke her hip while on an aged care outing in South Yarra. So, they took her to the Alfred Hospital on Commercial Road.

It only takes Stan a few minutes to be ready to leave but it takes more than an hour to get to the hospital. He sits on the tram and wills it to go faster. He remembers his father's funeral and he dreads another. At the junction of Elizabeth and Flinders Streets he exits and walks quickly up Flinders to Swanston Street where he slows down and looks up at the clocks on Flinders Street Station and remembers meeting friends at the beginning of long nights. He walks to the tram stop and looks over at Federation Square and he is still not sure if he likes the asymmetrical design. The 216-Tram arrives and he boards while still pondering the merits of Federation Square. His thoughts have returned to his mother when a uniformed man asks him for his ticket. Stan tries to explain that his mother is in an emergency situation at the Alfred Hospital but the inspector is not listening. He is escorted off the tram at the next stop where he is issued with an *on-the-spot-fine* of $75 and told to buy a Myki Card from the vending machine. The inspector watches to make sure he complies and then warns him about future infractions before telling him to enjoy the rest of his evening.

Stan's frustration is directed inward as he boards the next

tram. He is still fuming when he disembarks at the St. Kilda Road/Commercial Road junction and he walks the remaining few hundred meters to the hospital trying to calm himself. The evening is still hot, and even though Stan is dressed in shorts and T-shirt, the short walk has him sweating and the wind has him disheveled. When he approaches the reception, his hair is a cockatoo's nest. He forces a smile at the receptionist, "She's another wild day," He says before he gives his name and the name of his mother and asks for her room number. His mother is on the third floor. She has been there for 5 days.

He opens the door to her ward and four pairs of eyes turn his way before three pairs turn away disappointed.

"Son? ... Why are you here?"

"It's good to see you too."

"Now, now Stan, don't go getting antsy with me. I'm just surprised."

He walks to the bed and places his hand on her head. She brushes it off.

"Why didn't you call me?"

"You're not a doctor; you're not a therapist of any kind ... what can you do?"

"But, I'm your son."

She tells him that she is getting excellent care and that she is well fed so there was no need to call. Stan complains that he could have talked to her and she reminds him that he hasn't talked to her for years. Three pairs of ears are trained on this exchange and the attached heads nod in sympathy with the mother.

Stan sits beside the bed and his mother asks whether he brought chocolates. He makes excuses about rushing to get here. He doesn't tell her about being caught without a ticket.

"Five days does not sound like a rush to me."

Three heads nod in unison and Stan can only sigh as he gets up again and heads toward to door.

"Whe're you off to now?"

"Chocolates."

And he walks out the door and into the lift. He thinks about his family life and he shakes his head. "No wonder I left."

Ten minutes later he is back in the ward and old eyes accuse him of all things. He sits again and hands his mother a box of Chocolate All Sorts. His mother turns the box around and begins to pick at the cellophane wrapping.

"I would have a preferred Toblerone."

"But, Chocolate All Sorts was always your favorite."

"A long time ago dear, a long time ago."

His mother makes her choice and Stan offers chocolates to the other patients and soon they are all are sucking and chewing. Some are complaining that toffee is sticking to their false teeth but all are occupied so Stan asks about how the accident happened. His mother tells him how she was on an outing with her friends and she was sitting in a restaurant. She had ordered pan-seared scallops and was sipping on a chardonnay when her wheelchair rolled backward. She had forgotten to lock the wheel. As the chair rolled back, she tried to place the glass on the table but couldn't reach. The next thing she remembered was being on her back in pain, staring up at a pink Ned Kelly. And, without allowing time for questions, she turns her attention to Stan.

"What brings you back?"

He tells her that he came home to see her and she quickly volleys that back. She lets him get away with some vague explanations before they move to safer territory. They talk about how dry the weather has been and the test cricket series and the upcoming football season, territory that both feel comfortable in.

And, Stan's dream floods his conscious. The images are vivid and the reliving is painful. He performs his dream and thinks that he has lived twice.

The retired primary school teacher chimes, "I still sleep, wake, eat and shit."

"What?"

After a good hour, Stan finally rises from his chair and prepares to leave and his mother asks, "Have you visited your father?"

"He's dead."

"Unnecessary, son. Visit his grave ... it might help."

It is a lonely ride back on the tram and he stops off at Moonee Ponds Junction looking for a beer. The familiar pubs are in the same place but they are no longer familiar but he sits in the Junction Hotel anyway and drinks a few beers and the noise of poker machines compete with his scrambled thoughts. It is after midnight when he returns to Buckley Street and he is soon reacquainted with the depression in his old mattress.

CHAPTER 49

Talking to a Father

Stan wakes the next morning wondering where he is and he frowns when he realizes that he is in his childhood single bed. He showers before checking the fridge; it is as good as empty. He puts a few things in his little daypack, checks his Myki card is in his wallet and heads out looking for a breakfast restaurant on his way to the cemetery. His plan is to take a bus west along Albion Street to Nicholson Street where he will catch a tram to Bell Street and the cemetery is a short walk from there. Along the way, he stops at a café for bacon and eggs and he sits inside and watches the northerly wind trouble anything not locked down. Two young girls wearing Penleigh Girls Grammar uniforms sit at the table next to him and watch him eat around his egg yolks. He notices them watching just as he lifts the first yolk to his mouth and he tries to smile but his teeth puncture the yolk and his chin dribbles yellow. They laugh and look away.

At the cemetery, Stan walks around for a while trying to remember where his father is buried. A recognizable grave turns out to be someone else's and he eventually heads to the office to ask directions to Stanley Simpson's grave. He follows the map to the spot marked with an X and he reads the inscription that includes the dates of birth and death. "**Here lies Stanley Simpson,**

husband to Thelma, father to young Stan."

A concrete slab that is raised half a meter above the ground covers the grave. He sits on it. He looks up at the cobalt sky and wishes he could fly with the cirrus clouds that race south. He sits and he doesn't know what to do, what to say. He asks his father what he should say; no answer.

"I saw mum yesterday."

The silence has him stand and walk around the grave. Dust, from a fresh grave nearby, blows into his face and he closes his eyes.

"Remember the photo on the sideboard of you and me holding hands?"

The wind gains energy and dead flowers gather around his feet. He kicks them aside and again sits down on the concrete slab.

He then begins to talk about his childhood. It starts benignly enough, a little reminiscing. He moves through time until he reaches the age of 13 and Stan tells his father that this is the moment when things fell apart. It is the moment that Stan can never get past. Young Stan had won selection in a representative football team and he asked his father for advice. His father told him to play his opponent close, pull his jumper, elbow him in the guts and stand on his toes. Before that day, Stan idolized his father. He always sought advice and it was always given. Young Stan ran out onto the ground and found his opponent and immediately elbowed him in the guts. He continued to antagonize this young boy for three quarters until the boy turned and landed a haymaker on his chin. Stan was out cold. That day, Stan lost several hours of time, considerable self-respect and respect for his father. His father thought it was funny and often brought it up when friends visited. Stan stopped bringing friends home and stopped asking his father for advice. He tried to talk to his father about it a few times but his father just thought it was funny. He didn't want to know of

Stan's pain. He told him to grow up and be a man.

"I was 13 for fuck sake."

CHAPTER 50

A Promise

On the morning of February 7, Jinni swims some distracted laps before showering and dressing for the day. And she is soon boarding the tram that will take her to the Coburg Cemetery. Fifty-five minutes later she is walking up Bell Street and she stops at the cemetery entrance. The black, gothic gates are not inviting but she enters anyway. She finds the office and gets directions to the Farnsworth grave site. As she walks deeper into the cemetery, she passes a man dressed in blue sitting on a grave talking to the sky. He looks familiar but she thinks that it is probably just the blue clothes reminding her of Blue Park. She keeps walking and soon finds the single grave that holds Walter and Mary.

The man in blue is still visible and she sees him stand up and shrug his shoulders toward the tombstone before taking a 360-degree look around. Jinni thinks his visual sweep stops at her. She stares back for a short while before kneeling beside the grave of her homestay parents. She starts talking almost immediately, reminiscent of when she used to get home from school. She begins with the tram ride to the cemetery and moves through to her life in Seoul and her life in Busan. She finishes with thanking them for showing her possibilities; she apologizes for not keeping in touch and she promises to be more open with people and to smile. An hour passes before she stands and walks away. The man in blue has long gone. While she was talking, she hadn't noticed the wind and the heat. Now, she feels her hair sticking to her neck and she can't keep strands out of her mouth and eyes. The wind pushes her along as if it is encouraging her to move away from death back into the world of life. Fueled by the wind she increases her pace and she is quickly back on the street looking for a café.

CHAPTER 51

Mothers

The State of Victoria has been under water restrictions for three years. Residents are showering with buckets to collect wastewater for the garden, but home gardens are dying. Wealthier residents are having landscape gardeners re-design and rebuild their treasured patches with drought resistant plants. So, roses find themselves on scrap heaps and native grasses and shrubs flourish. Those residents who can't afford the modifications watch their children play in the hardened dust that was once lawn. Victoria's weather has been building for years but the last month has seen the sun and wind at its most damaging. Country Fire Stations are on red alert. The State has been under a "Total Fire Ban" for more than a week. And now, Victoria is being bullied by spot fires resembling devil's eyes. The wind from the north is birthed in Australia's vast deserts and it builds speed and destructive power as it flies south. Idiots drop lighted cigarettes and children play with matches and neglected power lines rub on neglected tree branches. Fires begin. But, Brisbane is in flood; the water is a long way from where it is needed and right where it can cause the greatest destruction. Australia is burning and flooding at the same time. It is a land of extremes. It is a land never far away from a natural disaster.

After the cemetery, Stan walks the streets. Every house and

every yard is different but exactly the same; measured gardens cry out for inspiration; fences, some brick and some wire and others wooden pickets, remind him of a Robert Frost poem about fences and their perceived purpose. He thinks about the normative nature of social existence. Children have dreams and adults have ambitions. Kids play in imaginary worlds, dreaming of great things; as adults, they settle for a salary and replicating their parents. Families and schools conspire to cut wings. And, the young Stan once dreamed about being a professional sportsman but settled for teaching PE.

Eventually, Stan returns to his mother's house to shower and to compose his mind before heading to the Alfred Hospital. But, the house keeps reminding him of his feud with his father. He picks up the photo of him and his father holding hands and turns it toward the wall. He picks up every photo in the house and tries to remember or imagine. Eventually, he takes a nap and his dream has him play the football game again.

He runs onto the ground surrounded by his teammates, skinny kids in shorts. They mob together and wish each other luck before they disperse to their positions. Stan runs to the back flank and shakes hands with his opponent. The rest of the dream sees Stan hunt the ball. He plays his own game and his moves have him smiling in his sleep. He has elite ability and his dream allows him to feel what should have been.

He wakes unsure whether to be angry or whether to walk forward and he remembers the dream that Vince related. He pushes his father off his back.

When he finally gets to the hospital, it is late afternoon. He greets the receptionist before going to the little shop to buy a stick of Toblerone. Then, he takes the lift to the third floor. He enters the ward and sees a nurse taking his mother's blood pressure. The retired primary school teacher informs him that she has eaten and had a nice shit. Stan just stares at her before enquiring of the nurse. The other patients nod a welcome and his mother tells him to sit down until the nurse is finished. When the nurse's tests are complete, she tells him not to worry, blood pressure is low but nothing to worry about. Stan holds the chocolate in his lap as he begins to tell his mother about having a beer at the Junction Hotel before moving on to this morning's activity. He tells his mum that he talked to his father but he doesn't go into detail. He just says that he feels a sense of release.

"Are you going to share the chocolate?"

Stan looks around and into a gummy smile. He peels off the wrapping and offers his mother the first piece. He then approaches each bed and helps each patient break off a section before returning to his seat and silence.

"So why did you leave home?" Asks the old teacher again and a chorus of support backs her up.

His eyes lock on his mother's, a pleading look.

"Life's as good as over son."

Rising from the chair, he walks over to the window and stares out at the park across the road.

"You really want to know?"

Stan understands he is reliving a dream but he tells the story anyway. He can't change anything.

And, when he reaches the bit about the Brussel sprouts, he again walks to the window and looks out at the serenity of the park scene, the calmness of it, the welcoming nature of it and he thinks of the threatening nature of the Himalaya. The vast mountains bleed danger; they are always threatening pain or worse. And, he had felt its uncompromising attitude to human life.

He continues with the story.

"Once I got back to Manali, Bobby Singh went into overdrive. He contacted the Himalayan Climbing Association and found out the names, phone numbers and addresses of the three climbers he suspected were on that climb twelve years before. By the time they got to Bobby's house in Defense Colony, New Delhi; Bobby had arranged for a meeting of the two surviving boys, now men, and the parents of the dead boy. I was the only member of my little party who was able to attend because the other three had flights to catch and jobs to go to. I had taken a month extra leave from my school so I was the representative of those who had found the body. I dressed in the best clothes I had brought with me; they weren't that smart, and Bobby Singh drove me to the deceased boy's parents' house. Bobby rang the doorbell and an elderly man with a balding pate, dressed in brown pants, white shirt and brown cardigan greeted us. Bobby made the introductions and then he excused himself. The house was an aging space that smelled a little of damp, sour sweat and many nights of curry. It was large, sort of typical Australian size, but not massive like the Singh family's houses. I was led into the lounge room and two men in their early thirties rose from their chairs to greet me. Their handshakes were firm but only one held my eye. A refined elderly woman wearing a sari of green and navy blue, almost black like the high-altitude sky, sat in an overstuffed armchair; she didn't rise but she smiled her welcome. The father of the dead boy guided me to a sofa and the two of us sat together, our knees almost touching. A servant brought over a tray and on it was a teacup, a small porcelain jug of milk, a silver bowl containing sugar cubes and a silver teapot draped in a knitted tea cozy of blues and reds. I picked up the cup and the servant poured me tea; I declined the milk and sugar and the servant retired to the shadows. For a few minutes the conversation was about where I was from and what I was doing in India. And then, abruptly, the mother asked me to tell what I had found.

I related an abbreviated version of events and the others in the room listened patiently until I arrived at the moment I removed the watch from the wrist of the corpse. The mother sat up straight in her armchair and the father put his hand on my knee."

"Do you have it with you?"

"I didn't want to say yes; the image of the withered wrist and long feminine fingernails flooded my thoughts, but the pressure of the man's hand on my knee forced me to pick up my little knapsack from beside the sofa and pull out an envelope and hand it to the father."

"Are you saying you wanted to keep the watch?"

Stan ignores the comment.

"The father stood and moved to the lamp over the side table and his wife joined him. I remained seated and the other two men and I talked quietly about Mulkila IV and trekking in general. The mother and father inspected the watch. They talked in subdued tones while everyone else retreated to their own thoughts. After what seemed like a lifecycle, they left the watch on the side table and returned to their seats. And then, they asked about photographs.

I had photos in my bag but I was reluctant to say yes. Their eyes demanded honesty. I wanted to lie because the image of the empty eye sockets and lipless grin invaded my present. I had photos of their dead son and I had no choice but to hand them over."

Stan stops talking and drinks more of his water. He stares out of the window; he focuses on nothing.

"I'm not sure I can continue ... no wonder I've never told this story in full before. I can do the abbreviated version and avoid the emotional bits ... but shit ... this is a big story."

Stan's mother is impatient, "I want to hear the rest of the story ... the reason for you leaving."

Stan spends more time looking at nothing in the park. It is just unfocused green.

"Ok, let me try to continue ... the photos ...

I again rummaged around in my bag and produced another envelope. It contained the photos I had had developed in Delhi that morning and the negatives of those photos. I again handed over an envelope I would have preferred not to share. And again, the mother and father rose as one and moved to the little side table. They held the prints under the lamp and I had to force myself to breathe."

Stan now moves away from the window and walks back to the chair beside his mother's bed. Before sitting, he refills his water glass and it takes him a while to start talking again.

"This is where it gets difficult. The pointy end is close ...

The members of this select gathering discussed what could be done with the body. Everyone was concerned that the corpse would become a photo opportunity for future climbers on the mountain. It was beyond safe helicopter altitude so that was out. One of the young men, the one who found eye contact difficult, had become a Himalayan trekking guide and he offered to lead an expedition to retrieve it. And, the other guy, who had become a ship builder in Goa, offered to finance it. The discussion explored whether it would be best to bring him down the mountain to be cremated in the traditional way. Cremating him on the mountain was out of the question because the wood would have to be carried up the mountain and the lack of oxygen at that altitude would prevent a fire burning fiercely enough to do the job completely. There was also a discussion as to whether it would be proper to bury him in another crevasse. The mother looked at me and asked what I would do. She asked what I would like my parents to do if it was me up there."

Stan needs to pause again. He can feel the cockroach stirring. He drinks again and just sits silently.

"You ok son?"

"Not really. I've never told this story in its complete form before and I've never told of its significance in my life. No, I'm not ok; it has been a burden and a blessing for the last ten years.

It's time to release it."

"We're listening."

"I didn't know what to say. I spoke of the powerful beauty of the location and I spoke about it not being the wish of the dead that was important; it is the needs of the living that must be attended to ... I don't know if what I said made sense. Shit ... I didn't have any wisdom."

"So, what did they decide?"

"This is where it goes a bit strange again. I don't know what they did."

The four old people look at each other and back at Stan before his mother speaks, "What do you mean, you don't know? Surely they told you what they did."

Stan rises from the chair and walks over to a side table and takes an apple from her fruit bowl. He bites deeply and uses the time to compose himself. He eats half the apple and places the remains on the tabletop before he continues.

"The conversation had gone beyond the point of working out what to do with the body and no decision had been made. I figured the conversation had reached an end, or a stalemate at least. I rose from my chair and shook hands with the two men. I cannot remember their names; in fact, I cannot remember anyone's name from that night. I walked over to the mother and shook her hand while she remained seated in her armchair. The servant offered me some cake to take with me but I declined and the father escorted me to the door. The two of us stood outside at the end of the driveway as I waited for a taxi or a tuk-tuk. The father thanked me for coming and sharing what I had found, seen and felt. I mumbled through some, 'no worries' rubbish and then, there was the sound of a door opening. The mother flowed over the space. She was angelic, all greens and high-altitude blues; her hair was grey and pulled back tight into a bun and she closed the gap and pulled me into a tight embrace."

Stan pauses and attempts to quench his emotional discomfort before continuing.

"As you know, I'm not the hugging type." He looks at his mother. "You were my role model ...

... I didn't know what to do with my hands. She did the embracing and I thought that it would end and I would be able to disengage and be on my way ... she didn't let go ... eventually, my arms rose and reached around her back. I returned her embrace. For a short time that seemed like a permanence, I felt connected to her. It wasn't sexual but our bodies had joined and so too had our emotions. Every synapse was open. We were one."

Stan can feel the embrace again and he savors it.

"And then she let go ... she turned around and glided back to the house and through the door that was being held open by the servant. She was gone and I was left standing in the driveway feeling warm and alive but alone ... I had never felt so alone yet so alive".

His mother remains silent; she is now staring at the ceiling as she looks inside but the retired primary teacher can't help herself, "That's why you left Australia? Looking for that same feeling?"

"Well, almost. Let me finish this tale ... I managed to flag down a tuk-tuk; I waved, somewhat absently, to the father as I headed into the night. I asked the driver to take me to Connaught Place on the edge of Old Delhi. By now it was almost midnight but the Delhi air rarely drops below warm and thick. I paid the fair without haggling; the driver probably paid for his son's education with what I handed over. I didn't care. I walked across the space that was trampled dust. It wasn't crowded like it gets during the day but there were still people around; there were still fortunetellers looking for the gullible ... I wasn't buying; there were still beggars looking for the easy mark ... I wasn't giving and there were shoeshine wallahs who wanted to shine my white tennis shoes ... I wanted what they had in the bottom of their shoeshine box, hashish."

Stan stood up from the chair and walked back to the fruit bowl; he picked up a bunch of grapes and took it to the window overlooking the park.

"I also bought a little hash pipe off the shoeshine man whose hair was dyed with henna and whose face was like a chocolate bar that had melted and solidified time and time again ... I probably paid for that man's son's education too. I walked off a short distance and sat in the dust with my back resting against a wall and stuffed my new pipe and the aliveness that I felt in the mother's embrace lingered on the edge of reality. I still had the alone feeling and the aliveness was fading; I could feel it ebbing. I lit the pipe. Smoke from the smoldering hash shrouded my little world and I tried to hold onto the power I'd felt in that mother's arms."

Stan looks out of the window and no one breaks the silence until the story continues.

"I had taken some pretty decent tokes on the pipe and I had closed his eyes. I could feel the woman's embrace; it was again fixed on my skin and when I opened my eyes, I was looking at a gaggle of children probably between the ages of 8 and 12. Some were trying to sell me things and some were just begging. I said nothing but I must have smelled of loneliness. As one, the haggling stopped; there was silence and the youngsters squatted in a semi-circle around me. And then, they were singing. These waifs with skin so dry it was cracking on their grime-flecked cheeks were singing to me."

"Serious?"

"Yep, they were singing ... They were singing a lullaby that I had heard Bobby Singh's niece and nephew sing to their newborn sister. It was a Hindi melody of welcome, of comfort and protection. And, these kids were singing it to a lonely man who kept stuffing his pipe and sucking it dry and the voices mingled with the hash smoke and drifted off into Delhi's immortal miasma.

"Eventually, I strapped my little daypack across my chest and pulled some coins and notes from my pockets and placed them in the dirt in front of me. I lay on my side and curled around my pack and fell into a dreamless sleep. When I woke, an almost full moon was sinking behind the buildings in the west and, in the east, light from an un-risen sun cast long shadows across Connaught Place. The urchins were gone as was the money I'd left in the dust but my pack was still secure on my chest, untouched. I stood on unsteady legs and felt the unevenness of the earth through my feet; I looked down to see that my tennis shoes had been stolen."

"So that's it mum; that's why I left Australia."

He looks at his mother but nothing is said and a voice from behind breaks the silence, "Are you serious? All because you had your shoes stolen?"

Stan ignores the old lady before continuing to the stories conclusion.

"I arrived back in Australia and started work again at the school. But, life felt muted. People surrounded me; people I knew and people I didn't but I couldn't find the energy necessary for community, no reason to continue. As I said before, my life had predictability, an inevitability that bordered on the suicidal. My synapses had closed. Every now and then I could feel the mother's embrace and its life flow but usually just in dreams. In my waking life, I saw people, friends and strangers alike moving in a known flow. I needed to get out of that current.

And, the mother and father of the boy I found on Mulkila IV, I never had contact with them again. I don't have their address or their phone number, nothing. That's why I didn't know what happened to the corpse.

No one here could possibly understand my experience; there was no one to talk to. Dad had the emotional capabilities of a Colt 45 and you hated to be touched."

Stan plucks grapes from a bunch and stares at his mother.

"As a kid, you stayed at work with students and colleagues till late. When you got home you had no time for me. Dinner with dad was like having dinner alone. Yet, this stranger in India, in one embrace, changed my life direction. When I returned to Australia I couldn't find the rhythm. It wasn't there for me."

Stan's mother has retreated deep within but a voice from another bed asks, "So why Korea?"

"Good point. I chose Korea because I knew nothing about Korea and I knew nobody in Korea. I felt that I could create my own flow."

"Why not India?"

"I knew it was illusory; I knew that my romance with India would keep giving false beginnings and my Indian friends would have protected me and taken me into their current. I instinctively understood this so I chose the unknown. I chose Korea."

"So how did it work out for you? Did you find the life and aloneness mix you desired?"

"Sometimes. I reckon I created my own stream; I was definitely alone but I rarely felt the life ... energy ... that synapse opening energy that I felt in the mother's clinch. I left Australia looking for a lively aloneness; regrettably, for the last year or so in Korea, I have only felt alone and lonely."

Nothing is said for a while until the old primary school teacher starts again. "I get the initial flight; I do ... but I reckon you could have returned to the known if the unknown was unsatisfactory. You have friends and family who care about you here."

"Maybe." And Stan returns to the chair and sits down and takes a drink. "I thought about returning many times. Every time I returned on vacation, I was tempted to stay. But, I'd set up a home in Korea. I'd bought furniture for Christ's sake ... and I'd become accustomed to the lifestyle. Korea had become an old sofa. I'd gotten so comfortable, I couldn't rise from the cushions."

"Sounds like you ended up finding or creating a replica of what you escaped from."

"That's what I have come to realize too."

"So, what now?"

"I don't want to do anything. I've just confessed to chasing an illusion. I'm sad about many things; I do know that I've got to start smiling again. I used to be funny ... I'm going to find my sense of humor and dust it off."

With that, he rests his hand on his mother's head and she neither accepts or rejects it and he says his goodbyes and walks to the door. Before he walks out, he looks back at his mother and says goodbye again and her vacant face asks when he will visit again. He tells her soon and as he does, he shakes her heavy shadow from his back.

CHAPTER 52

Only Bastards feel sorry for Themselves

Jinni spends the early afternoon of February 7 sitting at a café in the Prahran Market. It is out of the heat; the coffee is good and the wait staff is friendly. She sips on an iced Café Latte and continues to read Murakami's "Norwegian Wood." She is more than half way through the book and its dark theme of mental illness and suicide is countered by Murakami's sensual prose. The chapters are long and she can't wait for a chapter break. She needs time to reflect on what she has read so she places her bookmark between the pages in the middle of a chapter and closes the book. She tries to think about what she has been reading but her thoughts are invaded by memories and her visit to the cemetery. Eventually, she begins thinking about tonight and Miji's party and she recalls a line in the book where the protagonist was told that only bastards feel sorry for themselves. With this line running through her mind, she is determined to make the most of this evening and to follow where it may lead. She is going to smile at people and she is going to talk to people. And, in honor of Blue, she is going to wear a sleek, sky-blue dress she bought in Singapore.

She eats smoked salmon and smashed green peas on sour dough bread for a late lunch, and yearns for kimchi on the side;

afterwards, she packs away her things and heads back to *The Cullen* where she takes the lift to her room and she changes into her bikini before heading to the hotel pool. She swims a few laps as she goes through the day's events. The sun is still intense and she can feel it burning her back as she swims. Before returning to her room, she sits in the shade of an umbrella and before too long she doses off and soot swirls in an ominous willy-willy.

Miji's image emerges from the willy-willy; she is introducing a man dressed in blue. The image spins around and in and out of Jinni's sleeping mind. Miji is smiling and encouraging. She even thanks Jinni for coming.

CHAPTER 53

The Conflagration

At 7pm the air is heavy with the sound of helicopters landing on and taking off from the Alfred Hospital's helipad that straddles Commercial Road. The burns unit is almost empty. The mortuary is filling. The injured are suffering from smoke inhalation. The dead have been cooked from the inside; their body fluids boiled before their skin burned.

The action is frantic as hospital workers are flat out trying to save the lives of the victims. But, most are dead when they arrive. The fires in the Kinglake area released energy that was the equivalent to multiple Hiroshima sized atomic bomb blasts. The fierce heat has killed anybody within hundreds of meters of the fires. There was no escape for those who stayed behind. Other Melbourne hospitals are just as frantic. Wind changes and people's desire to protect possessions and property have devastated the little town of Marysville and its surrounds. Black ash is still blowing in the wind although the wind appears to be weakening.

Stan leaves the hospital and stares at the action. He needs to get away; visions of the tsunami return and he wants nothing of it. He makes the decision to walk through more cheerful memories from this side of the city.

He used to play tennis in Greville Street and that is where he heads. He walks west on Commercial Road with sirens, choppers, his mother and the Indian mother fighting for time and space. He turns right onto Punt Road and walks past the Freemason's Aged Care Center, where his grandmother died a long time ago; it is his grandmother who now jostles for center stage and he allows her this space. Her final words to him, a few days before she died, ring clear in his mind, 'Death is not another journey; there is no mystical light or reunion of lovers and loved. Death is empty; it is just death. So, get on with life.' She said these words while smiling. She was a funny old lady and he again vows to rejig his sense of humor. Her smiling face mixes with the wind as it blows debris and memories into the future. He deliberates on the idea that memory is the reincarnation spoken of by many Eastern religions. Do we return in reality or do we return as memory in future generations? With these thoughts flowing, he turns left at Wesley College into Greville Street. He walks past the College Lawn Hotel as the helicopters fly into the distance, and he remembers laughing with his old friend, Robert, over a few post tennis beers. He openly smiles and takes a mental note to give Robert a ring. Bits of his dream from the other night invade his thoughts and he even smiles at the vision of his mother and father dancing tango.

When he gets to Prahran Railway Station, his memory fails. The tennis courts are not where they are supposed to be, just after the railway line. Modern apartments have taken over the space and trendy restaurants spill out onto the street and laughter and conversation wash over Stan as he walks by. His head is on a swivel and he almost trips over a fire hydrant. He even laughs at that and smiles at the people who witness his almost misfortune. They smile back. He continues up Greville Street and turns left onto Chapel Street. He avoids colliding with groups of women and men who span the pavement as they move forward as one. He steps around the homeless man who squats on the concrete politely asking for loose change. Stan searches his pockets and returns to drop a dollar and a few silver coins into the upturned hat. He crosses the road and keeps moving past fashion shops, restaurants and bars. The wind flings dust into Stan's face and flakes of soot soil unused napkins and some tables harbor shock at the destructive power of the fires and other tables overflow with laughter over unknown events. Stan tries to stay on the light side of life.

At the same time, Jinni is sitting at the bar drinking her first Riesling. *The Cullen Bar* is half full; it is hard to celebrate when people are dying. The TV behind the bar is showing helicopters landing at the Alfred Hospital just down the road. It shows images of burned houses and burned livestock and wildlife. A fireman holds a water bottle to the lips of an exhausted koala and it drinks thirstily. Blackened bodies lay beneath blankets next to a burnt-out fire truck.

Jinni moves to the side of the curved bar so that she faces away from the TV. Her vision now looks through the interior of the bar and toward the entrance. She concentrates on the French Lounge music being played and the bartender smiles at her. She returns the smile and remembers her resolution to smile at and talk to people. Most of the groups and couples are glued to the TV screen. Most of the conversations are about the fires.

Stan turns left onto Commercial Road and a few hundred meters down the road he is stopped by a sign on the street advertising *Wet Hour* and this interesting twist on *Happy Hour* encourages him to step inside. He looks first at the horror on the TV before looking around the familiar yet unfamiliar hotel. His eyes are attracted to the paintings on the walls. A Tasmanian devil, all claws and dripping paint, menaces from one wall and on another wall, is the bushranger, Ned Kelly, in an armored helmet and heavy coat painted in shades of yellow and pink and Stan realizes that he is in the bar where his mother broke her hip. And then, he notices the Asian woman sitting at the bar. It is her skin that attracts his eye. She is smiling at him but he hasn't noticed. He is just staring at the color and smoothness of her skin. And then, he notices her smile and he almost withdraws but he manages a smile and the two smiles dance a little pas-de-deux. But, she returns to her Riesling and Stan, takes a seat at the open window. He steals the odd glance at the bar but the woman seems absorbed in her drink and she occasionally chats with the bartender.

The waiter saunters over to take Stan's order; he orders a Cascade Draft Beer and he looks again at the woman with skin the color of polished honey.

He brings back his dreams of Jinni and tries to do a face-recognition until the waiter places the beer on the tabletop. As he drinks, he is reminded of Vince and he misses him. Then, he begins to rehearse being funny. In his mind, he tells the story of trying to levitate and sleep at the same time? "I was staying at a dodgy hotel in Gulmag, Kashmir and the sheets were filthy ..."

Stan eventually stands and walks in the direction of the bar but the woman appears to be in deep conversation with the bartender so he veers off and heads to the bathroom. There, he looks into the mirror and practices his smile. He washes his face with cold water and practices again. The muscles begin to fall into a smile with just a little effort. He dries his hands before walking out and back into the bar. The woman is looking toward the chair he vacated and he approaches from the side. He stands next to her with his hands in his pockets pretending to look at the spirits on the shelves behind the bar. She looks up at him and smiles as she has told herself she would. Stan returns her smile and speaks.

"Hello"

And he looks back at the bottles and the reflection in the mirror is of a TV reporting on the horror in Kinglake. This has him look away and his eyes again find her face.

"If you like ... if you'd like to, you could join me for dinner. My mother says that the seared scallops are good ... I know this is a bit forward of me but ... you look like someone I've kind of met before ... in Korea."

"Well, I am Korean."

"Jinja?"

"Neh, Jinja"

"Anyang haseyo."

"Neh. Anyang haseyo"

"Jip ae odi isaeyo?"

"Busan aeyo"

"Busan? Jinja?"

"Join me? ... I've promised myself to be funny tonight; I even told my mother and grandmother that I would exercise my sense of humor. I might even tell you about the time I tried to levitate and sleep at the same time. Anyway, I'm determined to laugh ..."

"I made a promise to myself too and that was a promise to smile at people." And smile she does.

The TV continues to show images of burnt out houses and cars but neither is looking at the images. They have experienced their own disasters.

"I'll attempt humor and you smile whether it's funny or not." He held out his hand. "Do we have deal?"

She looks back at Stan and a gentle dreamlike image passes across her vision.

"Were you at the cemetery this morning?"

Stan stares at her.

She looks across at his table and makes a comment about the loneliness of his beer and she stands up, looks Stan in the eye and takes his still offered hand in a firm grip and shakes it. She then picks up her glass. "Lead the way."

When both are seated, Stan introduces himself and she replies,

"My name is Jinni."

EPILOGUE

Black Saturday: On 7 February 2009, in Southern Australia, as many as 400 individual fires were recorded. They became known as Black Saturday and they killed 173 people and injured 414.

Some of the fires were deliberately lit and three people were charged with arson causing death but no convictions resulted.

Indian Ocean Tsunami: The 2004 Tsunami devastated countries around the rim of the Indian Ocean and killed approximately 230,000 people. The devastation was so great that an exact number of dead will never be known.

Sampoong Department Store: The 1995 Sampoong Department Store collapse in Seoul, Korea killed 502 people and injured 937.

The owner, Lee Joon, was charged with criminal negligence and was sentenced to ten and a half years jail. His sentence was reduced to seven years on appeal. He died of health complications a few days after his release. His son, Lee Han Sang (Sampoong President) was charged with accidental homicide and corruption. He was sentenced to seven years. He now works for religious causes in Mongolia. Several city officials were charged with accepting bribes. They served prison terms of varying lengths. Other men sentenced were a number of Sampoong executives and executives of the company responsible for completing the building.

3,293 people were involved in the settlement, totaling $350 million. The Lee family was stripped of all their assets and possessions to cover the costs.

Seongsu Bridge: The 1994 Seongsu Bridge collapse killed 32 people and injured 17. Six cars drove off the broken bridge. One bus carrying mainly school children plunged into the waters of the Han River; 17 school girls died.

Poor workmanship, especially regarding welds plus loads heavier than predicted have been mentioned as causes of the collapse.

Subsequent examinations of all the bridges spanning the Han River found that most had structural problems due to poor workmanship and cost cutting

ACKNOWLEDGEMENT

This novel was written in cafes in Korea, Malaysia, Portugal, Australia and probably other countries too. So, to the cafes around the world that I sat in for long periods on a single coffee as I typed away on my computer, I thank you.

There are many people who have been supportive over the years of this project. Even the strangers going about their lives who didn't know I was watching and projecting.

A special thanks to James O'Sullivan for the use of his poem, "All His Belongings." And, for his revisions, encouragement and beery conversations.

To John Secombe for his friendship and willingness to spread the story around in its early stages. The feedback was critical to the finished product.

Peter Dorrell provided critical and emotional support as the project evolved. He also shared the story in its early stages. Again, the feedback was crucial in keeping the novel moving forward.

To Wendy Secombe for her editing and kind words.

Kathy Roots suggested the title for this book so I thank her for that.

Andy Boone read an early draft and encouraged me along the journey.

My wife, Sonah Lee, whose skin inspired the title, deserves a special mention for hanging in when the going got tough.

ABOUT THE AUTHOR

Gary Steel

Gary Steel is an Australian who hasn't been home for a long time. He holds a Master Degree in Applied Linguistics. He was a high school dropout and a high school teacher. He was a university professor of English and Communications at Korean, Japanese, Chinese and US universities. He was an elite sportsman and he continues to ride, run and swim. Gary climbed mountains in the Indian Himalaya and dived the ocean depths. He is a sailboat captain and he has sailed in the Indian and Atlantic Oceans and Mediterranean Sea. Gary has worked and lived abroad for more than 25 years and currently lives on Jeju Island, South Korea.

Made in the USA
Middletown, DE
05 February 2023

22990693R00166